ST. ANTONY'S FIRE

STEVE WHITE

ST. ANTONY'S FIRE

Copyright © 2008 by Steve White

A Baen Books Original

Baen Publishing Enterprises
P.O. Box 1403
Riverdale, NY 10471
www.baen.com

ISBN 13: 978-1-4391-3329-3

Cover art by Stephen Hickman

First Baen paperback printing, January 2010

Distributed by Simon & Schuster
1230 Avenue of the Americas
New York, NY 10020

Library of Congress Cataloging-in-Publication Data:
2008028783

Printed in the United States of America

10 9 8 7 6 5 4 3 2 1

To Sandy, who manages the increasingly difficult feat of making me feel young.

— PROLOGUE —

THE ENDLESS, SAGGING COASTLINE HAD A BREAK IN IT after all.

It was Antonio Alaminos who had spotted it, of course. The navigator had danced along the edges of the Gulf Stream with a skill that had caused some of the more ignorant common sailors to mutter darkly of pacts with Satan. And he had brought them safely through the narrow inlet between the barrier islands, into the bay where the three caravels now lay at anchor.

They had made landfall and set up a cross on the beach on the third of April, *anno Domini* 1513, at the height of the Easter season—*Pascua Florida*, "the Feast of Flowers," as Spaniards called it. Wherefore their captain-general, Juan Ponce de León, *adelantado* of Spain, had named this land "Florida" as he had waved his sword at it and claimed it for His Catholic Majesty Ferdinand, King of Aragon, Leon and Asturias and Regent of Castile.

Not, he reflected as he leaned on the quarterdeck taffrail of the flagship *Santiago* amid the humidity and the insects, *that King Ferdinand will ever be likely to find any use for such a pile of soggy shit.*

If pressed, he would have had to grant the place a certain beauty, with its riot of unfamiliar flowering trees. But only if pressed, for he came of a time and place and class of men who did not habitually think in such terms. It was gold he was after. Gold and slaves and . . . something else.

He sensed a motion at his left elbow. It was Diego Bermúdez, captain of the *Santiago*, a youngish man burning to equal or surpass the fame of his brother Juan, discoverer of the island of Bermuda. Alaminos, the pilot, joined them at the rail and stared across the still waters of the twilit bay at the darkling jungle beyond. After a moment, Alaminos gave a chuckle so low as to be barely audible above the noise of a million cicadas ashore.

"Have you ever noticed something about the things the Indians tell us?" Alaminos asked with the familiarity that had come to obtain between him and the *hidalgos* during the voyage. "Back in Puerto Rico, they told us there was a marvelous spring on the largest of the Bahamas that restored youth and vigor to old men. Of course, we learned better."

"Yes," said Bermúdez with a nod of sad accord. "We should have known better anyway. Springs on coral islands indeed!" He spat feelingly over the rail.

Five years before, in 1508, Ponce de León had conquered the island the Indians called Borinquen and renamed it Puerto Rico. He had been confirmed as its governor two years afterwards. But later he had been deposed by scheming rivals, as the island had stopped yielding the revenues to which the crown had become accustomed. But how could it be otherwise, at the rate the Indian laborers kept dying off from the pox that only left most white men with pockmarked faces? Odd. It couldn't even be God's judgment on them for their heathen practices, for they ungratefully went right on dying after being Christianized. Even more ungrateful was their propensity for rebelling and murdering their benefactors—which, of course, resulted in their dying even faster. And African slaves couldn't be brought in fast enough to replace them. There had been only one solution: find a new land, with more Indians—hopefully, healthier ones. So Ponce de León had equipped this expedition at his own expense.

"And then," Alaminos continued, "when we asked the Indians in the Bahamas about it, they told us about this wondrous island to the northwest." He chuckled again, without humor. "Whenever they find out what it is we're looking for, they always tell us that, yes, they've heard about it, they know of it . . . somewhere *else*. Somewhere over the next horizon."

Ponce de León frowned and ran his fingers through his frosted beard. "So you think they've just been telling us whatever will get rid of us? That there really is no fountain of youth?" Hearing no reply, he pressed on. "But didn't the ancients speak of such a fountain in the Terrestrial Paradise? Didn't the Englishman John Mandeville see it—and drink from it?"

"So he said," Alaminos admitted. "Of course, he said a lot of things."

Ponce de León ignored the last part. He leaned over the rail and stared through the subtropical twilight at the shore, indefinite in its marshiness. "Tomorrow morning we'll go ashore one more time and see what there is to find—maybe capture some Indians and have my son put them to the question. We can't give up the search."

He left unspoken the reason why they—or, to be strictly accurate, he—couldn't give up the search. At fifty-three, he was very nearly the oldest man he knew. And of course he ought to be thanking God for being alive and active at such an exceptional age. And yet he had felt the chill of oncoming winter in many ways. In painful joints, in shortness of breath, in the way the world was more and more blurred in his eyes . . . and in the increasingly frequent times he was unable to take pleasure from a woman—or, even worse, *uninterested* in doing so. (The concept of giving pleasure *to* a woman was simply too alien.)

No. It was unthinkable that he should never be young again.

"Tomorrow morning," he repeated, with even greater emphasis.

Juan González Ponce de León ran a hand through his sweat-soaked black hair as he turned from the terrified, bound Indian and reported to his father.

"I don't know. It's not the same language as the Tainos speak on Puerto Rico. But I can puzzle out some of it, the way you could in Italy if you only spoke Spanish. And he seems to be saying that there's *something* just south of here—something magical."

"A fountain?" demanded Ponce de León, with the gruffness he habitually used to disguise his pride in his son. Juan González had been with him in Puerto Rico, and as more than just an interpreter. He had been able to disguise himself as an Indian with only minimal staining of his skin—his Andalusian mother had obviously had some Moorish blood in her, if you went back far enough, although of course everyone politely pretended not to notice that. Spending time among them, he had gathered valuable information, at the cost of numerous wounds. Yes, having such a son was yet another reason he should be satisfied with his life. So why wasn't he?

"No, there's no word for that—or if there is, it's too different from anything in Taino for me to ask him. All I'm certain of is that his people are terrified of it, and avoid it. And . . . he seemed to be trying to tell me about corpses. But corpses that were not of men."

Juan Bono de Quejo muttered something in his native Basque. He was the captain of the *Santa María de Consolación*, the second of the expedition's ships, and was taking his turn to come ashore while Bermúdez remained aboard *Santiago*. "Demons?" he wondered aloud.

They all crossed themselves reflexively. Juan Garrido looked apprehensive, the whites of his eyes growing large in his dark face. The black Portuguese adventurer had been with Ponce de León in Puerto Rico and Guadeloupe, and had also served in Cuba. Everyone knew him to be a fearless and deadly fighter—against human enemies. "That would explain why the Indians stay away from it," he said. "Maybe we should too."

"And yet," said Ponce de León thoughtfully, "they are simple heathens. So they worship demons anyway. Isn't it more likely that this is of divine origin? That would frighten them more than the powers of darkness, in their ignorance of the true faith."

There was a great furrowing of brows as they all assumed unaccustomed expressions of deep thought.

These men were not generally given to the theological analysis that was the province of priests. But Ponce de León was a famously clever man. And his reasoning seemed to hold up. While they were still cogitating, he turned back to his son.

"Are you sure this couldn't be connected with the fountain of youth? Ask him if it has anything to do with water."

"I already did. At first he just looked blank. But then he seemed to be trying to tell me something about a pool that was not really water."

And, thought Ponce de León with a tingle of excitement, *the fountain naturally wouldn't look like ordinary water, would it?* He came to a decision.

"We'll investigate this. Tell the Indian we'll protect him from whatever is there. And make sure he understands what has happened to him up until now is nothing compared to what will happen to him if he doesn't guide us faithfully."

At first, they didn't even see the thing.

It wasn't that there was anything wrong with their eyes. It was simply that their brains refused to accept what their eyes reported.

The wreck lay amid the forest, in an area that was obviously second growth. It was impossible to avoid the impression that it had itself devastated the original vegetation, as though it had somehow fallen from the sky in a crash that had left it lying immobilized at a slight angle. But that, clearly, had occurred years ago, for the vines and the creepers and the moss and all the rest had begun to reclaim their own. Now it lay shrouded in greenery. But not so shrouded as to conceal its *wrongness*.

First of all, it was made of what seemed to be metal.

These men knew what could be cast in metal. Sword blades. Helmets. Armor. Ploughshares. Arquebus barrels. Even a cannon barrel, for the old bombards constructed of hoops and staves of wrought iron were already obsolete in the eyes of soldiers like these, *au courant* with the latest military developments. But this entire . . . vessel?—what *was* it, anyway?—was a single seamless casting, apparently in the shape of a disc as wide as a brigantine was long. It was a manifest impossibility.

And even granting that it could exist, it had clearly been sitting here long enough for the jungle to have begun to return. And yet *there was not a single speck of rust on it.* Its exterior surface was all the same uniform, gleaming, silvery smoothness, albeit bent and crumpled in spots and blackened on its underside, as though an intense fire had carbonized the metal there.

And how had it *gotten* here?

Ponce de León was the first to recover. He drew his sword and advanced on the apparition.

From the Indian came a shriek of terror. He strained forward against the rope that held him, shouting an appeal that transcended language—a desperate appeal to not approach the mysterious thing any closer. His screams brought one of his guards out of shock, and an arquebus butt descended on his head, silencing him. Ponce de León resumed his advance.

Without warning, a kind of rasping hum was heard, and a crack appeared in the impossible metallic surface —a hairline crack, surrounding a rectangular segment that proceeded, unaided, to lower itself on invisible hinges until it touched the ground, forming a ramp leading up to a doorway.

A low moaning arose from those behind Ponce de León. He turned, and saw his men on their knees, all frantically crossing themselves and fingering their beads.

"Remember," he shouted, "the black arts of sorcery cannot prevail against good Christian men!" He saw no purpose to be served by opening the question of just how good a Christian he, or any of them, was. Instead, he took in his left hand the crucifix he wore around his neck and held it up reassuringly. "But I cannot ask any-one to accompany me. I will go in alone."

"No, father!" wailed Juan González. "Don't risk your immortal soul!"

"That's right, master," Bono de Quejo put in, his voice charged with an urgency that thickened his Basque accent. "What will become of us if you are lost?"

"Our Lady and the saints will protect me," Ponce de León declared firmly. But, just in case, he drew his expensive state-of-the-art wheel lock pistol and cocked it. Then, sword in right hand, pistol in left, he walked toward the ramp that had appeared so miraculously, and ascended it.

This was a realm where nothing was—or could have been—made out of natural materials, in any Christian way. Even stranger was the light he was seeing it all by. He hadn't really expected torches. But there were none of the candle lanterns or oil lamps that gave light below decks on a ship. Instead, there were long panels of some-thing that was translucent and yet was not glass, glowing with a weird steadiness that lacked the flickering of a flame. And glowing without heat.

Very little of what he was seeing registered on him, cut off as he was from any familiar reference points on which his mind might have gotten a grip. He began to wonder if that was the true torment of Hell, for he knew with cold certainty that he would go mad if he tarried here too long.

He sternly reminded himself that the Adversary had no power to create anything, only the power to deceive. To believe otherwise was to fall into the Manichaean heresy. And all of this was certainly material—he periodically pounded a fist on something to confirm that. He could not believe that he could be taken in by a sending of this scale, for this long.

But every time he allowed himself to feel reassured, he happened onto one of the small but large-headed bodies, largely decomposed but with the skeletons still discernible.

Juan Ponce de León had fought in more wars than most men. He was nothing if not familiar with dead bodies, at all stages of decay. He knew very well what human skeletons looked like. And these skeletons were not those of men. His stomach heaved at the sight of their wrongness. He hurried on.

Then the awkwardly canted passageway opened out into a space that contained a framework holding one of the inhuman forms in a better state of preservation than the others. Like all of them, it was small; Ponce de León was accounted a short man, but his helmeted head barely had clearance in these spaces. He stared at the face, spindle-shaped like the rest but with desiccated parchmentlike skin still stretched over it. The huge eye-holes he had observed before were even more apparent, and the tiny mouth and the lack of a nose-bridge turned out not to have been illusions. Neither had the hands, with only three fingers and a thumb that was too long and wasn't at quite the right angle to the fingers.

He looked away, shuddering, and noticed what filled the center of the chamber. And he understood what the Indian had meant about water . . . but not quite.

The depression in the floor—he preferred not to dwell on the resemblance of its shape to that of a coffin—held something beside which all he had seen so far seemed normal and familiar. It was as though the air within it—no, not the air, something even more fundamental than that, something going to the basic rightness of creation itself—rippled in the way of disturbed water. He wrenched his eyes away, lest his soul drown in that unnatural pool.

His gaze fell on something he had not noticed before, amid all the strangeness. It was like one of the head-shaped effigies that hatters used to display their wares—almost comically ordinary, except for two things. One was that it was made of something that was neither metal nor wood nor anything to which he could put a name. And the other was what it held: a metallic headband or circlet, decorated with . . . but no, he was certain they weren't really decorations, although he could not guess what they were. It looked like it would fit on a man's head . . . or, he reflected, the head on one of the dead beings who haunted this place. It sat there, in front of the relatively well-preserved being, as though it was a coronet belonging to him. Perhaps even a crown.

All at once, he laughed uncontrollably. When he'd gotten his breath back, something compelled him to address the unearthly being as though it had been alive.

"Well, demon, or whatever you are, I've entered your realm, and you couldn't frighten me off. So you've learned something about the men of Spain! And while I may not have gained anything else—in fact, I'm sure I haven't, for this has been a fool's errand like all the rest of this expedition—I claim your crown, by right of conquest!"

He set down his weapons, removed his morion, and took the circlet in his hands. It was lighter than it looked. He placed it on his graying head.

All at once, his soul was no longer his own.

It wasn't that he no longer *had* a soul. That might almost have been better than this total inability to resist the great roaring voice inside his skull, all the while knowing he couldn't resist it. For a moment, his eyes met the enormous empty eye-sockets of the dead being . . . and he *knew*.

He knew what he must do. And he knew that the first of the things he must do was also his reward. And if his soul had still been his own, he would not have accepted that reward. He would have rejected it as the very breath of Satan. This, too, he knew. And that was the measure of his damnation.

He walked to the strange pool-that-was-not-a-pool and lay down in its weirdly swirling depths. And then he learned that there were even worse things than having no will. This penetrated not just his mind, but . . . what was the name of that pagan Greek philosopher who had postulated infinitesimal particles of which everything was ultimately composed? Oh, yes, Democritus . . .

Then his consciousness mercifully fled—the first mercy that had been vouchsafed him. And the last.

They waited, tormented by insects and tension, snarling at each other at the least provocation, or no provocation at all. As night approached and their patience began to stretch to the snapping point, Juan González Ponce de León prepared to call for volunteers to accompany him through that eerie portal in search of his father.

But at that moment, the figure of the captain-general appeared. With shouts of joy, they crowded around the ramp . . . and stopped.

If asked, they wouldn't have been able to explain what it was that halted them in their tracks. It was undeniably Ponce de León, looking no different . . . at least in any way they could have put a name to. But there was *something* different. Perhaps it was something in the way he moved, like a younger man. Or perhaps it was the expression on his face, as though it was someone else looking out through his eyes. Someone they weren't sure they knew, or wanted to know.

"Father . . . ?" Juan González spoke hesitantly into the silence.

Ponce de León laughed—and it wasn't really his laugh. "Have no fear, son, for we are not in the presence of the powers of darkness. Tomorrow, I'll show you all! And . . . I will found a church here, in thanks to God for His blessing!" He blinked, and all at once was almost as he had been—not quite, but close enough to allow them a feeling of relief. "But now we must return to the ships before nightfall." He led the way with a spring in his step that none of them had seen in quite a while.

But Juan Garrido lingered behind, held by the curiosity that his friends had always said would be the death of him. After the last of them had vanished into the woods, he looked around furtively, darted up the ramp, and entered the portal.

His comrades heard his soul-shaking scream of ultimate horror and despair behind them, and the noise as he ran with reckless speed through the underbrush. By the time they caught up with him, it was too late. He lay face down in a pool of blood, still clutching the dagger with which he had cut his own throat.

— ONE —

DON ALONZO PÉREZ DE GUZMÁN EL BUENO, DUKE OF Medina Sidonia and Captain General of the High Seas, had finally gotten over being seasick.

Some would say it's about time, he reflected ruefully. After all, he was commander of the greatest war fleet in history—the Armada of a hundred and thirty ships and thirty thousand men assembled by His Most Catholic Majesty Phillip II for the conquest of England and the restoration of the true Catholic faith to that benighted land.

His chronic seasickness was only one of the arguments he had used in his letter to the King, seeking to decline the appointment to replace the Armada's original commander Don Alvaro de Bazán, Marquis of Santa Cruz—who, some whispered, had been hastened into a not altogether unwelcome grave by the King's constant carping. In retrospect, he realized that letter had been a mistake. He should have slept on it, instead of instantly sitting down and penning a spate of self-deprecation. In particular, he should have known better than to plead inability to spend the lavish amounts a fleet commander was expected to contribute to an expedition out of his private purse. Coming from one of the greatest private landholders in Europe, a plea of poverty had been so patently spurious as to weaken the rest of his case, every word of which happened to be true.

Afterwards, realizing all this, he had pulled himself together and written a second letter stating forthrightly his real reason for not wanting the stupendous honor of commanding the Armada: the fact that he had no faith it could succeed.

Neither letter had had the slightest effect, of course. He knew full well the King's reasons for appointing him. First and foremost, he was the senior grandee of all Spain, inhabiting a stratum far above jealousy. None of the proud, touchy aristocrats who commanded the Armada's squadrons could possibly take offense at being called on to serve under him. Furthermore, in his capacity as hereditary Captain General of Andalusia he had directed the defense of Cadiz the previous year when the English pirate Sir Francis Drake had attacked it . . . and subsequently withdrawn, leaving the town unsacked. So the claim could be made that he had repelled *el Draque*, whose name Spanish nursemaids used to frighten naughty children. Nonsense, of course; Drake had simply sailed away as soon as he had done what he had come to do and set the Armada's schedule back by a year. It sounded good, though. And so his two letters had been wastes of paper and ink. The King had peremptorily ordered him to Lisbon to lead the Armada to what he had been practically certain was its doom.

The King had assured him otherwise. After all, the Armada sailed in God's cause, and therefore could not fail. And besides, one of the Gray Monks of the Order of Saint Antony was to accompany it, with certain equipment which was to be loaded aboard in the strictest secrecy.

The last had not reassured him as he knew it should have.

Partly, as he admitted to himself, his reservations were a matter of his family background. The Guzmáns had a tradition of enmity with the Ponce de Leóns, including old Juan, who had gone to his grave claiming to have discovered the fountain of youth in 1513. Admittedly, that grave had been an extraordinarily postponed one. But toward the end, his behavior had increasingly aroused almost as much comment as his lack of visible signs of aging. And the manner of his death, when it finally came, had occasioned whispered stories that no one wanted to believe. Equally disturbing had been the stories that had begun to filter back from the church he had established on the site. Shortly after its founding in 1540, the Society of Jesus had been directed to investigate the matter. The Jesuits sent to Florida had returned to Spain with a small, heavily cloaked figure, and petitioned the Church to found a new monastic order named after Saint Antony of Padua, the thirteenth century Franciscan known in his lifetime as "the hammer of the heretics." After a private audience, still shrouded in secrecy, the Holy Father had granted the request.

But it was more than just the Ponce de León connection—more than just a family feud. It was the

Gray Monks themselves, who were appearing in Europe in increasing numbers . . .

It was at that moment that the door to a certain cabin creaked open for the first time since they had left Corunna.

Medina Sidonia swung about, startled. The Gray Monk stood outside the door, with a pair of his human acolytes emerging behind him.

No, the Duke told himself sternly, setting himself a penance for the mental qualifier "human." The Gray Monks were human. They must be. Had not the Holy Father said so? After emerging from that private audience about which strange things were still muttered furtively, Pope Paul III had decreed that the man the Jesuits had brought back from Florida had indeed been just that: a man, possessing a soul. And if he looked peculiar . . . well, so did Indians or Africans.

And yet, the Duke could not stop himself from guiltily thinking, *it's not the same.* Indians and Africans might be ugly, but they were clearly of the moist, sweaty flesh of Adam. The Gray Monks' flesh didn't seem like flesh at all—dry, pale gray, unpleasantly thin-seeming. And the huge eyes were bottomless pools of undifferentiated darkness, utterly unlike those of any breed of men . . . or, for that matter, any beast. And the nose was an almost nonexistent ridge. And the mouth was a tiny lipless slit above the pointed chin. And then there were those disturbing hands . . .

No, he thought again, setting himself an additional penance. The Holy Father had spoken. For any good Catholic, that settled the matter.

"Father Jerónimo," he said, inclining his head with his customary grave courtesy.

"My son," acknowledged the Gray Monk in the sibilant way they always spoke, unpleasantly reminiscent of the hissing of snakes, as though they were forming human words without human organs of speech. He returned the nod, then looked up to meet the Duke's eyes. He had to look up. Medina Sidonia was not a tall man, but none of the Gray Monks stood much above four and a half feet. "You appear distracted."

"It is nothing you need concern yourself with, Father. Only a problem of navigation, and other such lowly matters."

"Ah, but anything that touches on the success of this Armada is my concern. After all, we sail in the service of God." It was impossible to read expressions on that face, and the unnatural, whispering voice seemed devoid of emotion. But the Duke could have sworn he detected a strangely inappropriate note of amused irony in the last sentence. "Besides," Father Jerónimo continued, "the King has commanded you to keep me informed of all developments."

This, the Duke knew, was true. His orders had included instructions concerning the Gray Monk which were strangely at variance with King Phillip's usual nit-picking passion for detail. In fact, they went beyond the instruction that had commanded him to follow the advice of Don Diego Flores de Valdés on the nautical matters of which he himself freely admitted he had no practical experience. These orders were open-ended, effectively making the Gray Monk the Armada's co-commander. He was to defer to the advice of Father Jerónimo in all matters in which the Gray Monk chose to interest himself. So far, these had proven to be no matters at all, which had enabled the unwelcome orders to recede into the background of the Duke's thoughts. But now the Gray Monk had emerged from seclusion, and the orders could no longer be ignored.

And besides, the Duke thought to himself in a sudden spasm of self-knowledge, he *needed* to vent his frustration and despair to someone, on this Saturday afternoon, the sixth of August, *anno Domini* 1588, when for the first time he knew beyond any possibility of self-deception that the Armada was going to fail, and that it had been doomed to failure from the first.

He abruptly turned away and walked across the quarterdeck of the flagship *San Martín*. Father Jerónimo followed, and bystanders nervously moved aside at the sight of him. He joined the Duke at starboard rail, and the two of them stared ahead at the coast of France, for they were only a few miles from Calais. Astern, the city of hulls and forest of masts that was the Armada blocked their view of the English ships that followed so inescapably.

"You know my mission," the Duke began, speaking as much to himself as to the Gray Monk, "for you were present at the council back in Lisbon where the King's orders were opened. I am to take the Armada up the English Channel and join with the Duke of Parma, clearing the sea of the English fleet so that he can cross over from the Netherlands with his army, reinforced by six thousand of the troops I've brought from Spain." *Crammed into every cubic yard of dark airless below-decks space*, he thought, *many of them seasick or with diarrhea*. He could often smell the nauseating, indescribable filth of their quarters up here on the weather decks. And their vomit and excreta seeped further down, through the storage holds containing the food they had to eat, and still further down into the bilges they lived atop. "Well, for the last several days I have known that I cannot accomplish the second part of those orders. The English ships are so much more nimble than ours that they can always keep the weather gauge, as the mariners call it. They can fight or avoid battle at their pleasure, bombarding us with the long-range culverins they have in far greater numbers than we, never allowing us to come alongside and board them as our soldiers wish."

"Still, you have fought your way up the Channel valiantly, suffering relatively small loss."

"Oh, yes. As long as we maintain our defensive formation, they can only nibble at its edges. But that makes us even less maneuverable, for we must keep formation with the worst tubs among the merchant ships the King collected to serve as troop carriers. We can't touch the English!" For a moment the Duke was unable to continue, choked by weariness and frustration. "No. I cannot clear the seas for Parma."

"Of course you can't, my son. Santa Cruz couldn't have. No one could have."

The Duke looked up sharply and met those strange eyes. As always, he could not read them. And he sternly ordered himself not to feel vindication at the Gray Monk's reference to the revered sea-fighter Santa Cruz, whose shoes the King had impossibly ordered him to fill. Anyway, the feeling only lasted an instant before black despair closed in over him again.

"Your words are a comfort, Father. But early this afternoon I learned that I can't fulfill the *first* part of my orders either. I can't join hands with the Duke of Parma as the King commands!"

"What do you mean, my son?" As before, the Duke distrusted his instincts in interpreting that expressionless voice. But was there a hint of mockery?

A moment passed before the Duke replied. He was running over in his mind the sequence of events that had brought the Armada to its present pass.

Their route from Lisbon had taken them out of sight of land only once, when they had crossed the Bay of Biscay from Corunna to the Lizard. So the voyage had never required deep-sea navigation. Instead, it had all been a matter of coastal pilotage, or "caping"—making one's way from cape to cape with the aid of the books of sailing instructions the French called *routiers*, a word which the English had bastardized into "rutters" in their usual way of plundering other peoples' languages. And the Armada carried the most advanced pilot's tool of all: the atlas of sea-charts and rutters compiled by the Dutchman Wagenhaer. ("Waggoner," in another typical English bit of linguistic brigandage.) All this the Duke had learned, trying to remedy his inexperience of the sea in preparation for his unwelcome task. But there was one thing he had not learned until this very day. And now he poured it forth to the Gray Monk because in his distress of soul he must pour it forth to someone. Wasn't that what a man of God was for . . . even when he was this sort of man?

"At ten o'clock this morning, we sighted the French coast, after having edged away from the English side of the Channel yesterday." Until then, they had hugged that side, on the express orders of the King. He had expected the sight of the Armada to ignite a rising of the English Catholics against the heretic bastard Elizabeth, for so he had been assured by English exiles who made their living by telling him what he wanted to hear. In fact, the only result had been to force the Armada to fight within sight of ports from which its enemies could be readily resupplied, while its own stocks of powder and shot ran lower and lower. "I have continually sent pinnaces to the Duke of Parma with letters urging him to be ready to meet us when we come within sight of his port of Dunkirk, although I have received no reply. But then, at four o'clock this afternoon, as we were already approaching Calais, the pilots informed me that they can't take us there! As Wagenhaer explains, there is a series of sandbanks running parallel to the Flemish coast, less than three fathoms deep—and extending twelve miles out to sea off Dunkirk. Ocean-going ships like ours can't approach closer than that."

"Only now they tell you this? But surely there must be a way through the banks."

"Only one very narrow channel. Wagenhaer warns that it is death to try to bring deep-draft ships though it without an experienced Flemish pilot. And we have none." The Duke mastered himself and continued. "So we can't fetch Parma's army as planned. The only hope is for him to come out and meet us. When I met with my council of war, most of them were for pressing on to Dunkirk anyway—they simply couldn't believe it!"

"Understandable." The note of irony in the Gray Monk's strange voice was now unmistakable. "But you overruled them?"

"Yes. I've given orders for us to anchor four miles short of Calais. We'll be there soon. Maybe the wind and tide will carry the English on past us before they see what we're doing and can drop anchor, so they'll lose the weather gauge." Even as he said it, he knew he didn't

really believe it. And Father Jerónimo didn't even bother
to comment. "I'll continue to send messages to Parma.
I've already asked him to send us armed fly-boats—the
light, handy, flat-bottomed vessels that are the only warships that can maneuver in the Dutch shallows. Now it
becomes imperative that he do so, and use the rest of
his fly-boats to bring his army out."

Father Jerónimo did something the Duke had never
seen him do before. He opened his tiny mouth a little
wider than usual—wide enough to reveal his disturbing
lack of normal teeth—and emitted a series of high-
pitched hissing sounds. Had such a thing not been altogether unthinkable, the Duke would have sworn he
was laughing.

"Parma has no fly-boats, my son. His 'fleet' consists of
river barges that can only cross the Channel in perfect
weather under your protection. If they tried to come out
and meet you, the fly-boats of the Dutch rebel Justin
of Nassau would sink them in the shallows where your
warships cannot go. After which Parma's soldiers would
have to swim back to shore in armor."

The Duke stared at him, aghast. "How can you know
this, Father?"

"I know many things, often by means you would find
mysterious. But there is no mystery here. I know it
because I am deep in the King's counsels . . . and he
knew it four months ago."

Medina Sidonia found himself without the power of
speech.

"Even last year," the Gray Monk continued, "Parma
was sending messengers to the King, emphasizing the
limitations of his barges. The King insists that all commu-
nications be channeled through him, in his office in the

Escorial. So naturally Parma informed him rather than you. Finally, in April of this year, Parma sent Luis Cabrera de Córdoba, who spoke to the King as boldly as any man has ever dared, explaining to him that the junction of the Armada with Parma's barges, the crux of the whole plan, is impractical. From which the King should have drawn the conclusion that the entire enterprise was pointless. But he pressed ahead, not bothering to inform you. He always assumes that God will send convenient miracles to dissolve any difficulties. Also, he is a man incapable of admitting a mistake, even—no, especially —to himself."

The Duke didn't even notice the Gray Monk's *lèse majesté*, which at any other time would have scandalized him. All he could think of was the pointlessness of all they had suffered already, and the even greater suffering that certainly lay in their future.

"Father," he heard himself say, "if you've known this all along, even back in Lisbon before we sailed, then why didn't you tell me?"

"Because from the beginning I have wanted us to come to this point." The dark eyes held absolutely no feeling. *If the eyes are the windows of the soul*, thought the Duke with a shudder, *what sort of soul am I looking into now?* "Shortly after the Lord High Admiral of England anchors off Calais, he will undoubtedly be joined by Lord Henry Seymour, who has been patrolling the Strait of Dover in case Parma should come out—even though the Dutch could have told him better. And I want them all together."

"But then we'll be outnumbered as well as out-gunned," protested the Duke.

"It is of no moment." All at once, the mocking amusement was back. "You see, the King is quite right: a miracle *is* going to enable this Armada to succeed in spite of everything. *I* am going to provide that miracle, using the devices that came aboard with me."

"What are these things? Holy relics?"

"Far from it. They have been brought from Florida over the past year. My acolytes and I will assemble them in a few of your pinnaces, which will then destroy the English fleet. Afterwards they will destroy the Dutch as well, if necessary. Then you will have the leisure to obtain the pilots you need from Parma and proceed down the coast to a point where Parma can join you simply by bringing his barges out of harbor at high water and drifting down on the ebb. And England, defended only by a militia of yokels, will lie open to Europe's best professional army, led by its best general."

"How will these pinnaces do what all my galleons have been unable to do?"

"It is very difficult to explain in your language. The devices send forth a stream of . . . very tiny particles which are the *opposite* of the particles of which the world is made. But that doesn't mean anything to you, does it? Let us say that their presence in the world is a wrongness; when they meet the stuff of the world, they and it both die, and in their dying they release a . . . fire? No, that's not right. It will be as though bits of the sun have been brought to Earth."

Medina Sidonia chose his words with care. "Father, my conscience compels me to say that I am . . . uncomfortable with this. I cannot but think that what you seem to be describing—destruction of the matter of Creation itself—is an impious tampering with God's works."

"What you think is of no consequence." All at once, the amusement and the discursiveness were gone, replaced by a cold emptiness—the very negation of the soul. "Remember, we are not truly equals. You know the King's command. And remember also what happens to those who defy the Order of Saint Antony. Surely you have heard stories. Be assured that they are true."

The Duke had indeed heard the stories, as the tentacles of fear had gradually spread across Spain and further into Europe. He held his tongue and looked into those enormous unblinking eyes, into bottomless darkness.

But then the moment passed, and Father Jerónimo's mouth opened in that barely perceptible way. This time the amusement held an indulgent note. "Besides, my son, why should you of all people object? Were it not for me, the Armada would fail . . . and you would be the scapegoat for its failure. Indeed, humans being what they are, they might over the course of time convince themselves that you were a fool and a coward, and that the Armada would have succeeded if only someone else had been in command. Utter nonsense, of course, as you and I both know. You are an organizational genius, without whom the Armada would never have set sail within the King's deadline. And your courage is beyond reproach, as you've consistently shown. You have done as well as anyone could have, trying to make a fatally flawed plan work while giving the King wise advice that he was too pigheaded to follow. Well, I will see to it that there is no injustice to your memory. Posterity will remember you, along with Parma, as one of the conquerors of England!"

"I lack all such ambitions, Father." The Duke's gaze strayed astern, toward the England he could no longer see. Family tradition held that the first Guzmáns had come to Spain six hundred years ago from England, of all places—Saxon adventurers who had plunged into the wars against the Moors and won a reputation as reliable and ruthless soldiers, wading through a sea of blood into the ranks of the nobility. He often wondered how that line of grim warriors could have produced himself, the seventh Duke of Medina Sidonia. He had never wanted anything more than to live in the Andalusian sun as the beneficent landlord of his vast estates, amid the orange groves and the vineyards that yielded the wines of Jerez—sherry to the English drinkers who had never allowed such trivialities as war to stop them from buying it. "I am here, not from any lust for glory, but only out of duty to the King."

"Well, then, if you prefer, I will enable you to succeed in doing your duty. And never forget your duty to God, as well. Must the English be consigned to eternal damnation as heretics because of your quibbles and qualms?"

It was a familiar line of argument. And its force could not be denied—at least not publicly. Privately . . . the Duke thought back to the freakish June storm that had scattered the Armada and left him sitting in Corunna, wondering for the first time if it was really the will of God that King Phillip add the crown of England to his collection.

He angrily thrust aside the insidious doubt. He *had* to believe that the Armada's cause was God's. Now, more than ever, he must believe it.

Of course the English weren't caught by surprise when the Armada's anchor chains came thundering down. They anchored smartly, a culverin-shot astern. Three hours later, Lord Henry Seymour's squadron joined them, and the following morning the Lord High Admiral called a council of war. The captain's cabin of the flagship *Ark Royal* was barely large enough to accommodate all those who had been summoned, especially now that Sir William Wynter, Seymour's Vice Admiral, had arrived.

At least we don't have to fit Martin Frobisher's big arse in, thought Sir Francis Drake. The boorish Yorkshireman would have been insufferable, having been knighted just two days ago. And there was the little matter of his having sworn to make him, Drake, "spend the best blood in his belly" over Drake's perhaps slightly irregular taking of the galleon *Rosario* as a prize. All things considered, it was just as well he wasn't present. Indeed, Drake's own presence at the council just might have something to do with his absence.

Drake dismissed Frobisher from his thoughts and focused his attention on Wynter, who was expounding what he thought was an original idea.

"And so, my masters," the grizzled Wynter concluded, "the Dons have anchored all bunched together, to leeward of us in a tidal stream—just the target for an attack by fire."

Charles, Lord Howard of Effingham, Lord High Admiral of England, nodded solemnly, for all the world as though everyone in the main English fleet hadn't already thought of fireships. Letting Wynter think it was his own idea was a diplomatic gesture toward Lord Henry Seymour, to whom Wynter stood in the same relation as Drake did to Howard, that of well-salted seaman to lubberly aristocratic commander. Seymour's hot blood was near the boiling point after his enforced idleness guarding the Thames against an illusory threat while others won glory in battle, and he needed all the soothing he could get. Howard had grasped that, as he did so many things.

God be thanked the Queen has such a kinsman, thought Drake, not for the first time. Howard wasn't getting any younger, and he might not have much more nautical experience than the seasick Spanish duke who commanded the Armada for the same reason of dazzlingly noble blood. But he did not lack decisiveness or good judgment—including the good judgment to listen to Drake. When Drake thought of some of the *other* blue bloods they might have gotten for Lord High Admiral, he shuddered.

"Your suggestion has much merit, Master Wynter," Howard said graciously. "It's in my mind that the Spaniards may well be even more than usually panicked by fireships, after their recent experience with the Hellburner of Antwerp." A grim chuckle ran around the table at the mention of the super-fireship that had sent a thousand of Parma's throat-cutters to their reward.

"All the more so," Captain Thomas Fenner put in, "because they know the Italian Giambelli, who built it, is now in England. What they *don't* know is that all he's doing for us is trying to put a boom across the Thames to keep them from coming upriver. They'll piss in their armor at the thought of fireships!"

"And," Drake added, "they'll cut their cables in their haste to be off, and put out to sea. Then the wind as well as we will be against them if they try to turn back and join with Parma. And once they're in the North Sea, in the season that's coming on, lacking anchors . . . well, my masters, the Duke of Medina Sidonia will wish he were at home among his orange trees—if, indeed, he hasn't been wishing himself there all along!"

There was general predatory laughter. The English had anchored off Calais in a subdued mood after the battles in the Channel. The long-range gunnery of which they'd had such high hopes had proven unable to do significant harm to the galleons' stout timbers, while the tight Spanish formation had prevented them from closing to short range. Now they saw a chance to break up that formation, and the close air of the cabin was thick with their eagerness.

The council broke up, and Howard and Drake saw Wynter off with many expressions of mutual esteem. As Wynter's boat pulled away toward Seymour's flagship *Vanguard*, Drake turned to Howard with a grin.

"If only he knew we've already begun to prepare fireships!"

"Yes. A pity the ones we sent for can't possibly arrive from Dover in time. But there's been no lack of volunteers to provide ships—like the five you've offered from your own squadron."

"It was the least I could do for God and Her Majesty!" Drake struck a noble pose.

Howard gave him a sour look. Drake was really hopeless at this sort of thing, although like everyone else (except Frobisher) he could never stay annoyed at the irrepressible pirate for long. "And of course the fact that you can claim more than the fair market value of those rotting hulks in compensation had nothing to do with it."

"My Lord! I am deeply hurt!"

"Oh, never mind. It's all one to me, as long as this works. And it *should* work, even though we shall have to do without Signor Giambelli's infernal machines." Howard's gaze strayed to the dark mass of the anchored Spanish fleet. "Only . . ."

Drake's expression abruptly hardened, and his eyes narrowed as they did when he sighted a threatening sail on the horizon " 'Only,' my Lord?"

Howard did not meet his eyes. "It's said they have a Gray Monk with them."

The August air seemed to get colder.

"Well, what of it?" demanded Drake after a moment, in a voice that clanged with defiance a little too loudly. "He hasn't worked any sorcery so far. Or if he has, it hasn't sunk a single ship of ours. Why should we be afraid of papist mummery from some unnatural spawn of Hell?"

"Of course, of course," Howard muttered. But he didn't sound convinced.

"Well," said Drake after another uncomfortable silence, "I'd best be getting back to *Revenge*." They made their farewells, and it was almost as it had been before.

But as he was rowed across the water to his ship, Drake could not rid himself of an oppressive feeling of foreboding. It made no sense. Everything he had said to the Lord High Admiral had been true and heartfelt. So whence came this vague sense of horrible and unknowable *wrongness*, as though something that had no business in the world was about to plunge the affairs of men out of the realm of reason and into that of madness?

By the time Lord Henry Seymour's squadron rendezvoused with the English fleet as Father Jerónimo had foretold, the Duke had already dispatched yet another pinnace with a letter to Parma. The following day he sent two others, each more urgently phrased than the last. Toward the end of the day, a message finally arrived—but it was not the long-awaited reply from Parma. Instead, it was from the Duke's own secretary, whom he had sent ashore to report on Parma's preparations. He now reported that Parma's army would probably not be ready to embark within a fortnight.

Father Jerónimo made light of it. "Parma has understandably lost faith in the plan. He has also grown disillusioned with a King who is niggardly with rewards. He is exerting the least possible effort. But when the news reaches him that the English fleet is destroyed, he will have no choice but to bestir himself. He will probably even regain his enthusiasm."

"But we can't remain much longer in this exposed anchorage. The weather could change at any time. Already our ships have had to drop a second anchor because of the tides. And the English are in a perfect position to let the wind and the tide carry fireships down upon us." The Duke couldn't suppress a shudder at the worst nightmare of naval warfare. Wooden ships were hard to sink, but they burned like torches.

"Of course. I'm sure they have already thought of it, and are preparing the fireships even now. But I have taken this into account. Under the circumstances, it would be natural for you to station pinnaces between the fleets, to grapple any fireships and tow them away."

"Yes, Father," nodded the Duke. "I've already given the order."

"Just so. The English will have no reason to suspect that those pinnaces are anything other than what they seem to be. But in fact they will be *my* pinnaces. So the surprise will be complete. And their shock, when they are eagerly anticipating putting us to flight, will be all the greater. So the appearance of their fireships—which

I would expect late tonight or in the small hours of the morning—will be our signal for the unleashing of the . . . miracle." Again came the tiny, ironic smile. "Would you like to be aboard one of the pinnaces, so you can witness what God has in store for the heretics?"

"My place is here on the flagship, Father." It was perfectly true, as far as it went. But in fact he wanted nothing to do with the engines the Gray Monk's acolytes had been assembling aboard the pinnaces. Engines? They seemed too light and flimsy for such a name, being largely constructed of the strange glass-that-was-not-glass he knew of from hearsay. He could not imagine how they could do anyone any harm.

Each pinnace would carry one acolyte, to operate the device. The small crews were all volunteers, and had been warned to expect supernatural manifestations. Father Jerónimo expected them to be paralyzed by terror anyway, but he had assured the Duke that at that point it would scarcely matter.

"I, too, should remain here," the Gray Monk agreed. "But we can watch from the quarterdeck. I think I can promise you rare entertainment!"

It was midnight when they caught sight of the lights that appeared at the edge of the English fleet, across the moon-shimmering sea. Eight lights, that grew rapidly in brilliance to reveal blazing ships larger than expected, sweeping rapidly down the tide toward the Armada's anchorage.

They watched from *San Martín*'s quarterdeck in horrified fascination. Most of the team the Duke had gathered around him to command the Armada were there: Don Diego Flores de Valdés, the seaman; Don Francisco de

Bovadillo, the senior general of the land troops; and Juan Martínez de Recalde, Spain's most respected admiral since the death of Santa Cruz and, at age sixty-two, like a father to the rest of them—especially to the Duke, who at thirty-seven was the youngest of them all.

These were men who stood out for courage even among Spaniards of their era, in whom courage was assumed. But they all shied away from the Gray Monk and made certain surreptitious signs. Father Jerónimo took no notice. He stared fixedly into the night and was the first to notice the oncoming fireships.

Diego Flores de Valdés cleared his throat and addressed the Gray Monk with obvious effort. "Ah . . . Father, as you know, our ships have been ordered to buoy their anchor cables and cut them, and stand out to sea, if any fireships get through the screen of pinnaces. Perhaps, just in case, we should alert them."

"There is no need," said the Gray Monk, never taking his eyes off the approaching fireships and the pinnaces that were converging on them—as they would have been converging on them in any case, in an effort to catch them with grapnels.

Somewhere deep in his soul, the Duke felt a . . . wavering in reality itself. As though a moment had come when the course of the world was unsteady, and was about to be diverted into uncharted waters—waters never included in God's design. He automatically rejected the somehow heretical thought.

"Now," he heard Father Jerónimo's hissing whisper.

Between the pinnaces of the screen and the English fireships, lightning flashed. But it wasn't lightning as God meant lightning to be. It followed a straight line, and it was more blinding than any lightning. And when it touched a fireship, that fireship did not catch fire or even

explode. It became a ball of fire, and the secondary erup-
tions of the combustibles it carried were mere flickers
of dull orange flame around the edges of . . . what had
Father Jerónimo said? Oh, yes: bits of the sun.

He was still trying to assimilate what his eyes were
seeing when the sound reached them—a thunderclap
that sent then all staggering backwards, clutching at
the taffrail.

"Mother of God!" gasped the hard-bitten soldier
Bovadillo. Recalde, whose health had not been good,
collapsed to the deck.

Only Father Jerónimo was unfazed. He spoke with the
calmness of one who was seeing only what he had
expected to see. "The acolytes have been told what to
expect, and they have their instructions. These weapons
are light, short-ranged ones, you understand—think of
the swivel guns your ships mount against boarders. But
at any time now the pinnaces should come within
extreme range of the English fleet."

At that moment, the unnatural lightnings began to
flash across the water to the dark mass of English
ships—which immediately ceased to be dark, as night
became a ghastly day. Ship after ship, at the touch of
what the Gray Monk had tried to describe—"antimatter," the Duke thought, even as the ultimate bringer of
evil was to be the "Antichrist"—erupted in that horrible
conversion of its own substance into the fires of Hell.

It only lasted a little while. As though from a great
distance, the Duke heard Father Jerónimo explaining
that the weapons could only put forth their lightnings
for a limited time. And it no longer mattered. What was
left of the English fleet was dissolving into a chaotic rout
as captains, insane with terror, cut their cables. It was

the fate they had planned for the Spaniards with their fireships. But often it proved to be too late, as flaming debris from the shattering explosions crashed into ship after ship, setting them afire—natural fire, the Duke thought numbly. Not the sort of fire he had just seen. He had seen Saint Antony's fire.

The Gray Monk turned to face their stares. He showed no emotion whatever as he stood silhouetted against the holocaust that had been the English fleet. "You must now send a pinnace to Parma without delay. The weapons will be . . . renewed in time to dispose of the Dutch, if necessary. So the way to England is now open." He turned to go to his cabin, then paused and gave the Duke his mocking look. "You seem disturbed, my son."

"What are you?" whispered Medina Sidonia.

"Whatever do you mean? The Holy Father has explained—"

"What are you?" the Duke repeated as though he had not heard.

"Does it really matter? And at any rate, it is not your concern. All you need to know is that this Armada is dedicated to the service of God, and that God has sent the miracle on which the King relied." The mocking look was unabated. "And therefore any means—any means whatever—that permitted this miracle to occur are God's means, and not for you to question."

"Including the powers of darkness?"

"Ah, but if they advance the cause of the true Catholic Church, how can they be the powers of darkness? Do not trouble yourself with these matters, my son. Merely do your duty, and spare yourself the torture of doubt. Onward, to purge England with fire and cleanse it with blood!" He turned with a swirl of gray robes, and was gone.

It must be true, thought Medina Sidonia in his agony of soul. *God moves in mysterious ways. Who am I to question them?*

And besides . . . if it isn't *true, what will my life have meant?*

Alonzo Pérez de Guzmán, whom men called *El Bueno*, "The Good," turned to his subordinates and proceeded, as always, to do his duty to his King and his faith.

— TWO —

THE SMOKE OF BURNING LONDON STILL CLUNG TO CAPTAIN Thomas Winslow as he rode his lathered, exhausted horse through the late-afternoon streets of Plymouth. Or at least he assumed he must smell of it, from the way people stared.

"What news?" some of the people called out. He rode on without answering, for the summons that brought him here allowed of no delay. And besides, they wanted reassurance and he had none to give.

He didn't pause as he rode past the Barbican, the district whose denizens specialized in separating sailors from their shares of prize money. The off-watch members of his own crew were undoubtedly there now, enriching the whores and tavern keepers with what little remained of the proceeds of their last voyage. He hoped they hadn't gotten into too many fights with tavern riff-raff who'd taunted them with cowardice because they were still in Plymouth.

He did, however, stop at the dockside where the *Heron* was tied up, practically alone. Even the man who had summoned him took second place to his ship.

"Boatswain!" he shouted without dismounting.

Martin Gorham appeared at the quarterdeck rail and touched the place where a forelock would have been if his hair hadn't receded. "Cap'n! Now God be praised! Are we to weigh anchor?"

"How stands the ship?" Winslow demanded without directly replying to a question he couldn't yet answer.

"Well enough, Cap'n. We've kept her in readiness to sail as you ordered, and it'll take me little time to haul the men out of the gutters." Only in the last generation had it become customary to refer to ships as female, but by now the usage was so well established that even old hands like Gorham did it. The boatswain turned to the watch. "What're you waiting for, you whoresons? Lower the gangway for the Cap'n!"

"Belay that," said Winslow. "I've no time. I must meet someone at the Red Lion."

"You'll not come aboard, Cap'n? But when do we sail?"

"Soon." Winslow hoped it wasn't a lie.

After the Spanish fleet had been sighted on July 25, everything that could float and fire a gun—even merchant ships that could do little more than "put on a brag"—had followed the Queen's warships out of Plymouth harbor. But *Heron*, a race-built three-hundred-tonner mounting a dozen guns, had stayed behind, and her captain had traveled to London, for he'd had his orders.

Gorham leaned over the rail and his ruddy face wore a beseeching look Winslow had never seen on it. "Cap'n, some of the rumors we've heard . . . some of the tales of what befell Lord Howard's fleet . . . the work of the Devil . . . Cap'n, what's *happening*?"

Winslow squeezed his eyes shut for a moment. Then he turned his horse's head away. "I'll tell you everything when I return," he called out over his shoulder as he rode off.

The Red Lion was Plymouth's best inn. The big half-timbered building was surrounded by watchful guards—surprisingly, for a great show of soldiers was not usually the way of the man Winslow had come to see. A letter in that man's hand, presented to the scowling guard captain, got him admitted with only a slight intensification of the scowl. A soldier led him to a large upstairs room.

Two men were in the room. One, wearing the long robes of a scholar, stood at a window, gazing westward at the harbor. Winslow thought he looked vaguely familiar, but promptly dismissed him from his mind. The other man sat behind a heavy oak table spread with papers—a lean man in his mid-fifties dressed in Puritan black that was relieved only by his white ruffed collar and a gold chain of office. His face was long and sharp-featured, with darkly sallow complexion and a neatly trimmed iron-gray beard. He gazed at the newcomer with hooded dark-gray eyes that missed nothing.

Winslow stood before the table and bowed. "Mr. Secretary."

Sir Francis Walsingham, Privy Councilor and Principal Secretary of State, had been knighted a decade before, but people still addressed him as "Mr. Secretary." Somehow, it sat more easily on him than "Sir Francis." They even called him "Mr. Secretary" in the third person, so completely had he made the office of Principal Secretary his own. The undefined nature of its duties and powers had been, to him, an opportunity rather than a vexation. If nothing was specified, neither was anything ruled out. Building on the foundation laid by his predecessor William Cecil, Lord Burghley, he had gathered more and more of the reins of government into his supremely capable hands. He had also developed something so new in the world that it did not even have a name. It would be a long time before anyone thought of the term "secret service."

"Greetings, Captain Winslow," he said, inclining his head in return. "I'm glad to see you here safe. You've ridden hard."

Winslow was suddenly and acutely aware of the state of his clothes, caked in dust and speckled with blown spittle from a succession of horses. "I came in haste as your messenger commanded." He reminded himself that it was never a good idea to try to withhold anything from Walsingham, and added, "I paused only to assure myself that all was well with my ship."

"And quite rightly, too. You must be exhausted. Sit down and pour yourself some wine." Walsingham indicated a flagon and goblets.

"Thank you, Mr. Secretary." Winslow lowered himself into a chair and poured wine with a hand whose shakiness made him conscious of the fatigue he had been holding at bay. He wanted to gulp the wine, but he made himself sip it slowly. It was well to keep one's wits about one when Mr. Secretary Walsingham wanted information . . . as he always did.

Long before becoming Principal Secretary—perhaps even before his stint as ambassador to France in the early

1570s—Walsingham had begun constructing a network of informers that extended far into Europe, and beyond into the Near East and North Africa. Indeed, some said he'd cultivated his first sources of intelligence in his early twenties while studying Roman civil law at the University of Padua, that hotbed of the new Machiavellian statecraft. Such would normally have been dismissed as beyond the range of human foresight. But in Walsingham's case it was actually believable. *Knowledge is never too dear* was his favorite saying, and he had spent most of his life acting on it. By now he sat at the center of a web that included at least five hundred paid spies of various kinds and degrees, from lowlifes of the London streets and the Southwark theatrical *demi-monde* to relatively respectable merchant travelers, and on upward to suborned diplomats and nobles, in layers of redundancy and labyrinths of compartmentalization. And then there was the support system of code-breakers, handwriting experts, forgers . . . and transporters of agents and messages, like Thomas Winslow, merchant adventurer of Plymouth.

"I already know," Walsingham began, "of what transpired after Parma's forces landed. But you were there. Could anything have been done?"

"No, Mr. Secretary. The Dons landed at Margate and advanced through Kent, south of the Thames. Our main army was north of it at Tilbury."

"Yes," Walsingahm nodded. "Her Majesty had planned to go to Tilbury and review the troops. I believe she intended to make a speech to them. But then the word arrived of what had happened to the fleet. She still wanted to go, but was dissuaded. At any rate, I have heard that the bridge of boats across the Thames was rushed to completion."

"Yes, Mr. Secretary. What human effort could do, was done. And it sufficed to get the troops across the Thames—as many of them as hadn't deserted." Remembering the horror that had run through the camps at the news from the fleet, Winslow wondered that they hadn't all deserted. He wasn't even certain he would have blamed them. These men hadn't taken up arms to fight the powers of darkness. "They joined the men of Kent, and made a stand on the Medway, near Rochester. But . . ."

"Yes," Walsingham nodded. "I have had reports of what happened to the Earl of Leicester's army."

Leicester! thought Winslow with a bitterness he dared not reveal. It was not for such as him to criticize a nobleman, even though he had spent years plying back and forth across the narrow seas with reports for Walsingham on how the war in the Netherlands was being lost thanks to Leicester's incompetence. *Well,* he reminded himself with a kind of vicious satisfaction, *Leicester's plump body is food for the crows now.* But the flame of rage within him lasted only a moment before guttering out, banked down by sodden awareness that it wouldn't have made any difference if the Captain General had been a soldier who had known what he was doing. He wouldn't have had anything to do it with.

There might have been a time, as the tales of chivalry asserted, when war had been a matter of individual heroics. Winslow doubted it. And even if it were true, that time was long past. Nowadays untrained men, however numerous and however brave, were meat for professionals like the Spanish *tercios*: regiments whose training meshed arquebus and pike into a single killing machine with a thousand bodies, one brain and no soul. That machine had ground up the militias of Essex and Kent at Rochester, and disposed of what remained of the Trained Bands of London at Kingston-upon-Thames, all with barely a pause. Then Parma had swung around to the north and marched east through Westminster, arriving at the gates of London a week after landing at Margate.

"I've had only fragmentary reports from London," said Walsingham, as though reading his mind. "Was it . . . ?"

Winslow found he must fortify himself with a swallow of wine before meeting Walsingham's eyes. "It was Antwerp all over again."

Walsingham winced as though he could hear the screams of the tortured men and raped women and children, and smell the stench of roasted human flesh. Everyone knew what had happened when that city had finally surrendered to Parma three years before.

"Ah, Mr. Secretary," Winslow spoke after a moment, "I have no knowledge of Her Majesty. In all the chaos . . . "

Walsingham's features smoothed themselves out into their usual mask of bland imperturbability. "Don't worry. We spirited the Queen away from London in time. That was why she had to be persuaded not to go to Tilbury. It was clear that Parma planned to sweep around London to the west, precisely for the purpose of catching her in his net." He paused, and when he spoke his voice was carefully expressionless. "You have no knowledge, I suppose, of my estate at Barn Elms?"

"No, Mr. Secretary," said Winslow miserably.

"Ah, well. There's not much doubt, is there? It was practically in Parma's path."

"As was my home at Mortlake, only a few miles away at Richmond," said the man standing at the window, whose presence Winslow had almost forgotten. "At least word was sent in time for our families to depart for the north." He turned and faced them, a tall man of about sixty, with mild blue eyes and a long but smoothly combed whitening-blond beard. His speech held a slight Welsh accent. "Hello, Thomas."

Winslow almost spilled his wine in his surprise, and half rose to his feet. "Doctor Dee! But . . . but I thought you were—"

"At Krakow, in the employ of Prince Albert Lasky, where you last saw me," Dee finished for him. "And so I was, until recently. I'd still be there, in the ordinary course of events. But in case it's escaped your notice, events have ceased to be ordinary. The Gray Monks began to take an interest in me."

A chill seemed to invade the room.

"They know a threat when they see one," Dee explained parenthetically, with his characteristic modesty. "Eventually, Prince Albert yielded to their pressure and expelled me. Several of his retainers had been found dead, their bodies in a condition I'll not describe. At least the Gray Monks didn't succeed in killing me. They did kill Edward Kelley."

Winslow murmured conventional condolences, but privately he regarded Kelley as no loss.

He had first met Doctor John Dee—eminent mathematician and linguist, astrologer to the Queen, experimenter in alchemy, and, it was widely whispered, sorcerer—years before, going to him for advice on navigational theory as had many others, up to and including Francis Drake. (In fact, Dee was no stranger to voyaging himself, having accompanied Martin Frobisher's arctic expedition of 1576, when his divining rod had proven embarrassingly unsuccessful at distinguishing real gold from the fool's variety.) Only later had he learned that they were coworkers in the Walsingham organization. Dee had reliably produced horoscopes showing the stars to be unfavorable to policies the Principal Secretary opposed, like the Queen's proposed marriage to the Duke of Anjou. He had also recruited certain of his fellow Cambridge alumni, notably the playwright Christopher Marlowe, as informants. Most importantly of all, perhaps, he had possessed in his vast library at Mortlake—doubtless ashes, now—the supposedly lost code book written by Johannes Trithemius a century before. Using that and his own linguistic gift, he had devised unbreakable codes for Walsingham. Indeed, when Dee claimed to have discovered the "Enochian" language in his efforts to summon angels, there were those who suspected that it was really just another code. Winslow knew better. Dee genuinely believed that he and Kelley, his medium, had revealed the native language of the angels. Winslow had thought that nonsense—everyone knew they spoke English!—and could never understand how so wise a man could be so gullible as to be taken in by an obvious rogue and trickster like the failed Oxford student Kelley, under whose influence he had gradually abandoned all his non-occult pursuits and departed for Krakow. He had continued to perform occasional services for Walsingham, however . . .

"I can see why you attracted the Gray Monks' attention," Walsingham remarked with a frosty chuckle. "Your prophecy of violent storms in the northern seas this year made it difficult for Phillip of Spain to get enough sailors for his Armada."

"I merely reported what the stars foretold," Dee declared loftily. "The storms will indeed come to pass. If our fleet had forced the Armada into the North Sea, with no way home to Spain save around Scotland and Ireland, its fate would have been sealed." He shook his head, dismissing the might-have-beens. "But yes, Parma doubtless considered the location of Mortlake when he planned his line of march. The location of Barn Elms, too," he added in a gracious aside to Walsingham. "I believe the Spanish ambassador once wrote, 'This Walsingham is of all heretics the worst.'"

"So he did. Seldom have I received a more valued compliment." Walsingham didn't need to add that he had read the diplomatic correspondence before King Phillip had. He laid his hands flat on the table in a getting-down-to-business gesture. "Well, they didn't catch either of us, did they? And now it is time to confer on the course of action for which God has spared us." He reached behind his chair and pulled a cord. A servant entered silently. "Ask Sir Walter and his companion to join us."

Winslow started, for he knew who "Sir Walter" must be: Sir Walter Raleigh, favorite of the Queen and Vice-Admiral of the West Country, responsible for the defense of the counties of Cornwall and Devon near whose common boundary they sat. More and more, he understood the veritable phalanx of guards around this inn. He also began to feel acutely conscious of his own modest social status. "Uh, with your permission, Mr. Secretary, I'll take my leave."

"No, Thomas." It was the first time Walsingham had ever addressed him by his Christian name, but it did nothing to soften his habitual understated tone of command. "You will remain. I know how weary you must be, but you are a full member of our council of war."

"I, Mr. Secretary?" Winslow's voice rose to an incredulous squeak.

"You." Walsingham adjusted a paper on the table as though adjusting his thoughts. "First of all, I must take you into my confidence. As I told you, the Queen escaped from London. I failed to mention that she is here."

"Here? In Plymouth?"

"Yes. It was the logical place to bring her. Of all parts of the kingdom, this is the most loyal. First of all, Devon is Protestant to the marrow. Secondly, the seafaring families that control Plymouth are Her Majesty's strongest supporters—and with good reason, since her 'Letters of Reprisal' gave legal immunity to Hawkins and Drake and—" Walsingham's lips quirked upward as he regarded Winslow "—other sea dogs." He paused significantly. "Haven't you wondered why I required you to keep your ship here at Plymouth, when you wanted with all your heart to sortie out with Lord Howard and Drake and the rest, and bring the Spaniards to battle?"

"I have, Mr. Secretary. I know now that if you hadn't I'd be dead and the *Heron* would be less than ashes, consumed by the fires of Hell. So I know I should feel gratitude to you—and maybe someday I'll be able to feel it. But I still don't understand."

I really must, Winslow thought, *be drunk with exhaustion, to speak so to Mr. Secretary. But what does it matter, now? What does anything matter?*

"Then understand this, Thomas. I needed to hold a stout ship, with a captain I knew I could trust, in reserve." Walsingham leaned forward, and Winslow could look nowhere but into those dark-gray eyes. "You are going to be the agent of Her Majesty's escape from England."

Winslow gulped the rest of his wine.

— THREE —

WINSLOW HAD NEVER MET SIR WALTER RALEIGH, BUT THERE was no mistaking him as he strode through the door. He was renowned for being extraordinarily tall—a full six feet—and handsome, with his wavy dark hair and exquisitely pointed beard. He was also a noted fashion plate even by the standards of Elizabeth's court, and while he now wore a cuirass in token of his active military status he managed to make it look like something for a courtly parade, especially with the splendid cloak that half-covered it. Winslow didn't know how much credence to give the story that he'd once spread a cloak like that over a mud puddle for the Queen to walk on. But be that as it might, it was easy to see why he had become a favorite of hers.

The man who accompanied him was nondescript by comparison—actually, most people were nondescript by comparison to Raleigh. He was of average height and build, plainly dressed, with a short beard and hair that was beginning to recede even though he looked to be only in his early forties. That hair was partially hidden by a bandage around his head, and Winslow's first thought was that he must have been wounded in the fighting against the Armada. But there was no blood in evidence; this was not a fresh wound.

Walsingham introduced Raleigh, and Winslow bowed as was proper. As he did so, he risked a surreptitious look at the exchange of glares that seemed to freeze the air of the room with the chill of a well-known animosity.

Walsingham and Raleigh were living proof that opposites did not always attract. Everything about the flamboyant courtier was an affront to the Puritan in Walsingham. Not that Raleigh was a mere playboy. He was a poet and friend to poets, and a founder of the "School of Night," devoted to the study of natural philosophy . . . including, some whispered, occult matters and the anatomy of stolen corpses. Walsingham wasn't narrow-minded in the way of those carping, arrogantly ignorant Puritan preachers who so often drove the Queen to exceed even her usual legendary capacity for profanity. Far from it: he was a patron of the theater (which most Puritans regarded as an antechamber of Hell) and an associate of John Dee. But the odor of atheism that clung stubbornly to the School of Night stank in his nostrils. And lately his distaste for Raleigh had acquired a very tangible basis.

Walsingham's greatest triumph in his self-assumed role as the Queen's watchdog had been the foiling of the Babington plot a year earlier. Hanging, drawing and quartering Anthony Babington and his equally dreamy

co-conspirators had been secondary to the obtaining of
conclusive evidence that Mary Stuart had been an acces-
sory to their plot to assassinate Elizabeth. Ten years
before, the Queen of Scots had fled to England to escape
the judgment of that country's nobles for her complicity
in the murder of her admittedly contemptible husband
Darnley and the attempted coup of her lover Bothwell.
Ever since, she had repaid her cousin Elizabeth's hospi-
tality by compulsively intriguing against her, and serving
as an all-too-willing focus for the discontent of Catholics
who regarded her as the legitimate claimant to the
English crown. As long as she lived and plotted, Walsingham had known Elizabeth could never sit securely on
her throne. But Elizabeth—understandably reluctant to
set a precedent for the execution of an anointed
Queen—had temporized and vacillated until her
"Moor," as she called the swarthy Walsingham, had provided her with Mary's blatantly treasonous correspondence with Babington. Even then, Elizabeth's inner
conflicts had been enough to cast Walsingham out of
favor after three strokes of the executioner's axe had sent
Mary's head thudding to the scaffold at Fotheringay
Castle.

The royal disfavor couldn't have come at a worse time
for him. The death in the Netherlands of his son-in-law
and close friend Sir Phillip Sidney had dealt a body-
blow to his personal finances, which were as chronically
unsettled as his health. (It was said that neither had ever
fully recovered from his ambassadorship in Paris, when
mobs of murderous Catholic fanatics had run amok on
Saint Bartholomew's Day and it had been far from certain that diplomatic status could shield a Protestant from

them.) He had counted on receiving at least part of Babington's forfeited estates from the Queen whose assassination he had prevented. Instead, she had given the lot to Raleigh.

Now Walsingham wore a carefully neutral expression as he resumed the introductions. "And, this," he said, indicating Raleigh's companion, "is Master John White of London."

"Master White!" Winslow exclaimed. "Of course I know of you. I've seen your marvelous paintings of the lands and peoples of America."

"Atlantis," John Dee corrected irritably. "Only the ignorant have fallen into the fad of naming the western continent after that Italian charlatan Amerigo Vespucci! I have conclusively identified it as the Atlantic island described by Plato."

"Didn't Atlantis sink?" Winslow inquired, all bland innocence.

For an instant, Dee seemed to expand as though gathering his forces for a crushing retort, and Walsingham smothered a chuckle. But then Raleigh intervened with an indulgent smile for his old associate in the School of Night. "Well, Dr. Dee, whatever we call the continent as a whole, I've named the province discovered by my expedition of four years ago 'Virginia,' after our beloved Virgin Queen. Master White was on that first expedition, and also the second one I dispatched the following year, as artist."

"Yes," said White, with a faraway look. "Nothing in my life can ever equal my first sight of that world, where all was new and untouched. I recorded everything: the plants, the animals, and the life of the Indians we encountered and befriended. But then . . . " His voice trailed off, and Winslow recalled what he had heard about the savagery and incompetence of Ralph Lane, military commander of the 1585 expedition, who had so antagonized the local Secotan Indians that the expedition had been left isolated in its fort on the island of Roanoke, grateful to be evacuated by Sir Francis Drake the following year. "Last year, when Sir Walter made me governor of the colony he dispatched to Virginia, I knew I couldn't undo the harm that had been done. But I hoped for a fresh start, for we were to settle further north, on the shores of the great bay the Indians call Chesapeake. But thanks to our treacherous pilot, Simon Fernandez, we were led into one difficulty after another, and finally left stranded on Roanoke Island, the last place we wanted to go. And then . . . " Once again White could not continue. He had, Winslow thought, the look of a man who had known too much sorrow and disappointment.

"Yes," Winslow prompted after a moment. "I heard stories—things went wrong, and you had to return to England for help. But weren't you supposed to return with a rescue expedition?"

"Oh, yes. Early this year I managed to obtain permission to try with two small ships. We departed in April. French pirates attacked us off Madeira. I received two wounds in the head, by sword and pike, from which I am still recovering." White gestured at his bandaged head. "At that, I suppose I should be grateful to God. The Frenchmen stole our cargo but spared those of us who had survived the fight, leaving us to limp back to England. By then, the Armada was expected and no ships could be spared for a second attempt. So the colonists still await rescue . . . including my daughter Eleanor Dare, and her daughter Virginia, the first English child born in that land."

"A sorry tale," nodded Walsingham. "Which, as it happens, is very pertinent to our discussion today. This is why you are here, Master White, in case you'd wondered."

"Actually, Mr. Secretary, I had," White acknowledged in his diffident way.

"Then let us proceed. Please be seated, everyone." The four of them pulled chairs up to the long table at whose head the Principal Secretary sat.

"I have," Walsingham began, "apprised Captain Winslow of what the rest of us already know. But to recapitulate: nothing in England can stop the Spaniards now—"

"The men of Devon and Cornwall will fight them all the way to Land's End!" Raleigh interrupted indignantly. "We will make them pay in blood for every foot of English earth! If they take the Queen, it will only be because not a man of the West Country still lives who can lift a sword or draw a bow!"

Walsingham waited out the dramatics, then resumed as though they had never occurred. "My sources of information indicate that Phillip of Spain plans to bestow the English crown on his daughter Isabella. We must not deceive ourselves. We are facing another reign like that of Mary Tudor. Only this time it will be even worse, because the Gray Monks will now extend their reach into England."

Everyone, even Raleigh, was silenced by Walsingham's usual pitiless realism. They all remembered the bad times of Bloody Mary when the air of England had reeked with the charred flesh of hundreds of Protestants. And they had all heard stories of the things that happened to those who opposed or even inconvenienced the Order of Saint Antony in countries under the rule or influence of Spain. The Puritans rejected the traditional Catholic demonology as a vestige of paganism, but they insisted that the Gray Monks were not men, if only because the Bishop of Rome—the Antichrist, in their eyes—had declared that they were. And it was said that both Spain and the See of Rome were becoming more and more the instruments of those weird beings.

"And this time," Walsingham continued inexorably, "there will be no Protestant heir for the godly to pin their faith on, as we did on the Princess Elizabeth in the days of Bloody Mary. If Her Majesty dies—as she will, if the Gray Monks and their Spanish puppets capture her—then all hope is gone. She must be taken to a refuge beyond England. The only question is where."

When no response emerged from the miasma of depression in the room, Winslow spoke up. "Uh, surely not the States of the Netherlands, Mr. Secretary. Without the support of a Protestant England, they cannot hold out much longer, stubborn though they are."

"No, they cannot. Likewise, the Protestant party in Scotland will never keep control over young King James without our backing, especially with a Spanish army just over the border."

"All too true," agreed Raleigh. "She must go to one of the Protestant principalities of Germany."

"But how long can they endure?" inquired Walsingham. "Phillip of Spain will surely aid his Austrian Hapsburg relatives in stamping out the true religion in the Holy Roman Empire. The Gray Monks already operate freely there, as Dr. Dee can attest. He was fortunate to leave the Empire inside his whole skin."

"The Cantons of Switzerland, then! Or the Lutheran kingdoms of Denmark or Sweden."

"That, too, only postpones the inevitable. Phillip has made clear his intention of exterminating Protestantism throughout Europe. And he has correctly identified England as the chief obstacle to his plans. Now, with that obstacle gone . . ."

"Well, what *do* you have to offer us?" demanded Raleigh, exasperated. "You seem to have ruled out all possibilities."

"Not quite all," Walsingham demurred. "I will now ask Dr. Dee to address the meeting."

Dee, like many other polymaths, had used a lucrative profession to finance the not-so-lucrative studies that really interested him. In his case, the profession was that of astrologer to the rich and powerful. Success in that field required a convincing show of authority. He had accordingly developed a style of hieratic portentousness, which he now let flow in full force. But the sorcerer's words were, by his standards, matter-of-fact.

"While I was still able to travel and work freely in Krakow and Prague, I made it my business to study the Gray Monks. I could not penetrate into the deepest secrets of their origin and nature; they have made it a point to conceal these matters. But, at the cost of considerable toil and danger, I was able to learn one thing: their real reason for desiring a Spanish conquest of England."

"What?" Raleigh leaned forward with a kind of truculent incomprehension. "But Dr. Dee, we all know Phillip's motives. Our sea dogs have raided his colonies and treasure ships, and our money and arms have kept the Spaniards bleeding away into the open wound of the Dutch rebellion. And he's convinced himself that he has a claim to the English throne on his mother's side—some nonsense about forebears who married daughters of John of Gaunt two hundred years ago. For a long time, all that stopped him was the knowledge that if he unseated the Queen from her throne he would have had to put Mary Stuart on it. Every papist in Europe, from Pope Sixtus on down, would have demanded it. And her family connections were with the French royal house, which Phillip couldn't love any less if they were Protestant. But then he got a promise from her to disinherit her son James and support his claim. And now, with the Scots Queen dead—"

"Ahem!" Dee gave Raleigh the kind of look customarily bestowed by a schoolmaster on a boy who had made an obvious mistake in his Greek construes. "If you will recall, I referred not to Phillip's motives for conquering England, but to those of the Gray Monks for enabling him to do so."

"Well . . ." Raleigh had the baffled look of a man who thought the answer to a question almost too obvious to put into words. "God's teeth, Doctor! They're papists, aren't they?"

"Are they, truly? I have reason to wonder about the genuineness of their Catholicism. I sometimes think they are silently laughing at all religion, while using it to manipulate humans. Be that as it may, I am quite certain that they don't care a fig for Phillip's political interests, much less his dynastic claims. They support him simply because he has the desire—and, with their help, the means—to destroy England."

"But why?" Winslow blurted. "You say they aren't even true papists. So why do they hate England so much?"

"I don't think they do. Indeed, I sense in them a void that holds neither love nor hate nor anything at all except a cold contempt for all besides themselves that lives. No, England is just in their way."

They all stared at the magus, except for Walsingham, who was hearing nothing new. Dee, who always relished being the center of attention, dropped his well-trained voice another octave.

"The hints that I have been able to gather together are maddeningly vague and obscure, as though they deal with matters that lie beyond mortal ken. But they all point in the same direction. There is even a clue in the saint for whom their profane order is named. All the Catholic world thinks Saint Antony of Padua was chosen because of his reputation as 'the hammer of the heretics,' and the Gray Monks have been content to let them think so. But there is a double meaning, for he is the patron saint of 'those looking for lost objects.' The Gray Monks are searching for something—seeking it avidly, almost desperately. I believe it has to do in some way with their origin, from which they entered our world."

"But Doctor," asked White reasonably, "if it's where they came from, then how can they not know its location?"

"I have no idea. But they now think they have learned, in general, where it is." Dee turned his hypnotic blue eyes on Raleigh. "It is in that region of Amer—I mean Atlantis where you, Sir Walter, have planted an English colony. Thus it is that we stand in their way."

"But," protested Raleigh, "I wasn't trying to thwart any deviltry of the Gray Monks when I dispatched my expeditions to Virginia! I sought to establish a base from which to raid the Spanish treasure fleets on their way from the Indies to Spain."

"Ah, but they don't know that. They can only regard us as a threat." Dee somewhat spoiled the effect he had created by lapsing into didacticism. "As well they might! My studies have established that England has a claim to those lands which far predates those of the Spanish and Portuguese, arising from King Arthur's conquest of Estotiland, a country which, as I have conclusively demonstrated, was located—" Walsingham gave a polite but firm cough, and Dee reeled himself in. "The point is, they must stop us English before we settle that coast and prevent them from carrying on their search. And the fact that we have colonists there now makes it urgent for them; we might find whatever it is they are looking for first."

"How would we know it if we did find it?" wondered John White.

"Who's to say?" Dee spread his hands theatrically. "But if it is as uncanny as I am coming to suspect it must be, then perhaps it will be something too extraordinary to be missed. And if we can destroy it, then perhaps we will cut off the Gray Monks' demonic power at its source. Or possibly we could take control of it, and bend that power to our own use."

"You've mentioned that last possibility before." Walsingham looked grave. "When you first raised it, I was troubled by its implications. Any traffic with the inhuman foulness of the Gray Monks must surely carry with it a risk to our souls."

"I admit the dangers," said Dee. "But if it is possible, have we any choice but to try?"

"Perhaps not. Indeed, we have few choices of any kind in this evil hour. If there is to be any hope at all for England and the true religion, the Queen must—"

"And what, exactly, is it that the Queen *must* do, my Moor?"

Winslow was sitting with his back to a side-door. It was from that direction that the sudden interruption, in tones of high-pitched female fury, came. So he could not see its source. All he saw was the men at the table getting to their feet with a haste that sent chairs toppling over, and then going to their knees—Raleigh and White practically falling, Walsingham and Dee lowering their aging joints a little more carefully. He could only follow suit. Once on his knees, he kept his eyes lowered and saw the hem of a voluminous skirt as its owner swept into the room.

"Well, Walsingham, you rank Puritan, what are you plotting behind my back?"

"I crave pardon for my unhappy choice of words, Your Majesty. But I seek only to secure your safety, and the rescue of the realm."

"Ha! More likely you seek the advancement of your fellow Puritans. Sweet Jesu, but they bore me with their unending demands for further reformation of the Church of England of which *I* am the supreme head on Earth! God's blood, isn't it already reformed enough?"

"Soon, Your Majesty, I fear it will no longer be reformed at all."

Winslow expected thunderbolts, but he heard only a snort which he could have sworn was half amused. "Oh, get up, all of you!" the Queen commanded in a voice that was merely imperious.

As Winslow rose, he saw the Queen hitch up her farthingale and settle into a chair with its back to the westward-facing window, with the blaze of sunset behind her head, so he could make out no details—only a fringe of pearls around hair that the setting sun turned even redder than its dye. A pair of ladies-in-waiting moved into flanking positions as she surveyed the five men.

"Sir Walter, thick as thieves with Walsingham! Well, let no one say the days of miracles are over! And you, Dr. Dee—I might have known. But who are these other two schemers?"

"Master John White, gentleman of London, Your Majesty," answered Walsingham. "And Captain Thomas Winslow, merchant adventurer, only just arrived from London."

"London." The royal head with its ruddy nimbus turned in Winslow's direction. "So you were there when . . . ?"

"Yes, Your Majesty," he mumbled. "By God's mercy, I escaped ahead of the Spaniards, unlike so many others."

"Many, indeed." The head lowered, and when she spoke again it was to herself and to her memories. "Sweet Robin," she whispered.

Leicester, Winslow realized after an uncomprehending moment. And it came to him that she was seeing in her mind's eye the young Robert Dudley whose bold Gypsy charm still lived, for her, inside the fat, florid, wheezing earl Winslow himself had known. That insolent rogue would have won her youthful hand if any man could have. But she had never once been able to put out of her mind the headless corpse of her mother Anne Boleyn and its grim lesson in what could befall a woman who gave control of her fate to a man as all women had to do . . . all women besides herself.

Now her sweet Robin was dead, and her own youth was dead too, for she could no longer pretend that she was the girl who had loved him.

"Your Majesty," Walsingham said before the silence could stretch beyond endurance, "we must not deceive ourselves with false hopes. Such army as we could muster is dead or fled, and Captain Winslow has confirmed our worst suppositions about the fate of London. The men of the west and north will resist valiantly, I'm sure," he added hastily with a glance in Raleigh's direction. "But they cannot prevail. If you remain in England, it can only be to fall captive to the Spaniards . . . and therefore to the Gray Monks."

The Queen rose to her feet, and the last glare of the sunset outlined her entire body. "You would have me abandon my people to their fate?" she asked in a dangerously quiet voice.

"Your Majesty, there is no choice—"

"Bad enough that I let you persuade me not to go to Tilbury and speak to the troops there," she continued, overriding him. "God, how much I wanted to say to them! I wanted to tell them that that I was not afraid to come among twenty thousand armed men, despite the cautious counsel of such as you, Walsingham. I wanted to tell them that I knew I had nothing to fear, because I loved them and I know they loved me because they loved England *and I am England*. No: that *they and I are England*, and that we are joined in an inseparable bond. 'Let tyrants fear,' I wanted to say to them. I wanted to tell them . . . oh, how did I have it worked out in my mind? 'I know I have the body of a weak and feeble woman, but I have the heart and stomach of a king, and of a king of England too, and think foul scorn that Parma or Spain or any prince of Europe should dare to invade the borders of my realm.' Or . . . well, something like that. I was still working on—" She came to a flabbergasted halt as the roomful of men fell to their knees again.

"Before God, madam," whispered Walsingham, "I regret that I did let you go to Tilbury! Only . . . ." The realism that Elizabeth knew was indispensable to her even as it infuriated her reasserted itself, and Walsingham rose slowly back to his feet. "No, Your Majesty. I do not regret it. You would have given our nation something to cherish as part of its heritage—but there would have been no nation left to cherish it. You might have summoned up from the soul of England something that could have stood against Parma and his hired killers, but nothing could have stood against the foul and unnatural sorcery of the Gray Monks. And if you had died, England's last hope would have died with you. You must"—Walsingham unflinchingly used the forbidden word—"depart England, to Sir Walter's colony of Virginia, from whence Dr. Dee believes you may well be able to return in triumph to the liberation of your people. That is why Captain Winslow is present, for his ship will convey you there." Walsingham took on a crafty look. "My only concern is whether Your Majesty will be up to the hardships of the voyage."

"What?" Walsingham quailed—or seemed to quail—under the royal glare. "How dare you? I'm a year younger than you. And I can dance a galliard and ride a horse for miles while you can barely stand up without your joints creaking, or pass an hour without the flux sending you running lest it gush forth!"

"Your Majesty's unabated vigor is an inspiration to us all," Walsingham murmured.

The Queen advanced toward Winslow, and as she left the sunset-glare of the window he could finally see her face clearly: the face of a sharp-nosed, thin-lipped woman of fifty-five, caked in white makeup, with dark-brown eyes that speared his very soul. "So, Captain, do you think yourself up to the task Walsingham has set you of getting me across the ocean alive? Or am I too decrepit an old crone?"

Afterwards, Winslow could never clearly remember what went through his mind. But he looked up and met those dark-brown eyes, and spoke from his soul because he could not do otherwise. "No, madam. You are Gloriana, and you are ageless."

Silence slammed down on the room. After a moment, the Queen gave a short laugh. "God's toenails, Captain Winslow, but you're a pretty flatterer! Sir Walter, you had best have a care for your laurels in the courtier's art!"

"I protest before God, madam, that I do not flatter," Winslow heard himself say, in a voice that shook with emotion. "My upbringing has not been in any arts."

Elizabeth of England leaned closer, and her eyes penetrated to depths Winslow hadn't known he possessed. "Devil take me if you don't remind me of Drake, Captain Winslow." She turned to Walsingham. "I suppose Drake . . . ?"

"Yes, Your Majesty," Walsingham said somberly.

"Ah. Of course." The Queen said no more. There was little speech to be spared for grief, in this season of death. "And who is to accompany us, Walsingham? You, for one, I'm sure. If you fell into their hands, the Inquisition would devise something truly special."

"No doubt, Your Majesty. And Dr. Dee and Master White must also come, for it is by means of the former's learning and the latter's experience that we hope to find what we seek in Virginia."

"As you say. Lord Burghley is too old to endure a voyage even if he were here, and I know he has already departed for his estates. The Spaniards will find him there, of course, but they'll probably put him to work administering the country for them. They know he served my half-sister Mary as best he was able, because at bottom his concern all along has been for the right ordering of the realm." The Queen turned to Raleigh. "And you, Sir Walter?"

"My place is here, Your Majesty. As Vice Admiral of the West Country, I will endeavor to hold these counties against your return from across the seas."

"You are so certain of that return, Sir Walter?" A note of tenderness entered the Queen's voice.

"As certain as I am of the loyalty to you that is the only thing Mr. Secretary Walsingham and I have in common—indeed, probably the only thing that could have made us sit down together at the same table."

"You really must guard against these attacks of honesty, Sir Walter. They will be the ruin of you as a courtier." The Queen straightened up, and everyone in the room stood straighter. "So be it, then. I leave the preparations for the voyage in your hands, Captain." She started to turn away, then paused and took another look at Winslow. "By God, but you put me in mind of Drake! I hope I'm not mistaken. For the sake of the realm, I hope I'm not mistaken." She swept away. England departed.

"Well, Thomas," said Walsingham after a moment, "how soon can you be ready to sail?"

Winslow thought furiously. "Mr. Secretary, I know the Dons aren't far behind us. But we can't undertake this voyage without preparation. The stores—"

"Letters in my name should get you what you need."

"All well and good. But no one in his right mind ventures across the Atlantic with a single ship—especially this late in the year. What if something befalls that one ship?"

"Set your mind at rest. I have arranged for a smaller vessel to accompany the *Heron*."

"But what about shallops? I remember from Master White's accounts that we'll be traversing shallow waters."

"That also has been attended to." Winslow wondered why he was even surprised, knowing the man with whom he was dealing. "I suggest you see to your ship. We sail with the morning tide."

— FOUR —

"NOW, BOATSWAIN," SAID WINSLOW IN A VOICE THAT sounded almost as harried as he felt, "you must understand that we are going to have the Queen herself aboard, and two of her ladies-in-waiting—Mr. Secretary Walsingham managed to persuade her that we could carry no more than that. You must understand that these are not . . . ah, they're not the sort of women with whom the crew are accustomed to associating. So there are going to have to be some, well, changes in the way the men customarily behave. I'm thinking in particular of the language that occasionally escapes them in moments of stress."

"Oh, have no fear, Cap'n," Martin Gorham assured him with great seriousness. "I'll allow no God-damned profane talk among the men. If any of these sons of noseless whores fail to observe the niceties, I'll hand 'em their balls to use as holystones!"

Walsingham's eyes twinkled. He was what was known as a worldly Puritan. "With your example before them, Master Boatswain, their deportment can hardly fail to be exemplary."

"Thankee, yer lordship," Gorham beamed. "Rest assured that every swinging dick of this crew will be a model of prim and proper behavior." An eruption of shouting confusion on the dockside caught his attention, and he leaned over the rail. "Have a care with those casks, you pox-eaten lubbers!" he bellowed, and with a hurried "Excuse me, Cap'n," he hastened off.

"Actually," John Dee remarked with a twinkle of his own, "I suspect the sailors could learn a thing or two from Her Majesty about the art of swearing."

Winslow was in no mood to be amused. He had begged Walsingham for more time, but the Principal Secretary had been adamant. Time was a luxury they did not possess. The Spanish army would be coming west toward Plymouth as soon as Parma could flog the aftereffects of the sack of London out of it. Furthermore, Dee was certain that the Spaniards would lose no time in sending a naval expedition to Virginia—probably major elements of the Armada, as soon as they could be refitted and reprovisioned. He was confident that certain new navigational theories of his would enable *Heron* to use the shorter, more northerly longitudes, bettering the usual time for such a voyage and avoiding the Spanish islands of the Canaries and the Indies. Winslow was only too willing to follow his advice. Spaniards aside, he had no desire to dawdle in the tropical seas that, this time of year, were already spawning hurricanes. In fact, they would arrive off the treacherous coast of Virginia at the height of hurricane season. And the longer their departure was delayed, the worse it got.

So they had toiled through the night, and Winslow had passed beyond exhaustion into a state beyond the reach of fatigue. One of the first matters to be settled had been that of accommodations. The Queen and her ladies-in-waiting would, of course, have the captain's cabin. Winslow would move just forward of that into one of the mates' cabins, which he would share with Walsingham, Dee and White, evicting the current occupants to the forecastle, and so on, with the lowliest sailors sharing the 'tween deck with the soldiers who were aboard simply because it was unthinkable for the Queen to go anywhere without a guard of honor. Sanitary arrangements weren't as much of a complication as some might have thought. Chamber pots would naturally be provided in the captain's cabin, from whence they could be taken directly out onto the stern gallery to be emptied into the sea. (A single experience, Winslow thought grimly, would teach the ladies-in-waiting the wisdom of doing so from upwind.)

As for provisions, Walsingam's letters, delivered by soldiers pounding on doors at night, had proven marvelously effective at persuading ship chandlers to be flexible about their business hours. The loading had gone on through the night, and was only now coming to completion under the boatswain's bellowing supervision. In addition to the usual stores, they were bringing a consignment of copper implements. White had explained that the Indians of Virginia set great store by copper, and had been impressed by the Englishmen's relatively advanced techniques for working it.

Storage requirements for the additional provisions had left no space to store the two shallops Walsingham had procured in the usual way, disassembled in the hold. Instead, they would have to be towed, running the risk of losing them in heavy weather. But it could not be helped, for the light, shallow-draft boats were indispensable. Only they could approach Roanoke Island, whose inaccessibility had been its main attraction to Raleigh, in search of a base for privateering.

Nor was that the only problem caused by the overloading of the ship. The 'tween deck was so cluttered with men and cargo that there was no room for the guns—sakers and minions, with six culverins in the waist—to recoil. So Winslow had ordered them tied down, which meant in effect that they could be fired just once, for in the heat of battle there would be no practical way to reload them. He fervently hoped that *Heron* would meet no threats more formidable than sea scavengers who could be frightened off by a single broadside.

As promised, Walsingham had engaged an auxiliary vessel: *Greyhound*, an aging sixty-ton caravel captained by one Jonas Halleck. Winslow had never met the man, and had barely had a chance to exchange courtesies with him in the torch-lit chaos of the frenetic night. He could only trust in Walsingham's well-known ability as a judge of men.

Now, finally, the loading was coming to completion in the dawn light under the boatswain's blasphemous urgings, and a carriage was approaching along the dockside, followed by a cart. Soldiers cleared a space, and Sir Walter Raleigh descended from the coach, offering a hand. No spread cloak, Winslow noted. The Queen took it, and as her feet touched the dock all grew unaccustomedly quiet.

She had dressed as plainly and practically as she ever did, as though for riding. Any encouragement Winslow felt from that died a swift death at the sight of the number of chests being unloaded from the cart. He wondered where, even in the relatively commodious captain's cabin, they could possibly fit. But then Raleigh conducted the Queen up the gangway, and as she came aboard everyone knelt.

"Arise, Captain Winslow." Elizabeth seemed to be in a high good humor. "It's hardly fitting that you should kneel here. Ever since that bold rascal Drake took it upon himself to shorten Thomas Doughty by a head, English sea captains have asserted a kind of monarchy aboard their own ships."

"Only under God and Your Majesty," Winslow demurred as he rose. "And as for Thomas Doughty, from everything I've heard of that voyage his head hadn't been doing him much good anyway."

"I wasn't mistaken about you, Captain: you're another saucy rogue like Drake. You'd best hope I'll be able to forgive you anything, as I always could him."

"I only hope you'll forgive me the cramped and uncomfortable quarters that are the best *Heron* can offer, Your Majesty."

"Bah! You're as bad as Walsingham." Elizabeth paused to spear that worthy with a glare. "Anyone would think I was made of spun sugar! Have the two of you forgotten that I was once imprisoned in the Tower? If I survived that, I think I can survive your fine ship, Captain Winslow."

Except, Winslow thought, *you were in your early twenties then. And the Tower of London didn't pitch and roll and lurch with the waves. And it wasn't loud all day and all night with the constant creaking of a ship at sea. And it wasn't headed into the height of hurricane season. And it couldn't sink.*

"You may show me these 'cramped and uncomfortable quarters,' Captain," the Queen interrupted his thoughts.

"This way, Your Majesty," said Winslow with a bow, offering her his arm. "My cabin is yours."

She took the sight of it very well, he thought. But then she turned to him and said, "Very fine, Captain. Only . . . where is the *rest* of it?"

"This *is* 'the rest of it,' Your Majesty," he explained miserably.

"Ah. Thank you, Captain." Elizabeth Tudor kept her features composed and swallowed once. "But if this is your cabin, where will you be sleeping?"

"In the mates' cabins, through which we passed just before we entered here, Your Majesty."

"What? You mean *that* is all the space you'll have?"

"Actually, Your Majesty, I'll be sharing it with the Principal Secretary, and Dr. Dee, and Master White."

"Ah. Thank you, Captain," the Queen repeated with a gracious nod of dismissal. As Winslow withdrew, he heard a low, "Jesu! I never fully appreciated my sea dogs until now."

As he emerged on deck, Raleigh was taking his punctiliously polite leave of Walsingham. Then he turned to White with more warmth. "Master White, I pray to God that you'll find my settlers in good health on that wretched island! I still don't fully understand why they ended there, and not on the shores of the Chesapeake Bay as I intended. You say it was the pilot, that renegade Portuguese rogue Simon Fernandez—"

"Yes, Sir Walter. We thought we had reason to trust in his experience. After all, he had been on the expedition of 1585, when one of the three inlets through the barrier islands was named 'Port Ferdinando' in his honor. But from the first, it was as though he was creating delays and difficulties. Then he loaded us up with foul water and poisonous fruit when we stopped for provisions in the Virgin Islands, with which he was familiar. And once we arrived at Virginia, he made mistakes someone who knew those waters never should have. And finally he abandoned us where we could only die—on Roanoke Island, where we were only supposed to pay a call on the small garrison that had been left there, before proceeding on to the Chesapeake Bay."

Raleigh gave a headshake of angry frustration. "Well, Fernandez died with Lord Howard's fleet, which was too good for him if what you say is true. We'll succor the colonists now—and all of England with them, if Dr. Dee is right. Captain Winslow, I wish you a prosperous voyage. You carry the hopes of our country . . . and the most precious passenger in the world." With a last glance aft, toward the captain's cabin, he departed. White watched him go, then excused himself.

Dee turned to Walsingham and raised one eyebrow. "It *does* seem a very strange story, doesn't it?"

"What do you mean?" Walsingham's tone was odd, Winslow thought—deliberately flat and emotionless. And it wasn't like the Principal Secretary to be willfully obtuse.

"The fate of Raleigh's colonists," Dee persisted. "How could so much have gone so wrong? One would almost think the expedition was deliberately wrecked. And not from without, either, but betrayed from within."

Walsingham tried to turn away. But Dee moved in front of him and held his eyes with that hypnotic blue gaze of his, while Winslow looked on, bewildered.

"And," Dee continued in the same quiet but relentless way, "I happen to know that Simon Fernandez was one of those you had a hold over. In fact, he owed you his life. In 1577, he was a pirate wanted for murder by the Portuguese. He was arrested, but for some strange reason released. And a year later, instead of hanging as he so richly deserved, he was piloting Sir Humphrey Gilbert's expedition to the New World!"

Walsingham pushed past Dee and stood at the rail, staring out in silence, while Winslow began to think the unthinkable.

"Why?" Dee asked very quietly. "Raleigh's aim was to strike at Spain—and you are the most consistent enemy Spain has ever had, or probably ever will have. I know what you think of Raleigh, but surely personal dislike couldn't make you—"

Abruptly, Walsingham whirled to face Dee, and for the first time in Winslow's experience his features, always so carefully controlled, were a mask of anger from which the magus flinched back. "Do you truly believe that I have no greater ends in view than petty personal jealousy or spite?" He mastered himself, turned back to the rail, and spoke tonelessly without facing them. "For more than ten years, I have been playing a very delicate, very subtle game against the King of Spain—a game for the safety of England and Her Majesty, to say nothing of the true religion. Everything has been painstakingly balanced. All our moves against Spain have had to be coordinated with all the others, their effect precisely measured and their consequences carefully considered. And then came Raleigh, with the Queen's favor and ideas too large for him. He was uncontrollable, like . . . like . . . " Walsingham thought a moment, then turned to Winslow and spoke with seeming irrelevance. "Thomas, a ship's heavy guns are attached to the bulkheads by cables. I'm told that sometimes, in battle or storm, those cables break and the gun is free to roll back and forth across the deck with the rolling of the ship, too heavy for anyone to halt, crushing all in its path until it finally strikes a bulkhead hard enough to smash through and fall into the sea."

"Uh . . . that's true, Mr. Secretary. A loose cannon is one of a seaman's nightmares."

"Yes, that's it: a 'loose cannon.' A useful phrase, which I'll have to remember." Walsingham resumed staring out beyond the rail. "Raleigh's plan for establishing a base in what the Spaniards consider their territory for the purpose of raiding their treasure fleets had no part in my design. It could have upset everything. It had to be stopped."

Winslow stared. All he could think of was that there had been a hundred and seventeen colonists, twenty-eight of them women and children. And . . .

"Master White's little granddaughter Virginia Dare," he heard himself say.

Walsingham winced as though from a sharp pain, and would not meet Winslow's eyes. "My service to Her Majesty has required many things of me that will always weigh on my conscience. After a time, the conscience becomes accustomed to the burden. Too accustomed, perhaps. Small additional weights are too easily assumed . . . like the weight of a newborn infant."

"And in the end," Dee said slowly, "you lost your game after all. England is fallen."

"Only because of a factor that no one could have predicted or accounted for: the Gray Monks. Had they not entered the world from God or the Devil knows where, I swear I would have won my game, and the Armada would even now be leaving its wrecks on every coast of Scotland and Ireland." Walsingham gave a chuckle that had no humor in it. "If I had known then what I know now, I would have done everything in my power to promote Raleigh's venture. For he—blindly, ignorantly —was striking at one place where the Gray Monks can be hurt. And now his colony holds England's last hope."

"If his colony still exists," said Dee somberly. *Despite your best efforts* was a qualifier that hung silently in the air.

Before anyone could think of anything else to say, Martin Gorham came puffing up the gangway. "Pardon, Cap'n, but all is aboard. And the tide is rising."

"Just so, Boatswain." Winslow began to give orders, and the controlled chaos of the night seemed to reawake. Soon the ropes were let slip and *Heron* began to edge away from the dock.

Standing on the poop, Winslow looked over the port rail and downward. Elizabeth stood on the stern gallery, as if to catch the last possible glimpse of England. Suddenly, she looked up and called out to him.

"Captain! It seems we've forgotten someone."

Winslow looked back along the dock. A young man was riding a horse—none too expertly, and both were clearly exhausted—along the seawall, trying to catch *Heron*.

"Stop!" the man cried. The sailors responded with a gale of laughter. "I mean, ahoy! Or whatever will serve to halt you."

"You're too late, fellow!" Winslow called out. "You'll have to take your chances with the Dons."

"But I bring urgent dispatches for the Principal Secretary!" the man shouted, not so much dismounting from his horse as falling off. "You must take me!"

Walsingham leaned over the rail. "What 'dispatches,' buffoon? From whom?"

"From Christopher Marlowe, in London," the man gasped, running along the dock to catch up with *Heron*.

"Marlowe!" exclaimed Dee. "Not just anyone would know he was one of your agents."

"No, indeed. And I'd rather not leave those who do know behind, for the Spaniards to put to the question." Walsingham turned to Winslow. "Thomas, perhaps we'd best look into this further."

"Boatswain!" Winslow ordered. "Cast a line!"

A line swung out just as *Heron*'s stern cleared the jetty. The man grabbed it and was swept off his feet, landing in the water to the further hilarity of the sailors, who hauled him aboard. He collapsed in a wet heap on the deck.

"God bless you, Captain," he gasped. He appeared to be in his early to mid-twenties, of no great stature, with brown hair already beginning to exhibit that slight receding from the temples which presaged middle-aged baldness. His expressive mouth was surrounded by a thin youthful attempt at a mustache and beard. His only remarkable feature was his eyes: hazel, large and extraordinarily luminous. "I can only pay you with thanks—the exchequer of the poor." He momentarily took on a look of concentration, as though he was filing that turn of phrase away in some compartment of memory for future use, before resuming. "But I'm sure the Principal Secretary will reward you."

"I am the Principal Secretary," said Walsingham, pushing past Winslow, "and kindly permit me to be the judge of where rewards should be dispensed. Now, how is it you happen to know Christopher Marlowe?"

"I only arrived in London a year ago, Mr. Secretary. Since then I have worked in a variety of fields—"

"What a surprise," Dee remarked in an undertone.

"—including acting, in which capacity I'm not altogether ill-regarded. It was thus that I made the acquaintance of that eminent playwright. I have some small ambitions in that direction myself, you see, and—"

"Yes, yes, get to the point!" Walsingham demanded testily. "What of Marlowe? Does he still live?"

"I cannot say he does not, but I doubt that he does. He attempted to depart London ahead of the Spaniards, but ran afoul of a patrol and was wounded. I happened to be the only one available to whom he had confided his . . . second career as an informant. So he entrusted these to me." The young actor held out a sealed satchel he had been carrying slung over his shoulder. Walsingham took them with an absent murmur of thanks and departed, in close conversation with Dee.

Winslow looked aft. Plymouth harbor was receding astern. He turned to their somewhat wordy new arrival. "Well, it's too late to put you ashore. I don't suppose your 'variety of fields' has included seamanship."

"Ah . . . not exactly, Captain."

"Somehow I thought not." *More overcrowding!* he thought disgustedly. "Well, Boatswain, can you find something to keep a landlubber occupied?"

Gorham looked dubious. "I suppose so, Cap'n."

"Good." Winslow started to turn away, then had an afterthought. "Oh, by the way, what's your name?"

"Shakespeare, Captain," said the new crewman, ducking his head. "William Shakespeare, lately of Stratford-upon-Avon in Warwickshire."

— FIVE —

FOR MOST OF THE VOYAGE, THEIR WEATHER-LUCK HELD. Heading southwest, they avoided the northern tempests John Dee had foretold, and which he continued to insist would have been the Armada's ruin had it been forced past the Straits of Dover into the North Sea. Then, while still well north of the Canaries, they took a starboard tack and struck out into the trackless spaces of the Atlantic.

Columbus and everyone who had followed him had swung far to the south and let the currents and the prevailing winds carry them to the Indies. But Dee insisted that his projected route, more direct if not so effortless, would be quicker if it worked at all. Of course, he could not determine their longitude accurately—an inability that irritated him extremely, even though the problem was equally intractable to everyone else. But he assured

Winslow that their progress was as his theories predicted, and everything seemed to bear him out.

The Queen, far from burdening Winslow with complaints, seemed to be actually enjoying the voyage, and thriving on it. The only feminine whining came from the ladies-in-waiting, and most of their complaints concerned the looks they imagined the sailors kept giving them, which may not have been entirely imaginary; they were both distinctly middle-aged, but seamen acquire new standards of beauty. Walsingham, whose health was never robust, suffered stoically, as it befitted a Puritan to endure without complaint whatever inflictions God saw fit to send as tests.

Even Shakespeare managed to make himself fairly useful. *Heron*'s hurried departure had left them short of fresh-caught landsmen, and the grudging help of the Queen's guards didn't altogether make up the difference. The young actor was willing to learn, and fared better among the sailors than Winslow would have expected. He'd probably had experience with decidedly mixed company in the theatrical stews of Southwark.

Once, on a day of exceptionally fine weather, Winslow was strolling the upper deck amidships, where Shakespeare was working at the daily chore of manning the bilge pump. "So, Will, shall we make a seaman of you yet?"

Shakespeare paused, leaned on the pump, and sighed. "At the moment, Captain, I'd give a thousand furlongs of sea for an acre of barren ground." His features took on the look they sometimes did after he'd said something: an instant of intense concentration followed by a quick, satisfied nod. "Never again will I venture so far from home."

"Oh, come! You're no stay-at-home—you left War-wickshire for London. What was it? Many things send men to sea. Desire to see the world, or a nagging wife, are frequently named."

"You see through me, Captain. In truth, it was both of those. At eighteen I married a woman six years my senior. We had three children—a daughter, and then boy and girl twins. But afterwards . . . " Shakespeare sighed again. "If there be no great love in the beginning, heaven may decrease it upon better acquaintance." Concentration and nod. "I left, and for a time supported myself as a schoolmaster, and in other ways, before joining a company of actors. But I've also supported my family, sending them money the while."

"A common enough arrangement," Winslow nodded. And so it was, as young men moved to the burgeoning metropolis of London like iron filings to a magnet.

"So common as to include yourself, Captain?" Shakespeare inquired.

"Eh? No, I have no wife. I could never have supported a family while working my way up from the forecastle. And since I've achieved my captaincy . . . well, the occasion has never arisen." Winslow suddenly wondered why he had let himself be drawn into conversation by the lowliest member of his crew. Of course, Shakespeare was also an educated man, which made it difficult to know how to deal with him, as he lay outside the usual social categories. And there was something about him that encouraged confidences—indeed, drew them out. Still . . . "Well, back to the pump," Winslow commanded, strangely aware that he sounded stuffy, and even more strangely embarrassed by the fact. He moved on.

Yes, he reflected, turning his mind to other things and gazing at the placid sky, *the weather has favored this voyage. God must approve of the quest on which we are embarked.*

It was, of course, exactly the wrong thing to think. The gods of the sea, far older than the one God who had supplanted them and all their kin, hate nothing so much as self-satisfaction in mortals.

Winslow knew they were in for a storm when the clouds began scudding across the sky from west to east. That also told him that the coast on which they might be wrecked was not too far remote. He could only order the sails hauled in and hope for the best.

When the storm struck, it did not disappoint. Gales buffeted them for days, and rain choked the decks with water that sloshed back and forth as the ships pitched and heaved. Even many of the experienced seamen were sick, and the landsmen suffered terribly. Walsingham had, at this worst possible time, gotten the flux from drinking water that had gone bad as it always did on long voyages. The combination of that and seasickness left Winslow and Dee fearing for his life. The Queen was sick too, but bore it tight-lipped. The ladies-in-waiting were in too much agony even to complain.

John White suffered as much as any of them. But through it all he had only one obsessive concern: the towed shallops. If those craft were lost, he declared, they all might just as well have stayed in England.

The only member of their company who seemed to find any redeeming feature in the storm was Shakespeare. During one brief lull in the rains, Winslow was inspecting the weather deck when he saw the young actor clutching the handle of the bilge pump and retching. But when his stomach was emptied, his look was the familiar one that suggested he was committing a line to memory. Over the moaning of the winds and the rumbling of the thunder, Winslow caught: "And thou, all-shaking thunder, strike flat the thick rotundity o'the world!" Shakespeare gave a particularly self-satisfied nod.

"So you can find inspiration even in this, Will?" Winslow shouted over the noise.

Shakespeare looked up, wiped the residue of vomit from his mouth, and actually smiled. "Oh, yes, Captain. How could it be otherwise, in the midst of something this . . . vivid?"

" 'Vivid!' You might have other words for it if we're shipwrecked. Most of the islands people used to think dotted the Atlantic have turned out to be fables, but you never know."

"Ah—fables. The very word! Just think: we might be shipwrecked on a fabulous island of magical beings!"

"I'd prefer that we not be shipwrecked anywhere, thank you very much."

"But think of the possibilities!" Shakespeare took on a faraway look that a renewed gust of wind and rain did nothing to disturb. "A magician, living on the island in exile . . . and his daughter, who has never seen men other than her aged father, and knows only monsters and faërie . . . what a brave new world, she would think, that had such people in it . . . "

Winslow sighed, gathered his cloak around him against the renewed rain, and resumed his inspection.

When the storm finally lifted, *Greyhound* was nowhere to be seen. But a shore lay ahead. John White peered at it.

"Cape Fear," he announced.

"Good name," Gorham was heard to mutter.

"Congratulations, Dr. Dee," said Winslow. "We've arrived only a little south of our destination."

"Only a little distance," White cautioned, "but a great deal of difficulty. I well recall my second voyage to these shores, with their riptides."

His dourness was justified. The winds were still contrary, and they wasted days beating around the hazardous shoals of Cape Fear before they could begin following the coast northward. The smells wafting seaward from the marshes and pine forests to port tantalized them.

Presently, they sighted the barrier islands. The weather was still blustery and unsettled, and when a break in the sandbars appeared Winslow was sorely tempted to take *Heron* through it into the sheltered waters of the sound beyond.

"No, Captain," insisted White. "I recognize that island over there—Wococon, the Indians call it. On the second expedition, we tried what you're thinking of. Believe me, these waters are far more hazardous than what we went through at Cape Fear. All we accomplished was to run aground, under the pilotage of that rogue Simon Fernandez. No, we must continue up the coast to Port Ferdinando." He said the name with obvious distaste. Walsingham, who had recovered sufficiently to stand on the quarterdeck with the rest of them, was carefully expressionless.

"But from what you've told us, *Heron* can't enter there in safety any more than here."

"No. But if you anchor just outside Port Ferdinando, you can actually see Roanoke Island in the distance. The shallops won't have far to go . . . although honesty compels me to say that the going is treacherous."

"Is there any other kind along this damned coast?" Winslow demanded irritably. But when he made eye contact with Walsingham, the Principal Secretary nodded. Their hopes rested on White's hard-won knowledge. "Very well," he said without any great enthusiasm. "We'll proceed northward."

They continued up the coast, constantly taking depth soundings, while Winslow watched the horizon for *Greyhound*. He had hoped the storm would have carried the smaller ship to the same stretch of coast, but so far there was no sign of her, and he began to fear the worst.

Soon they were passing another barrier island that aroused White's memories of the earlier voyages. "Croatoan," he told them. "Birthplace of Manteo, the Secotan Indian who was such a help to us, and who journeyed to England with us after our first expedition here, four years ago." His face wore its frequent expression of uncomprehending hurt, of blighted hopes. "It was almost as though we had ventured into the Garden of Eden, or the Golden Age of which the pagan poets tell. The Secotan welcomed us with civility and friendship. Granganimeo, brother of King Wininga of the Secotan, made us welcome. Both are dead now, thanks to that madman Ralph Lane, who left this land in chaos."

"And yet," Winslow ventured, "didn't you go to Croatoan last year, after you and the colonists had been left on Roanoke Island?"

"Yes. My first task as governor was to order the houses repaired in Lane's fort, which fifteen of his soldiers had been left to hold when Drake evacuated everyone else. All we found of them was the bleaching skeleton of one. Once that had been attended to, I persuaded Captain Stafford, commander of the pinnace that had been left to us, to take some of us, including Manteo, to Croatoan. Manteo had many kindred still living there, including his mother. I needed to know if the Croatoans were still disposed to friendship toward us, in spite of everything Lane had done. At first I despaired, for they seemed hostile, and fled when we went for our guns. But then Manteo called to them—they hadn't recognized him in his English clothes, you see—and after that all was well as soon as we pledged not to plunder any of their food as Lane had. They promised to intercede for us with the rest of the Secotan—the people of Secota and Aquascogoc and Pomioc and other places. But in the end, the Croatoans couldn't mend the damage done by Lane's murder of Wininga. We were attacked. One of us, George Howe, was killed. We retaliated—I should have resisted the demands for that, but I didn't, to my shame. By the time I went back to England for help, Croatoan was the only place left where our people had any hope of finding friendship."

"Thanks to Manteo," Winslow observed.

"Indeed. Aside from the birth of my granddaughter, my only pleasurable memory of my final days of Roanoke Island is that I was able to reward Manteo in some measure for his faithful service. You see, Sir Walter had decided to exercise his powers under Her Majesty's grant and make him feudal lord of Roanoke, to hold that coast in Her Majesty's name while we went north and settled on the Chesapeake Bay as originally planned. So, after he was baptized, I exercised my powers as Sir Walter's deputy and declared him Lord of Roanoke and Dasemunkepeuc."

"Uh . . . Das . . . ?"

"Nobody else could pronounce it either," White admitted. "So we just called him Lord Manteo. He is now his people's governor as Her Majesty's vassal. I look forward to seeing him again almost as much as I do to greeting my own people."

The weather continued unsettled, and at the northern end of Croatoan Winslow sent the shallops to do soundings in search of a breach. But the shoals were too labyrinthine, and White was no help here. So they worked their way onward to the north, with infinite caution now that *Heron* was a vessel alone, containing all their lives as well as the hope of England.

Finally they sighted what White, with visible joy, declared to be Hatorask Island. Beyond was the open water of Port Ferdinando. To the west of it stretched the shallow waters of the protected sound. And in the distance, a speck against the mysterious continent beyond, an island could be glimpsed. White stood at the port rail and stared at it longingly.

"Roanoke Island," Winslow stated rather than asked.

White nodded, without taking his eyes off that barely visible island.

"Well," said Winslow, squinting at the westering sun, "it's too late to try for it now. Tomorrow morning we'll launch the shallops."

White nodded again, as though barely hearing. Winslow doubted he would get much sleep.

In the morning, Walsingham and Dee both wanted to be in the shore party, the former from a sense of duty and the latter out of sheer curiosity. Winslow, asserting his authority as captain, overruled them. He knew the passage, however short it seemed, would not be without its risks. Only able seamen—including Winslow himself —would accompany White in one of the shallops. The

other would go in the opposite direction to nearby Hatorask, for the fresh water of which they were desperately
in need.

"Fire the sakers and minions," he ordered Gorham,
"with a few seconds spacing between each shot. That
should let them know we're here."

"Yes," White agreed avidly. "They'll probably
acknowledge by building a fire on the shore."

The guns' crashing report echoed across the water,
filling the air with the rotten-eggs smell of burned powder and sending flocks of startled seabirds screeching
aloft. The landing party got awkwardly into the boat. The
weather was still more unsettled than Winslow liked, and
the boat pitched alarmingly in the choppy water. A man
fell over the side, and it took time to retrieve him. It
took still more time to maneuver away from *Heron*, and
when they approached the Port Ferdinando breach it
became apparent that the inrushing water of the rising
tide, which they could see breaking over the bar, had
turned the channel into a churning cauldron. They hung
on grimly, the men straining at the oars while Winslow
struggled to keep the craft bow-on into the swells lest
they capsize.

Finally they crossed the breach, and Winslow could
spare a glance at the distant island in search of the anticipated signal fire. But no smoke was to be seen.

It took hours to row across the unsettled waters of the
sound. All the while, White stared fixedly ahead as
though by sheer will he could force the appearance of
smoke. Finally the shallop ground ashore onto the sand
of Roanoke Island.

No one was in sight. The lack of any human sound
made the noise of the wind and the waves and the birds
seem like dead silence.

"Well, Master White," said Winslow, a little too loudly, "do you know where you are?"

"I think so." White's features were a study in mixed eagerness and bewilderment. "The settlement should be in this direction. It's where Lane had built his fort. We found it dismantled after being left here, but built new cottages there."

They set out along the sand and scrub, following the shore around the north end of the island, skirting the aromatic forest of loblolly pine. Presently, White sprinted ahead, scrambling up a sandy bank he clearly recognized. Before the rest of them could catch up to him, he had stopped dead.

There was a clearing ahead. But that wasn't what White was staring at. Just in front of him was a tree. Carved in its bark were the letters "CRO."

"What does it mean, Master White?" demanded Winslow. "Is it in a code?"

"No." White shook his head. His face was a sea of conflicting emotions, but he spoke calmly. "At the time I returned to England for help, the colonists were considering going to the mainland and moving to some place perhaps fifty miles inland, away from danger from the Secotan villages Lane had provoked into being our enemies. In order that I could find them on my return, it was agreed that they would carve the name of the place they had gone on trees, or on the doors of their cottages. And if they were in distress, they were to carve beside it a Maltese cross. There is no such cross here!" For an instant, hope came uppermost in the chaotic struggle his face reflected.

Winslow shook his head. "But where is 'CRO'?"

"I don't know. It is meaningless. So if they are gone . . . *how will we find them?*" White's look of hope vanished in panic like the sun going behind a dark cloud. With an inarticulate cry, he sprang forward. Winslow and the seamen could only follow.

This time, White was on his knees. His face reflected a despair too absolute for weeping.

A clearing was before them, holding a crude wooden palisade, dilapidated, overgrown with weeds, and quite obviously deserted. No one, Winslow estimated, had been here for at least a year.

"My daughter Eleanor," White whispered. "And her husband Ananias Dare. And their baby girl Virginia. And the baby boy born afterwards to Dyonis and Margery Harvie. And all the others. Gone. Even the houses. Gone."

Disinclined to disturb such utter desolation, Winslow walked around him and looked around. Nothing.

The sailors also dispersed about the clearing, looking about curiously. Inside the palisade they found a scatter of items—iron bars, shot for the sakers that had been left behind, and other items that might well have been left behind as too heavy to carry. All was overgrown with grass and weeds.

Suddenly, one of the men called out to Winslow. "Cap'n! These here look like fair letters. Can you . . . ?"

"Let's have a look, Grimson." Winslow walked over to where the illiterate sailor was pointing—a post by the right side of the entrance to the palisade. He stared for a moment, then released a whoop of laughter. "Master White! Come here. I think this is a sight that will make your heart sing."

White stumbled to his feet and joined Winslow. At first he simply stared. Then he fell to his knees again, but this time in an attitude of thanks to God. And this time his tears flowed.

"Croatoan!" he shouted. "Of course! That was what 'CRO' meant, but someone never had the chance to finish it. So now we know where they went. And . . . *no Maltese cross!* They are safe, with our Secotan friends on Croatoan Island!"

The sailors crowded around White, pummeling his back and shouting rough congratulations. He stood up and faced Winslow, his face a blazing sun of joy. "Captain, now we know where they are. If only we had fired signal guns when we passed Croatoan! But we must go there at once!"

— SIX —

IN FACT, GOING TO CROATOAN WASN'T AS SIMPLE AS THAT. Winslow tried to explain that to his listeners in *Heron's* cabin, but with difficulty. Walsingham and the Queen were landlubbers of the deepest dye. Dee's knowledge of navigation was in advance of his era in many ways, but his practical experience of the sea—until recently, at least—was limited to his voyage to Baffin Island with Martin Frobisher. And John White, who had crossed and recrossed the Atlantic more times than all but a few men, was afire with an eagerness that made naught of obstacles.

"You must understand," Winslow told them, "that we've already passed north of Croatoan. And the weather is still unsettled. The sound was choppy when we rowed the shallops back. Master White can tell you how difficult that was. I've doubled our cables, because I think a storm is coming soon—I can feel it in the clammy air." He sought for the words that would convey to these people a seaman's sense of the sea and its moods. He knew its mood now. He knew it in the roiling channel of Port Ferdinando.

"But Thomas, won't the wind be with us now, sailing southward?" asked Walsingham.

"It should be—but I'm not relying on that, in these disturbed seas. We'll have to stay close to Hatorask Island, lest those same winds blow us beyond Croatoan so that we'd have to fight our way back northward against contrary winds. That will mean risking the shoals as we try to work our way past the point of land south of Kenricks Mounts."

White's eyes pleaded with him. "Captain, my daughter and granddaughter and all the others are there. We've come so far, and are now so close!"

"I know. And with all my heart I want to risk this venture. But I cannot forget the fact that *Heron* is alone on this treacherous coast. And I cannot ignore what she is carrying . . ." Winslow's gaze strayed to the head of the table, where the Queen sat in silence.

"Captain Winslow," she said quietly, "are we agreed that my faithful subjects are on Croatoan Island, awaiting succor?"

"Such seems to be the case, Your Majesty."

"And you would have me abandon them out of fear for my own safety?" Elizabeth shook her head. "Sovereignty is more than power and privilege, Captain. It carries a burden as well. For most monarchs, most of the time, the trappings of power and privilege hold the burden so far at bay that it can easily be forgotten. But it is always there. And now fate has stripped me of those trappings and left me here off this wild weather-beaten coast, all alone with the burden. Those few score English subjects on Croatoan are my kingdom now—all the kingdom I have left." She rose to her feet, and the others perforce rose with her. "I do not wish to go before my Maker knowing that I failed, out of fear, to bear the burden to which I was born."

"Also," Dee put in with uncharacteristic diffidence, "they may have discovered that which the Gray Monks are seeking. For all we know, that was why they removed to Croatoan. As long as that possibility exists, we must pursue it."

"Very well," sighed Winslow. "We'll make the attempt."

They lost two anchors off the Kenricks Mounts point, as the ship plunged in the swells and Winslow fought to keep it from running aground on the bar. By sheer instinct, he steered *Heron* along a deep channel between the shoals until they were past Hatorask. There was a lull in the weather as they brought Croatoan in sight—although not a lull Winslow liked, for it was the sort that portended a storm. Nor did he like the fact that he had only two anchors remaining, in hurricane season. He dropped one of them and was about to order the firing of a signal gun when a lookout cried, "Sail ho!" and pointed southward.

Squinting into the distance, Winslow made out a flag with the cross of St. George. So had others, for cheers rang out. It was *Greyhound*.

The lull continued long enough for Captain Jonas Halleck to be rowed across to *Heron*. Winslow had only met him briefly before they had departed Plymouth. He was a stocky man in his early forties with a thick salt-and-pepper beard framing a weathered face. Winslow recognized him as a member of a vanishing breed of sea captain: illiterate, tough as brine-soaked leather, full of growling disdain for the rutters and the other new printed navigational aids that he couldn't read. But he knew how to estimate latitude, using the cross-staff, to within thirty miles on a good day.

"After the storm eased, we raised the coast well to the south," he rumbled, still averting his eyes from the exalted company in *Heron*'s cabin. The crowded meeting also included Gorham, whom Winslow had decided it would be well to invite, and who was practically digging his toes into the deck in his embarrassment at his social inferiority. There was barely room for the steward who kept their wine goblets full. "I feared we would encounter the Dons, in those latitudes. And indeed, we sighted one of their sails. But he was on a south-southwest course, running before the wind, and already astern of us."

"Still," Walsingham muttered, "it means they're patrolling this coast. And if you sighted them, it's possible that they sighted you as well. So it's also possible that, as soon as that captain makes his report, they'll know we're here."

"I doubt if it will affect matters much," said Dee. "If my sources of information are to be trusted, they'll be coming to this coast in force anyway."

"I assume that is meant to reassure me," said Walsingham dryly.

"At all events," Halleck resumed, "by God's grace we worked our way up the coast and rounded Cape Fear safely, despite the riptides. But one thing I must tell you. Looking astern as we came up from the south . . . Well, I have feel for these things. And I swear that there's a hurricane brewing down there. I can smell it."

A hurricane, with the Spaniards maybe coming behind it, Winslow brooded.

"Your Majesty, my lords," he said somberly, "if a hurricane catches us off this coast we'll be blown God knows where, and may very well not be able to return this season. If we are to attempt a landing on Croatoan, it must be now."

"Yes," said Walsingham with a decisive nod. "And this time, Thomas, I *will* accompany the landing party."

"And I," Dee put in hastily. "If whatever uncanny thing the Gray Monks seek is on Croatoan, I will be the most likely to recognize it for what it is."

"And I will also go, Captain," stated the Queen. She held up a hand to silence any protest. "I wish to feel solid land under my feet again. And if I understand Captain Halleck, those who go ashore may well be in better case than those who remain aboard ship, waiting for the hurricane."

Winslow started to open his mouth, but then closed it . . . and not just to avoid *lèse majesté*. The fact was that the Queen, besides being the Queen, was absolutely right. She would stand a better chance ashore—always assuming that White was correct about the friendliness of the local Indians. And he doubted that Walsingham would survive a hurricane aboard ship, even on the large assumption that the ship itself survived.

"Your Majesty's wishes are my command," he said smoothly. "But I cannot be responsible for the comfort or dignity or safety of your ladies-in-waiting. They must remain aboard ship." He gave the boatswain a significant look. Gorham returned it. No words were necessary. The ladies-in-waiting would be left alone in the Queen's absence.

For an instant, Elizabeth seemed about to take exception to the word *must*. But then she subsided and nodded shortly. "Yes. You are right, Captain. But my guards shall accompany me, for the sake of the royal dignity."

And the squad of soldiers, commanded by a young but competent-seeming lieutenant named Fenton, might well come in handy, Winslow reflected. "Of course, Your Majesty. All shall be as you command. And at any rate, there'll be little use for any men but experienced mariners aboard the ship in the storm." He held out his goblet for a refill. As he did, he noticed the identity of the steward: Shakespeare, performing one of the tasks Gorham had decided he could probably manage. Moved by a sudden, obscure impulse, he added, "For the same reason, we'll take Master Shakespeare ashore. I suspect an actor would be even less use in a storm than soldiers." There were chuckles around the table.

"Captain Halleck," Winslow resumed, "while I am ashore with the landing party, you will be in command of the fleet." He forced himself not to smile at the word *fleet*. "If a hurricane does indeed strike, you will endeavor to ride it out. But if the survival of the ships is at stake, you will run before it. Do I make myself clear?"

"Aye," Halleck rumbled, meeting Winslow's eyes. They both knew that might well mean that the landing party, including the Queen, would be out of reach of succor for a year—not that any help was likely to come from conquered England next year, or ever. But neither saw any need to mention it.

"Very well," said Winslow. "We'll go ashore in the morning. Boatswain, see to the preparations. And fire the signal guns."

But, as at Roanoke, there was no answering fire ashore.

It was the rising sea that let Winslow know, with sickening certainty, that they were in for it. He knew that feeling, that coiling, tightening tension. Beneath the sullen surface, nature was gathering its forces and mustering its malevolence, building up to an explosive release. When it came, he knew it would be sudden.

They were barely ashore on Croatoan when the wind shifted with an abruptness that even the landlubbers among them noticed. The Queen turned to Winslow with a look of concern. She pointed at the forest beyond the beach.

"Should we take shelter under the trees, Captain?"

"No, Your Majesty. There's going to be much lightning. We must stay here in the open." He turned to the sailors. "You know what to do. Lieutenant Fenton, I'll be obliged if your men lend a hand."

The sailors needed no further instructions, for they knew what was coming. With the clumsy but willing help of the soldiers, who could sense the imminence of danger, they upended the boats and stretched a sailcloth between them, creating a large, crude tent. Despite the waxing wind, they were all slick with sweat in the damp tropic air that wind was bringing with it from the womb of hurricanes.

"Your Majesty," said Winslow, indicating the cramped space in the shelter, too low to stand up, "I regret the indignity, but—"

"Faugh!" The Queen scrambled under the canvas awning. She had barely done so when the whistling sigh of the wind abruptly rose to a roar, and the sailors assigned to hold the ropes at the sail's corners barely managed to hold on.

The hurricane was like an elemental principle of malicious fury as it came blasting up the coast. The howling, shrieking roar of the wind rose still higher, but it was drowned out by a continuous cannonade of thunder. Lightning stabbed with insensate violence, and rain fell in sheets that periodically drenched them despite the muscle-straining efforts of relays of men to hold the ropes down. For what seemed an eternity of misery, they huddled under the canvas. During a lull in the din, Winslow heard Shakespeare, close beside him, mutter, "I will shroud here till the dregs of the storm be past." Even at this moment, the young actor gave his quick brow-furrowing nod, like a clerk filing something in its proper place.

Finally the storm passed, leaving in its wake an eerie combination of damp air and clear sky. The hot afternoon sun shone down on a beach littered with the detritus of the storm. Aside from themselves, the island seemed empty of humanity.

They stumbled to their feet as the sailors drew back the canvas and began to fold it, letting the sun warm their shivering bodies and dry their wet clothes. With a dead lack of hope, Winslow looked seaward. He was not disappointed in his pessimistic assumptions. Not a sail was to be seen on the horizon. *Heron* and *Greyhound* were wherever the storm had taken them. He dared to hope that place was not the bottom of the ocean.

"Well, Master White," he said heavily, "it seems we must go in search of your colonists. Dr. Dee, perhaps you should come too. Lieutenant Fenton, you and your men will remain here on the beach and guard Her Majesty and the Principal Secretary."

"You would leave us here while you go adventuring, Captain?" the Queen inquired archly. "I believe I've had quite enough of this beach for the present."

"Very good, Your Majesty. But please follow well behind us with your guards and listen for any cries of alarm from us up ahead."

"What dangers do you anticipate, Captain, on an island inhabited by friendly Indians and our own loyal subjects?"

"Hopefully none, Your Majesty. But I cannot forget that there was no reply to our signal gun."

On that somewhat dampening note, they struck out into the forest of loblolly and live oak, heavy with the scent of wild muscadine grapes. Presently they ascended the top of a sandy ridge. All at once, White could stand it no longer. "Hallo!" he shouted. "It is I, Governor White, father of Eleanor Dare, and I have returned as I promised. Come out!"

And, slowly, figures that had been invisible because of their motionlessness began to emerge from the surviving woods.

The sailors clutched their weapons and formed a defensive crescent as the Indians silently approached. They looked like John White's paintings come to life: nearly naked brown-skinned men whose black hair was shaven on the sides, leaving a crest on top. Their black eyes, squeezed into slits by their high cheekbones, peered out from elaborately tattooed faces. They were armed with bows which didn't look very powerful to Winslow's eye but which, he imagined, would do well enough at this range.

For a moment, the tableau held. Then the Indians parted, making way for an individual who had the same racial characteristics as the rest of them, including the tattoos, but who differed from them in two important ways. First, he was smiling. Secondly, he was wearing the remains of an English taffeta blouse covered by a doublet that had quite obviously never been washed in its entire not-inconsiderable lifespan.

Winslow and his sailors could only stare at this apparition. But John White, after an incredulous instant, bounded forward with a joyous whoop and embraced the Indian, who burst into an English-sounding laugh and returned the hug, repeatedly exclaiming, "Old friend, old friend!" Then White cleared his throat, assumed a pose of formality, and turned back to his nonplussed companions.

"Captain, Dr. Dee, I crave pardon for so forgetting myself in the excitement of the moment. We are in the presence of nobility. Allow me to present you to Lord Manteo of Roanoke and Dasemunkepeuc."

After the barest hesitation, Winslow bowed. Dee and the sailors followed suit. Manteo inclined his head with a gracious dignity that would have done credit to Hampton Court.

"And will you not introduce us as well, Master White?" came the Queen's voice from behind them as she stepped forward. Lieutenant Fenton and his soldiers, not knowing what to make of the scene but knowing bows and arrows when they saw them, started to raise their weapons. The Queen halted them with a peremptory gesture and stood before her feudal vassal.

Manteo stared intently at the bedraggled woman in the still-damp riding outfit, so different from the elaborately gowned and made-up figure to whom he had once been presented at court. Then his eyes widened with dawning recognition and he fell to his knees.

"*Weroanza* Elizabeth!" he cried. Then he turned, still kneeling, to his fellow tribesmen. "*Weroanza* Elizabeth!" They all dropped their bows and practically fell on their faces.

"What is he saying, Master White?" Walsingham wanted to know.

"It is their title for Her Majesty, Mr. Secretary." White seemed embarrassed.

"Yes, but what does it signify, exactly?"

"Well, er . . . it means 'Big Chief Elizabeth.' "

For an instant Winslow thought the Queen was going to explode with the effort of holding back a delighted guffaw. "Well," she finally gasped, smoothing out her features and taking a deep breath, "on my return to England I shall assuredly ask Parliament to add that to the list of my official titles." She looked down into the beaming, tattooed brown face and bestowed a smile that could have won the heart of a Puritan. "Arise, Lord Manteo. It gladdens us to greet our loyal subjects of Virginia. And know this: while you have had wiser and mightier Big Chiefs, you have had none who loved you better."

Manteo, his face transfigured, rose. He turned to his fellow tribesmen and translated. They leaped to their feet, waving their bows and shouting "*Weroanza* Elizabeth," although the name was barely recognizable on their tongues. Winslow could barely hear Shakespeare muttering behind him, but he caught the words *most royal*.

"But," the Queen continued when she could make herself heard, "we would also greet our loyal *English* subjects on this island, where we have been given to believe that they sought refuge among you."

"That's right!" John White, in his eagerness, came close to committing the inconceivable solecism of interrupting the Queen. "We saw the word 'Croatoan' carved on a tree on Roanoke, to let us know they had come here. Where are they? My daughter Eleanor Dare and granddaughter Virginia Dare, and all the rest?"

Manteo's face fell, and he spoke in his careful but very good English. "Some of them came here, yes. Your daughter and her infant were among them. But now they are gone."

"Gone?" White's features froze. "You mean dead?"

"No. I mean . . . gone." Manteo looked deeply troubled. "What happened to them was a wrongness. Something that should not happen, for it violated God's laws."

"The Gray Monks!" gasped John Dee. He stepped forward eagerly. "Tell us! Describe what happened."

Manteo's eyes slid away. "One of the Englishmen remains here, in our village. You should ask him. Perhaps he understands. As for me . . . well, you know I am a good Christian."

"Of course, Manteo," White soothed. "Did I not preside over your baptism last year?"

"Then you know I do not speak lightly when I say it was like something out of the old, dark, stupid ways before you brought the true faith to us. It was like something that God—the God of this world—never meant to allow."

"I fear he may be right," Dee murmured.

Manteo's village was as John White remembered: a fence-like palisade surrounding almost twenty longhouses roughly constructed of poles and draped with rush mats that could be rolled up to admit light.

They passed through the palisade in silence and proceeded between the longhouses and past the central firepit. All of them but White stared at the residents, especially the women: even more heavily tattooed than the men, and with breasts partially exposed by the knee-length deerskin garments they wore. Those garments left them quite naked behind, as the sailors did not fail to notice the first time one of them turned around.

The stares they got in return were of a curious quality: not stares of amazement, for English people were no longer a novelty here, but rather of apprehension, as though the English had become linked in these people's minds with uncanny and ill-omened things.

Manteo, who was rapidly proving himself as indispensable as White had said he was, broke the mood by announcing the identity of the red-haired English woman, and shouts of "*Weroanza* Elizabeth" rang out. Then he led them to one of the longhouses. The sailors and soldiers sank gratefully to the ground outside and ate the food the Indian women brought. But the Queen, Walsingham, Dee, Winslow and White followed Manteo into the smoky interior, where a man in the remnants of English clothing lay on a pallet. He was scraggly-bearded and unhealthy-looking, and his left leg was wrapped in some kind of large leaves.

"Dick Taverner!" exclaimed White.

The man lifted himself on one elbow and stared through the gloom. "Master White?" He shook his head. "No, it can't be. The fever must be back."

"It's I, Dick. I promised I'd be back, didn't I?"

"But . . . you said you'd be back in three months. How long has it been? We gave up on you."

"I tried, Dick. As God is my witness, I tried. But much has happened in the world beyond this coast. Which reminds me . . . " He cleared his throat and spoke with awkward formality. "Your Majesty, I present your loyal subject Richard Taverner."

Taverner's expression passed into something beyond bewilderment as the Queen stepped into his line of sight. "The fever . . . " he mumbled, blinking stupidly. But then he shook his head violently and stared. "No . . . I've gone mad in this place."

"You are not mad, Master Taverner," said the Queen with a smile, "and I honor you for remaining faithful. . . . No, be still!" she added hastily as Taverner tried with obvious pain, to bring his legs under him and kneel.

"But . . . but," stammered Taverner as he sank gratefully back down, "how can it be that Your Majesty is here?"

"I dare say Lord Manteo has wondered the same thing." The Indian's expression gave ample confirmation. "But I have waited until we could speak privately, for these are not the tidings you wish to hear. I have come seeking refuge." The Queen took a deep breath. "You must remember that war with Spain was in the air even before you departed England last year."

"Yes, Your Majesty. The Scots queen was two months dead when we set sail. The air was full of rumors of the Armada the King of Spain was preparing. Just weeks before our departure, Sir Francis Drake had set out from Plymouth. Everyone said he was to attack the Armada before it could sail."

"Aye!" The Queen's eyes flamed. "Drake sailed into Cadiz harbor like the daring corsair he was. As he himself said afterwards, he 'singed the King of Spain's beard.' " The fire in her eyes guttered out. "But it was all for naught. Drake delayed the Armada's sailing, but it sailed this year. And as God is my witness, we would still have seen it off, if we'd had only men to contend with! We were defeated not by men, but by unnatural sorcery."

Taverner's face took on an even more unhealthy shade. "The Gray Monks?"

"Yes. Our fleet—Drake, Lord Howard, everyone —was consumed in St. Antony's fire. There was nothing left to prevent the Duke of Parma's forces from landing in England, and nothing in England could stop them." The Queen motioned Walsingham and Winslow forward. "My Principal Secretary persuaded me that my duty to my people required me to escape from England aboard captain Winslow's ship. We came here because my advisor Dr. Dee believes the Gray Monks are in search of something among these islands—something that may hold the key to their power."

"The Gray Monks," Taverner repeated in tones of horror. "Sorcery. Yes. That would explain what happened here."

"But what *did* happen here?" demanded White. "Where are the others?"

"Yes," Dee urged. "You must tell us everything."

Taverner took a deep breath. "When you did not return, Master White, we divided. Most of the men went inland, led by those of the Assistants who didn't have wives and children dependent on them, to try to find the Chesapeake Bay where we were meant to settle. God alone knows if they still live, and where they are if they do."

"The 'Assistants'?" Dee queried.

"Men appointed by Sir Walter to assist me in governing the colony," White explained impatiently. "Go on, Dick."

"But only able-bodied single men went with them. It was decided that married couples and their children should go to Croatoan, where thanks to Manteo we could hope to find friends, among whom we could seek shelter."

"My daughter Eleanor," White said eagerly. "And her husband, and her infant daughter Virginia Dare."

"Aye. And the others with children: eleven children and seventeen women in all. Also twenty-one of the men, husbands and certain others—including me, for I had laid open my leg and it had grown inflamed. As you see, it's never healed. So I had to be carried in a litter by some of Manteo's men. We were marching inland, toward this village, when we reached a clearing. No, not a clearing, really—just an area of second-growth woods, much younger than what grew around it, as though it had been somehow cleared many years ago . . . but not by fire, for the outlines of it were too regular.

"All at once, my litter bearers stopped. Manteo said it was because his people always avoid that area—they say it's bad luck. While he argued with them, the English people kept on going and . . . and . . . "

"Yes?" Walsingham prompted. "Continue."

"You'll think me a liar, your lordship. Or mad."

"Tell them, Richard," said Manteo. "I will vouch for you."

Taverner swallowed. "As the people walked into that strange area, they began to . . . to *fade out*. But only for an instant, so short I would have missed it if I hadn't been watching them. Then they were *gone*, without a trace!" Taverner looked from face to face with a pleading look. "As I am a Christian, Your Majesty, I swear it's true."

"It is true," said Manteo solemnly. "And I too am a Christian. When I was a boy, old men claimed their grandfathers had told them that something like a tremendous thunderclap cleared out that area and then roared on southwestward. And ever since then, there have been stories of people disappearing there. But this is the first time that anyone has seen it happening."

"This must be it!" Dee's voice trembled with excitement. "Anything so monstrous can only be the work of the Gray Monks!"

"No doubt," said Walsingham with his usual calm thoughtfulness. "Or . . . could it be that this event of which the Indians' forefathers spoke was nothing less than the entry of the Gray Monks into the world? Remember, Florida is southwestward of here."

Dee stared at him, for not even his imagination had reached so far.

"But where did they enter from?" Winslow breathed. "Hell?" No one answered him.

"Well," said the Queen, shattering the silence, "I would see this uncanny place." And before anyone could react, she was sweeping out of the longhouse. The others could only scramble after her.

"Your Majesty," Winslow called out to her back, "I can't allow you to endanger yourself this way!"

"*Allow* me?" she stopped and whirled around to face him with an abruptness that almost made him fall over backwards. Rage blazed in her eyes. "You may have authority over everyone on your ship, Captain, but now we are ashore. You do not command here."

"But Your Majesty," wheezed Walsingham, catching up, "your life is too precious to—"

"By the blood of almighty God, am I the only one here who *isn't* an old woman?" The Queen turned from them contemptuously. "Lieutenant Fenton, you and your men will accompany me. Lord Manteo, lead the way. The rest of you," she added witheringly, "may remain here if you choose." And she was off again.

Repressing an oath, Winslow gestured to his sailors. They fell in behind Fenton's soldiers, forming up around Walsingham, Dee and White. Shakespeare formed up with them, gamely enough; someone had found him a boarding pike. Hopefully he knew the difference between stage fighting and the real thing. Winslow took his place in front with the Queen, Fenton and Manteo as they left the village and plunged into the forest.

The area was as Taverner had described it, and Winslow felt his neck hairs prickle at the indefinable wrongness of it. Even the Queen was visibly taken aback for a moment. Then, shoulders back, she strode forward. The others could only follow.

Manteo was the only one to hold back. His Christianity was too new to have wholly banished the older beliefs from his mind—all the more so inasmuch as he had seen confirmation of those beliefs with his own eyes less than a year ago. So he hesitated . . . and saw the English begin to fade from sight rapidly.

"*Weroanza* Elizabeth!" he screamed, and in defiance of all the generations of his ancestors he gathered himself to spring forward.

But then the too-sharply defined space in the forest was empty. And Manteo, all vestiges of Christianity vanished, fell to his knees and howled desolately.

— SEVEN —

ODDLY ENOUGH, IT NEVER OCCURRED TO WINSLOW TO think he was going mad.

Afterwards, when he had time to reflect, he decided that was because he knew this was something not even the maddest of human minds could have dredged up from its reservoir of fears and fantasies. Monsters and devils, perhaps. Perhaps even the sight of the world being consumed by fire or flood. But not the world fading away, losing its color and becoming blurred and colorless—except for his companions, who remained as before, in sharp contrast to the unnatural twilight world around them. Sounds were fading too, for Manteo's cry seemed to come from a vast distance and then go out altogether.

111

Besides, it only lasted for less than a minute. Manteo going to his knees was the last thing Winslow saw. Then the world vanished altogether and there was . . . nothing.

Just that. Nothing. Not even blackness. He was afloat in an indescribable void which held only the others who had accompanied him. And even they could not be seen. There was no word for the way in which he was conscious of them, for it had nothing to do with the ordinary senses. Nor could he tell how close they were, for there was no such thing as distance. Nevertheless, in some way his language held no words for, he knew they were receding from him, passing beyond his ken.

He screamed. He could not even hear himself scream.

But then, he could not see himself either. His consciousness, his soul, was disembodied and adrift, all alone in nothingness.

He had never thought Hell would be like this.

But then, in the same fashion as before, he sensed that the others were reentering his frame of reference. Which, in turn, meant he *had* a frame of reference again. The infinite emptiness was acquiring a kind of texture.

As abruptly as it had vanished, reality reappeared, and his companions were there in the same sharp contrast of color and solidity against the dim gray world around them.

Only . . . it wasn't the *same* world.

Winslow could see that at once. This rolling landscape was nothing like what had surrounded them on Croatoan Island before it had faded away. That was obvious even before reality firmed up and regained light and color and sound.

They stood on a hillside in what looked like late-afternoon summer sun, overlooking a wide valley that stretched off to the hazy limits of vision, a countryside of many streams and lakes, with a scattering of low pale-tinted structures among foliage that more than half concealed them. Even at a distance, there was something peculiar about the trees. Winslow spied a flock of birds. They didn't look quite right either.

They all stood stock-still, staring about them and then staring at each other in silence. No one screamed. What had happened to them had been too quick, and too foreign from all normal experience, for ordinary terror or panic. In a corner of his mind where he could still be amused, Winslow noted that for once Shakespeare had nothing to say.

It came as no surprise to him that the Queen was the first to break the hush.

"Have we died, Doctor Dee?" she inquired in a rock-steady voice.

The brutally direct question brought the magus out of shock. "I think not, Your Majesty. I see no choirs of angels, as one would expect in Heaven. And this land bears even less resemblance to . . . the other alternative."

"Then where are we?" the Queen demanded.

"And how were we transported to this place?" added Walsingham, whose recovery of his mental equilibrium was as unsurprising to Winslow as the Queen's.

"The faërie lords have spirited us away by magic!" came the quavering Welsh-accented voice of one of Lieutenant Fenton's soldiers. "We're under timeless Elf Hill!"

"Enough of that talk, Owain!" rasped Fenton.

"I fear, Lieutenant, that it holds as much or as little likelihood as anything else," said Shakespeare with a small, tremulous smile.

Winslow voiced a thought that had entered his mind from he knew not where. "Can this be where the Gray Monks came from? Perhaps we've entered their world in the same uncanny way they entered ours."

They all stared at him.

"It would explain much . . . " Dee muttered to himself.

"I see none of them about," observed Walsingham, ever the voice of realism.

"Well," said the Queen briskly, "lest they arrive, we should seek shelter. I believe I see buildings in yonder valley. Perhaps we can even find the colonists who departed from Croatoan as we did, or at least word of them."

"A moment, Your Majesty." Something in Winslow's voice made even the Queen pause. He stood for a moment, looking around him, committing to memory what this ridgeline and that copse of trees looked like from where he stood. He had gone on raids deep into Spanish territory, and had learned to fix locations in his mind. After a few seconds he blinked, and turned to meet the Queen's quizzical look.

"I know not by what miracle or sorcery we came here, Your Majesty. But I beg you to recall that it has happened more than once on Croatoan Island—*at the same place.* I wonder if this place where we have appeared holds the same divine or magical potency. If so, we may wish to return to it."

"In order to return to Croatoan, you mean," Walsingham stated rather than asked.

"I think it may well be so, Mr. Secretary. And, should it become necessary, I am confident that I will know when I am here at—" he gave the Welsh soldier Owain a wink "—Elf Hill."

The Queen smiled. "As good a name for it as any, Captain. And now, let us proceed."

As they walked down into the valley, Winslow saw that he had not been mistaken about the strangeness of the trees. None of them was like any he had ever seen in any land to which he had voyaged. The leaves were a variety of odd shapes, and their characteristic yellowish-green color lent an autumnal look to what felt like summer. Many of them were hung with unfamiliar fruits which no one felt the urge to sample.

As they descended into the valley, they came among the buildings. But there were no people as they had hoped. These structures, built to the tenets of a strange, curving architecture out of materials Winslow could not identify, were long abandoned and mostly collapsed. In many cases, they had clearly been seared and smashed by titanic forces of some kind. That had been a very long time ago, for the forest had taken over the ruins. But this was a different kind of forest: trees of various colors and shapes, blazing flowers, feathery shrubs, an overall look of diverse exoticism.

It reminded Winslow of a garden left untended for too long, allowed to run riot. And that, he decided, was precisely what it was. This had been a city unlike any he had ever known, with no differentiation between city and parkland. And after the city had been devastated, the ubiquitous gardens had overspread their bounds, invading the crumbling buildings.

"One thing at least I am now certain of," John Dee murmured, peering at a huge violet-and-viridian flower.

"Yes?" Winslow queried in the same hushed tone.

"I had thought we might have been spirited to some remote and unknown part of our own world, perhaps even beyond Cathay. But this—" he made a vague gesture indicating the runaway vegetation "—is no part of creation as we know it."

They proceeded in silence along the old thoroughfares, now cracked and weed-choked but still discernible. The soldiers and sailors, deployed around the Queen and the other noncombatants, were tensely watchful. But the only motion they glimpsed was that of occasional small, unfamiliar animals scurrying through the underbrush and darting into cracks in walls.

It took a moment before Winslow realized that he was hearing a sound that was neither the chittering of the animals nor the cries of birds. It failed to register at first, for it was a kind of sound neither he nor any of the others had ever heard—a low, buzzing hum like nothing in nature, and like nothing produced by man. It took another moment before he spotted the source of the sound, as the sunlight flashed on a distant metallic craft that was sailing through the sky.

At first he could only stare. One by one, the others followed his stare and, like him, were struck dumb by the manifest impossibility their eyes reported.

But then he saw that the flying metal boat had changed course and was headed in their direction.

"Run!" he cried, shaking off his paralysis.

"Take shelter in here!" urged Lieutenant Fenton, indicating a large burned-out building across the way, its roof largely fallen in. Winslow wasn't sure how much good that would do . . . but, on reflection, it was far from clear that running would do any good either. He joined with Fenton in herding everyone through the great building's wide entryway and the gaps where its walls had crumbled.

The sorcerous flying boat swooped in on them with soul-shaking rapidity, coming to a halt above the street and hovering by the same magic that allowed it to fly (for it had no masts or sails). Then, its humming sound rising to a whine, it settled to the street in a cloud of disturbed dust. Its size now became evident: perhaps sixty feet long and twenty wide. It was in the form of an open-topped raft, so its occupants also became visible . . . and all at once the terror aroused in Winslow and the others by the uncanny vessel itself was as nothing.

"The Gray Monks!" gasped John Dee.

Winslow had never met a member of the dread Order of St. Antony, but he had heard enough stories to recognize the diminutive hairless beings with the huge dark eyes. Yet these were not wearing the gray habits that had given them their name. Instead, they wore close-fitting garments of some unfamiliar silvery material, seemingly all one piece, from neck to toe. *If they have toes*, thought Winslow in a flash of supreme irrelevance. As the raft settled to a halt and the whining sound diminished and fell silent, several of them hopped down onto the street. The tubular implements they carried looked like no guns of Winslow's experience, but they held them like guns as they deployed in a crescent facing the ruined building. Behind them, a larger version of those implements was lowered over the raft's gunwale and set up on a three-legged base under the supervision of one of the oddly dressed Gray Monks. But the drably brown-clad pair who did the work, and who behaved in the unmistakable manner of slaves, were . . . something else.

They were no taller than the Gray Monks, standing no more than four and a half feet, but size was their only point of resemblance. At first glance, they looked like miniature men, wirily built, with long hair in shades of reddish brown. But their arms and legs were longer than those of men—not absolutely, but in proportion to their bodies. And their beardless faces—whose color was a lighter reflection of their hair's, as though the latter's pigments had seeped into it—were of a strange cast: narrow jaws, tilted cheekbones and eyebrows, and large pointed ears.

The word *elfin* entered Winslow's mind even as he heard Owain stammer, "See, I *told* you!"

"Stand fast!" Fenton commanded his men. They formed a line inside the barn-door-wide entryway and hurriedly measured priming powder into the pans of their arquebuses. Then they clamped the slow-burning matches into the serpentines. The sailors flanking them gripped their assortment of weapons. Winslow—slowly, so as not to precipitate anything with an abrupt motion —drew his blade. In keeping with his social pretensions as a ship owner, it was a gentleman's backsword: straight, basket-hilted, single-edged to give the blade enough weight and strength to chop bone.

One of the Gray Monks, with gold insignia of some kind on the chest of his silvery garment, stood at the rail of what Winslow thought of as the craft's quarterdeck. He had always heard that they spoke in a thin, whispering hiss that did not carry well. This one spoke into an implement like a squat horn, which amplified his words. It didn't make them understandable, however, for they were in a language like none Winslow had ever heard in even the most cosmopolitan seaports. But he knew a demand for surrender when he heard it.

"I wonder why they don't speak to us in Latin?" Dee sounded puzzled.

"We'll try answering them in that tongue," said Walsingham, who proceeded to do so.

The only result was that the Gray Monk in the ornamented garment, with an unmistakable gesture of exasperation, gave an order to his subordinates in another, even stranger-sounding language. They began a purposeful advance on the ruined building.

Winslow wasn't sure exactly what happened, for Fenton gave no order. Maybe a soldier's nerves snapped, or maybe a stray spark caused an accidental discharge. But an arquebus crashed out, and the rest of the soldiers, their nerves already stretched to the snapping point, fired a deafening volley. Heavy lead balls smashed into several of the approaching Gray Monks, who staggered backwards. But, even through the rotten eggs-smelling cloud of smoke, it was clear that there had been no other effect. The strange silvery suits had a magical quality of invulnerability.

Then the Gray Monks began to return fire. But it was not gunfire as the Englishmen knew it. Winslow saw a line of crackling light from one of the strange weapons spear a soldier's chest, which emitted a burst of pink steam through the hole that had been burned in his armor, as though the blood and water of his body had been instantaneously superheated beyond the boiling point.

There was no time for thought. With a wild cry, Winslow sprang forward, and the sailors followed him. So did the soldiers, dropping their useless firearms and drawing their short swords. The Gray Monks' fire wavered, as though the sudden charge had caught them off balance. Winslow struck the weapon of one of them aside, recovered from the swing, and brought his backsword around in a slash across the Gray Monk's torso. The blade sliced through the silvery material, and a fluid that did not look like normal Christian blood spurted. As the Gray Monk collapsed, squalling, Winslow spent some very tiny fraction of a second wondering how his sword had done what arquebus balls had not. Was the potency of the suit's magic somehow related to the speed of that which struck it?

There was no time for further speculation as he charged into the melee. The Gray Monks were recovering from their surprise and bringing their magic weapons to bear. But at knife-range they had little time to aim them. And the English were mad with sudden release. They had found themselves powerlessly in the grip of a situation they could not comprehend, with no useful way of striking back. Here, at last, was something they could understand.

Winslow saw Fenton leap past him and thrust his sword through a Gray Monk where the heart would have been on a man. There was none of the gush of blood that such a thrust should have occasioned, but it seemed to serve well enough as the Gray Monk sank to the ground. Their eyes met for an instant and Fenton flashed Winslow a grin as he sprang forward again . . .

And then they were face to face with the large weapon on the three-legged stand. And the Gray Monks had plenty of time to aim it.

Winslow saw it swinging toward Shakespeare, who was emerging from the fray with a bloody boarding pike.

With a cry, Fenton sprang forward, interposing himself, seeking that weapon's crew with his sword.

There was a dazzling flash, and Fenton's head and chest cavity simply exploded into a grayish-pink shower that sprayed Winslow's eyes.

But he could still see, blurrily, as the weapon swung around and one of *Heron*'s sailors ceased to be. And then another . . .

He stumbled to his knees under another shower of gore, and squeezed his eyes shut. *This is the end,* his innermost soul cried from the pits of despair. *We cannot prevail. We were foolish to try. England is gone . . .*

Then, penetrating to the depths to which his soul had sunk, came the sound of wild cries.

He opened his eyes. Warriors were leaping up behind the line of Gray Monks, attacking it from the rear with mad abandon. Warriors of two kinds. Some were of the elfin sort he had previously seen as slaves . . . but these were obviously anything but slaves. A few of them were armed with the same weapons as the Gray Monks, whose magic silvery garments evidently provided no protection against them. The rest carried a kind of two-handed slashing sword with which Winslow was unfamiliar, but which they wielded with obvious skill. They cleared the Gray Monks away from the heavy weapon and wrestled the slaves of their own sort down, tying them with no more force than was necessary to overcome their strangely listless struggles.

But the other attackers were human—human and to all appearances Englishmen, even though they wore the same sort of odd tunic-and-trousers outfit as their allies, in the same range of earth tones, and were armed with the same combination of weapons, although their edged blades seemed designed to exploit human reach and strength.

But what Winslow mostly noticed about the new human arrivals was that their leader was a woman.

She leapt into the Gray Monks' midst with a two-handed curved blade calculated to maximize the effect of its wielder's upper body strength. And she leapt with a twisting midair motion and a series of slashes he could not follow. Then she landed on her feet . . . and a Gray Monk to her right was clutching the blood-spurting stump of his right arm, while another Gray Monk to her left was sinking to his knees trying to hold in his spilling inhuman guts.

With the barest pause, she was in motion again with the same blinding speed, bringing her blade around in a wide, flashing figure-eight . . . and the two Gray Monks' heads were sliding down from their severed necks and falling to the dust before their lifeless bodies slumped down to join them.

For a moment Winslow simply stared, with a nonverbal thought that could only have been rendered as, *What a woman!*

But then he remembered that a battle was still in progress. He sprang to his feet and led a final charge. The Gray Monks still aboard the flying raft started to take it aloft. But the elflike beings aimed the heavy weapon they had captured at its underside, toward the stern. The sizzling tunnel of light that marked the weapon's passage stabbed forth, and with an internal explosion the vessel lost control and crashed into the foliage of the ruined city.

Winslow found himself face to face with the female leader of his new-found allies. She looked to be about nineteen or twenty, with a body that was fully female but whose litheness could only be the product of years of strenuous campaigning. Her hair was a very dark chestnut, pulled back into a thick braid lest it blind her eyes in combat. Her features, while regular, were too strongly marked for conventional prettiness, and her skin was unfashionably tanned. Her eyes, green with only the slightest flecks of hazel, met his boldly.

Unable to think of anything else to do, he smiled.

She smiled back . . . and, with the same incredible speed she had shown before, whipped out a throwing knife from her belt and hurled it at his head.

He didn't have time to blink, much less to duck. But as soon as he was aware it was happening, the knife had flashed past him, and the woman, still smiling, was indicating with a jerk of her chin that he should look behind him.

He turned around. A Gray Monk, who had been pointing a weapon at his back, was sagging to the ground. The knife hilt protruded from his left eye.

He turned back to the extraordinary young woman and spoke with no expectation of being understood. "It would seem you've saved my life."

"So it would seem," she answered dryly, with a nod.

His jaw dropped. "You speak English!"

"I *am* English! So are we all, who found ourselves here after coming through the wound the Grella ripped in creation at Croatoan."

Out of the corner of his eye, Winslow saw John White stiffen.

"Then, my child," came the Queen's voice as she approached from the ruined building, "perhaps you know who *I* am."

Winslow fell to one knee, followed by others around him. The young woman stared with huge eyes. "The Queen? No, it can't be!" But she fell to her knees. "It must be true. You are as the elders described you. I was brought up on tales of England. Only . . . shouldn't you be older? And how can it be that you are here?"

"I am here seeking refuge. It's a long story."

"Then I fear it must wait. We cannot remain here. We barely have time to do what must be done." She indicated her followers, who were methodically splashing each of the dead Gray Monks with some fluid and setting them afire, as though it was necessary that they be consumed and not merely killed.

One of the small, wiry beings ran up to the young woman, and they conversed for a moment in what Winslow recognized as the language the Gray Monk had first used to hail them. Then she turned back to the Queen. "We have less time than I thought. The Grella are returning."

"You used that word before," Winslow said. "Do you mean . . . ?" He indicated the silver-clad bodies around them, and she nodded.

"We know them as the Gray Monks," said Walsingham.

"So the elders have told us. But whatever you call them, they're coming in greater force. And this time they won't land. They'll stay aloft and sear the area with fire, and drop bursting shells that turn the air to poison. We must take shelter with the Eilonwë." She gave the Queen a beseeching look. "Your Majesty, we *must* hurry."

"She is right," the Queen nodded. "Lead on, girl!"

They followed their new nonhuman allies—the Eilonwë, as they were evidently called—through the overgrown ruins. The sun was low in the sky when they came to a low half-collapsed structure so covered with vegetation as to be almost indistinguishable from a hill. A vine-shrouded entryway opened onto a ramp that slanted underground. Two of the Eilonwë produced small torches that produced light without fire—Winslow was rapidly growing inured to magic—and led the way downward.

Presently they came to an open space whose boundaries were lost in the shadows. "We should be out of danger now, and can pause for a rest," said the young female warrior, who didn't seem to need it—she wasn't even breathing hard.

"Then explain something to me, before we accompany you any further," said John White, stepping in front of her. "You claim to be one of the English settlers who went to Croatoan. But I knew all of them. I know what every young woman in the colony looked like. And I don't recognize you. I don't recognize any of your companions. *Who are you?*"

"First, answer this," said Dee in a voice that countenanced no denial. "You spoke of 'the elders.' What did you mean by that?"

"Why, our parents. The generation who brought us, their children, into this world where we have fought the Grella for nineteen years."

Surely, thought Winslow, *she must have meant something else. I couldn't have heard that correctly*.

But Dee must have heard the same thing, for he was staring at her. "*Nineteen years? What lunacy is this? The colonists disappeared from Croatoan less than a single year ago!*"

A stray memory awoke in Winslow. "And didn't you say something about how the Queen ought to look older? What did you mean by that?"

She nodded slowly. "So it's true after all. The Eilonwë must be right about the nature of time. We've had trouble believing it, for seems like madness. But it must be true. I myself am living proof of it, for I was carried into this world as a babe in arms."

"Who are you?" White asked again, barely above a whisper, speaking like a man who must ask a question even though he fears the answer.

"Who am I? Why, sir, the Eilonwë call me Alanthru rael'Khoranie. But my English name is Virginia Dare."

— EIGHT —

"WHY DO YOU STARE AT ME, SIR?" VIRGINIA DARE FINALLY asked, shattering the silence.

John White fell to his knees, and a convulsive shudder ran through him. "Because I last saw Virginia Dare on the twenty-seventh of August, 1587–only a little over a year ago. She was nine days old. Her mother, Eleanor Dare, was standing in the surf at Roanoke Island, waving farewell to me as I departed for England, for she was my daughter. She held my granddaughter up, giving me a last glimpse to store in my memory. And now you tell me you are she!" He buried his face in his hands. "God, God!" he moaned.

Virginia Dare went to her knees facing him, and took his hands in hers. "You are John White, my grandfather? All her life, Mother told me of you."

White winced as though from a pain that was not unexpected but nonetheless cruel. " 'All her life'? You mean . . . ?"

"Yes, she is dead," said Virginia Dare in the voice of one to whom death was a commonplace. It was a voice that accorded ill with her youth. "So is my father Ananias Dare. They were killed by the Grella, although their bodies were never found. Most of the elders are dead by now. We've had a hard life here, hunted like animals. It's only thanks to the Eilonwë that any of us still live." Her expression softened, and a sad smile trembled into life. "If Mother was alive now, she'd be almost as old as you!"

"But how can this be?" spluttered Dee. "Insanity!"

"I tell you, we're under Elf Hill, where time stands still!" Owain's voice quavered.

"To the contrary," said Walsingham, who could no more stop his brain from applying logic than he could stop his lungs from breathing. "It would seem that time moves *faster* here, if Mistress Dare has lived nineteen years, growing into a young woman, while less than one year has passed for us."

Owain looked bewildered, and more than a little crestfallen.

"So," Winslow ventured, "perhaps only minutes have passed in our world while we've been here."

"Very good, Thomas," Walsingham murmured approvingly.

"But this is absurd!" stormed Dee. "Not even the Greeks ever indulged in such incredible speculations! Nowhere in the writings of the ancients is there anything to suggest that—"

"Perhaps I can clarify matters."

The new voice silenced them all. Its English held none of the repellant, serpentlike hiss that the Grella imparted to human languages. Indeed, it had a not-unpleasant musical quality. But it was not a human voice.

More of the magical fireless torches were emerging from the shadows, revealing a new group of Eilonwë. At their head was one who, unlike all the others they had seen, was unmistakably old. His hair was snow-white, and his brown face bore a network of fine wrinkles which made it look even more alien. And his movements lacked the more-than-human fluidity of the other Eilonwë.

Virginia Dare stood up and went to him, speaking urgently in the Eilonwë tongue. He gave a silvery laugh. "Out of courtesy to our new arrivals of your nation, let us speak in English, Alanthru . . . I mean, Virginia. And please introduce me."

She turned, and spoke with a formality beyond her years. "Your Majesty, this is Riahn tr'Aliel, the leader of the Eilonwë of this region. Almost alone among his race, he has learned English."

"I have always been fascinated by languages," the elderly Eilonwë explained in his fluent but indescribably accented English. "And your tongue posed a unique challenge, being totally unrelated to any I had ever encountered."

Winslow sensed a stirring of interest—and fellow-feeling —in Walsingham and Dee, each of whom could plausibly claim to be England's foremost living linguist. And in any company but theirs the Queen would have been considered extraordinarily multilingual. Winslow himself could barbarously mispronounce a number of French phrases, but the only foreign language in which he was really conversant was Spanish. It had its uses in his line of work. Academic language masters would have blanched at those uses.

"But Virginia," Riahn continued, "did I understand you to say *Your Majesty?* Or did my limited experience of your language mislead me?"

"No, it did not," said Walsingham before Virginia Dare could answer. His office of Principal Secretary settled over him like an invisible cloak. "You are in the presence of Elizabeth, by grace of God Queen of England, Wales, Ireland and France, and Defender of the Faith."

"As little as I may look it at the moment," said the Queen with the irresistibly charming smile she could bring to bear when she chose. "And I rejoice to greet a fellow sovereign."

"Oh, no, Your Majesty," Riahn demurred. "I am no hereditary monarch, such as Virginia's parents and the others of the generation that knew England described to me. I am . . . But it's all rather complicated, and it's the least of the things I need to explain to you. So let us hurry to a place where I can explain them at leisure. It is night outside, and this tunnel emerges a goodly distance from the scene of your earlier fight, where the Grella have converged."

"And," Winslow remarked, knowing he was presuming beyond his station, "we can't stay in here forever."

The Queen's eyes met those of her Principal Secretary. Walsingham, after the barest hesitation, nodded. The Queen turned back to Riahn. "Very well, Sir Riahn. You may lead the way."

They continued along the tunnel for some distance before emerging into a cloudless night, under the stars and a three-quarter moon whose silvery light made the overgrown ruins seem even more haunted. The Eilonwë led the way, flitting through the night with silent grace, with Riahn at the head, for all his evident years. It was as though they fled through Arcadian groves in the company of elves.

Shakespeare must have felt it. As they ran, Winslow heard him murmuring with more than his usual intensity. "Over hill, over dale, through bush, through briar, over park, over pale, through flood, through fire, I do wander everywhere swifter than the moon's sphere." He gave a more than usually emphatic and self-satisfied nod.

Abruptly, they arrived at the foot of a curving, graceful sweep of what had been an impressive stairway of cracked alabasterlike white stone, leading up to the moss-hung façade of what must have been a truly monumental example of the architectural style they had seen before: elliptical roofs supported on shallow arches. All was crumbling into ruin now, but the moonlight and the encroaching vegetation had worked a kind of magic, transforming a derelict structure into an enchanted place of shadow and starlight.

Appearances were deceiving. Once they entered, it became apparent that the building had been converted to covert use, with drably functional partitions dividing its cavernous interior into rooms and corridors, transformed into a kind of day by the Eilonwë's fireless light. Some of the sailors and soldiers muttered uneasily, but Virginia Dare obviously took it in stride and they couldn't show fear before a girl who had none.

The enslaved Eilonwë, still moving with a strange lack of either cooperation or real resistance, were led away. The rest of them proceeded to a large central chamber furnished with low tables and couches, where people, Eilonwë and human alike, greeted Riahn. John White stepped forward as though in a dream and confronted a man who looked to be in his fifties.

"Ambrose Viccars? Is it truly you?"

"Master White!" Viccars smiled in his gray beard, deepening the wrinkles at the corners of his eyes. "Yes, it's me. I'm one of the last of the elders left. Word was sent ahead that you had come here, and that Her Majesty is with you." White confirmed it, and Viccars went to one knee, while Winslow wondered just how word had been "sent ahead."

Viccars introduced a few others whom White knew . . . or had known, nineteen of their years before. "My own dear Elizabeth is long dead," he said with the fatalism they'd previously observed in Virginia Dare. "She and our son Ambrose Junior—you remember him, don't you?—were killed by the Grella."

"I'm sorry," said White, grasping him by the shoulder.

"We'd had two other children since coming here. The older, a boy, is a fighter now."

"Aye," Virginia Dare interjected. "He's avenged his mother and his older brother many times over, as I can testify."

John Dee cleared his throat loudly. "Yes. Well, unless my memory is at fault, Riahn, you promised an explanation of certain matters. Like the fact that Master Viccars, and Mistress Dare, and all the other English among you have lived nineteen years in a single year."

It was as though Dee had broken a dam. They had all been holding their questions inside, for there were simply too many questions to deal with. But now they all came flooding out, and afterwards Winslow could never remember who had asked which one.

"How did the colonists come to be here?"

"How did *we* come to be here?"

"How did the Gray Monks come into our world?

"What *are* the Gray Monks?"

"What are *you*?"

"What *is* this place?"

"What . . . ?

"How . . . ?"

"Why . . . ?"

Riahn raised a silencing hand. "I know this is all very difficult for you. And it is difficult for me to explain in your language. First, let me ask you something. How did your . . . journey here seem?"

They all turned to Dee, who described the fading-out of the landscape of Croatoan, the infinite void, the reappearance of the world—or, at any rate, of *a* world. By the time he was done, Viccars and the other former colonists were nodding.

"Yes," said Riahn with a nod of his own. "It confirms our conclusions about your race." He took a deep breath. "You must understand that there are many worlds. I'm not speaking of the other planets of space—"

"The *other* planets?" Dee queried. "So you are saying that Copernicus is right after all? That the Sun, not the Earth, is the center of the universe, and the Earth is but one planet revolving around it?"

"Ah . . . that is a matter which we must take up at another time. I am speaking of worlds which do not lie elsewhere in space but which exist parallel to each other, in more dimensions that the four we know—"

"Four? But Euclid clearly states that there are three."

"*Please!* You must let me finish without interruptions."

"Possess your soul in patience, Dr. Dee," commanded the Queen. "I would hear this out."

"These parallel realities, as we must call them," Riahn resumed, "are similar in many ways—especially in astronomical matters. For example, you doubtless noticed the moon tonight. It is the same size to which you are accustomed, and takes as long to complete a revolution around the Earth. You will find that the year is also the same. You may also have noticed that the constellations are familiar. And you have surely noticed that you weigh the same as ever."

"Well of *course*—!" Dee began before remembering the Queen's ban of silence.

"There are differences, however. Geography, for example. You will see what I mean when I show you a map of *this* Earth. Likewise, living things differ—as, for example, the differences between you and us, or between both of us and the Grella. But the single most important difference is that time passes at different rates in different realities. Of this, you have seen the proof." Riahn gestured at Virginia Dare. "And," he added hastily as the Queen began to open her mouth, "please do not ask me the *why* of any of this. We understand that no more than you do. Perhaps the Grella understand it, for they have learned how to pass from one reality to another.

"At certain locations, the fabric of reality is in some manner weak. Long ago, the Grella, on whatever world to which they are native, discovered that by a brutally powerful application of energy at one of these points it is possible to . . . burst through into another reality."

"We English have good reason to know of their powers of sorcery," the Queen nodded grimly.

"If I understand you correctly, then you are wrong. This is not, uh, sorcery, but rather an application of the . . . well, the mechanic arts, in which the Grella are far more advanced than we—which, if I may say so without giving offense, means they are *very* far in advance of you. As far as we know, they are the only race ever to discover how to . . . tear the fabric between realities. Since making that discovery, they have been spreading like a plague from one world to the next. After subjugating a world, they use their arts to search it for another of the 'weak points' of which I have spoken. Then they move on to devastate yet another world."

"As they have devastated yours," said Winslow quietly, recalling what he had seen.

"Indeed." Riahn's equanimity was almost chilling. "For thousands of years, we have lived as you see: fugitives lurking among the crumbling ruins of our own ancient civilization, able at best to strike back occasionally. But during that time, we have gradually gained some of the knowledge of the Grella—such as what I am telling you now. One of the things we have learned is that almost two thousand years ago, shortly after completing their conquest of our world, a Grella exploration craft was lost—presumably as a result of finding one of the 'weak points,' forcing its way through it and, for some reason, being unable to return. The Grella here in our world have never found that point again.

"Then, nineteen years ago, the English inexplicably appeared here. They told us that your world has become afflicted by the beings you call the 'Gray Monks.' "

"The Grella!" Dee exclaimed. "So *that's* it! This craft of theirs, a flying craft like the one we have seen, emerged into our world at Croatoan Island and suffered an accident, reaching the Spanish lands to the south before crashing. Only . . . you said this happened two thousand years ago."

"Two thousand years ago *here*," Walsingham said suddenly. He closed his eyes, and the turning gears of his brain were almost audible. "That would be about a century ago in our world. In other words, about a quarter-century before Ponce de León landed in Florida."

"But what were they doing in Florida during that quarter-century?" Winslow wondered.

"Quite probably they were dead," Riahn stated matter-of-factly, then continued into the stunned, uncomprehending silence. "They have . . . machines that can control the living body on a very basic level—a level you do not yet suspect exists, for it lies in the realm of the invisible. Among other things, it enables them to take control of the mind. The Spaniards must have somehow come under the control of these machines, then followed commands to restore the Grella to a kind of life. That, too, can be done." He stopped, suddenly noticing the looks on his listeners' faces.

"Now I know why their bodies had to be burned," Winslow heard himself say.

"No," said Walsingam in a strangled voice. "Resurrection from the dead? *Them?* No!"

"But does it not explain a great deal?" Riahn asked gently. "We have been given to understand that the Grella have extended their influence over your world by taking control of a powerful religious organization—"

"The church of Rome!" Walsingham spat. "What could be more natural? It is the embodiment of all that is corrupt—the Whore of Babylon! The Gray Monks found their natural home there, in the cesspit of the Vatican!"

"I perceive that you are of a different persuasion," said Riahn urbanely. "And I would not presume to dispute your assessment of that Church's predispositions, of which you are in a better position to know than I. But even so, the mind control of which I speak must have expedited matters. Also, we have heard tales that the Grella's Spanish discoverer thought he had discovered the secret of renewed youth . . . but in the end wished he hadn't."

"Ponce de León," Winslow breathed. They'd all heard the stories.

"After enslaving his mind, it would have been typical of their sense of humor to give him such a 'reward.' For, as I have said, this renewed life is not true life. It lacks a certain indefinable essence—"

"The soul?" Dee's query sent a chill up the spines of all the humans.

"We have learned that term from your compatriots. It will do as well as any other. The same is even more true of the restoration of life to the already-dead Grella in your world. Indeed, it is our belief that this has been performed, not once but many times, on all the Grella now extant, leaving them the empty abominations they now are. They must have ceased to have offspring ages ago."

"This mind-control evil of which you speak," Winslow began hesitantly. "We saw slaves of your people serving the Grella. Are they . . . ?"

"Yes. Their lot is worse than slavery as you understand the word, for they cannot even *wish* to rebel or disobey. And after a time it culminates in a particularly ugly form of madness. We have . . . healing techniques to release them from their mental bondage. Sometimes it works and sometimes it doesn't," Riahn finished fatalistically.

"There's one thing you haven't explained," said Dee stubbornly. "If the Grella must use their devilish arts to force their way through the barrier between one 'alternate reality' and another, how is it that we English—first the colonists, and now us—simply blundered through it?"

Riahn opened his mouth to speak, but could not seem to find the words. Then, after another false start, he turned to one of the low tables and took a sheet of paper and a kind of stylus. "I do not know if I can explain this in your language. It is difficult enough in *my* language. But let me try." He drew two circles. "Imagine that these represent your reality and ours, even though as I said before we are dealing with many dimensions, while the surface of this paper has only two." Dee nodded at the last part, as though Riahn had finally said something he could fully understand and agree with. Riahn, ignoring him, drew concentric dashed circles around each of the solid ones. "The area between the circles is the extradimensional void through which the gap between realities can be bridged. As I have explained, this can only be done at certain points." He drew an X-mark on the perimeter of each of the solid circles. "At these points, the Grella can tear the fabric of reality and force their way through." He drew a brutally solid line from one X-mark to the other. "In so doing, they weaken the 'fabric' at those points even more. Once they do so, you humans—for reasons we cannot pretend to understand, for they involve some unique quality of your race—can pass through as you have done, simply by entering the affected area. First you enter a realm we call the 'Near Void.' " He indicated the zone immediately surrounding the solid circles, within the dashed circles. "Here, judging from your descriptions of your experience, you can observe the material world in a blurred, colorless way while being yourselves invisible to its denizens. But then you pass on into the 'Deep Void,' where time and space are meaningless."

"The infinite emptiness in which we found ourselves adrift," Dee breathed.

"Precisely. You are then drawn into the other reality's Near Void, and finally into that reality itself. This, as I say, seems to be a unique quality of you humans. At least the Grella seem to know nothing of it. Their 'brute force' approach evidently bursts directly into the Deep Void. We have no explanation for this difference."

"If they lack souls . . . " Dee looked up from a reverie and met Riahn's eyes. "Can *your* people do this?"

"I cannot say, for we have never had the opportunity to try."

"Why not? You could try at the same place where the English first appeared."

"Ah, but we don't know where that is."

Ambrose Viccars spoke up. "When we arrived here, we were dizzy with shock. It didn't help that it was night here at the time. Many of us thought we had died. Others thought we had entered a world of madness. A couple really *did* go mad, and never recovered. None of us were in any condition to think straight. So we simply set out, trying to find Manteo and his people, who, we thought, *must* somehow still be nearby. We blundered on and on before encountering the Eilonwë. After that, of course, we had even more to get used to! And when we found out that the Gray Monks, as we knew the Grella, ruled this world . . . Well, what with one thing and another, we lost sight of where the spot was. And we've never had the leisure to try and find it."

"I can find it," Winslow stated positively.

They all stared at him, with a great variety of expressions on their faces. In some cases, one expression followed another across the same face.

"You mean," Viccars finally managed, "that we can go home?"

"No."

That voice stopped them all in the midst of their chaotic thoughts, for the Queen had listened in intent silence for a long time. "No," she repeated. "I doubt not your words, Sir Riahn, nor do I doubt that you can do what you say, Captain Winslow. But there is no home for us to return to. I promised Mistress Dare the tale of why I am here. It is a heavy tale. The Armada that was rumored when you left England, Master Viccars, finally sailed. The Gray Monks—the Grella, I should say—gave it a victory it should never have won. England is fallen. London is ashes. I fled to the New World because Dr. Dee believed that the secret of the Gray Monks' powers was to be found there. Well, he was right. But I see no way for us to use that secret against them. Does anyone?" She stood up and looked around at each face in turn, finally turning to Walsingham. "Well, my Moor?"

Walsingham shook his head slowly, then bowed it. Winslow had never thought to see him looking so utterly defeated. "We could go back to Croatoan, Your Majesty, and stay with Manteo's people. But it would only be to await the arrival of the Spaniards and their Grella masters, for they are coming in search of the way back to this world, from whence they can bring more of their fellow to complete the subjugation of our world to their soulless reign."

No one else spoke, for the air of the chamber was too choked with wordless despair to hold sound.

— NINE —

SOMETHING THAT WAS NOT REALLY A BUTTERFLY FLEW past Winslow's field of vision as he lay on the hillside at the edge of the woods and gazed across the valley of the ancient Eilonwë city toward Elf Hill.

He still thought of it as that, and since he had started using the term all the humans had come to adopt it. But this was the first time he had looked on it since their initial emergence into this world. For a while after that emergence, the Grella had been thick as fleas on a dog in the area where one of their patrols had been wiped out. Later, there had been no time as they had adapted to the fugitive existence the Eilonwë and their human allies led among the tunnels and the ruins. There had been too much to learn.

One of the things they had learned was that the Eilonwë were divided into a multitude of *sheuaths*.

(Nations? Tribes? Clans? Something else?) They were united in their hatred of the Grella, but in nothing else. Riahn led the *sheuath* in whose territory the portal to Croatoan lay, though by what right he led them was not clear—it was not hereditary monarchy, certainly. His *sheuath* had always advocated active resistance to the Grella—a tendency that had become more pronounced since the English had joined it—but it acted alone. Certain others felt the path to survival lay in passive concealment, avoiding the notice of the alien masters as much as possible, and even those favoring active resistance had their own ideas as to how to go about it. Such was the way of the Eilonwë, and Winslow couldn't help thinking it was a way that might have smoothed the Grella pathway to conquest.

They had also learned that what had seemed to them the magic of the Eilonwë—flameless torches, devices for sending voices winging across great distances to carry messages instantly, and all the rest—did not really involve the black arts. It was simply what the Eilonwë had managed to retain of the mechanic arts their ancestors had possessed before the coming of the Grella, and could now produce in their small hidden workshops.

Riahn had put it to them in the form of a rhetorical question: "Is an arquebus or a compass magical?"

"Of course not!" Dee had huffed.

"Ah, but your own forefathers would once have thought it so."

Dee had looked blank, as had everyone else. Technological change was an idea that had only just begun to enter into their world. It was still so new that it had not yet had time to become a part of their mental universe. Tools had always changed so slowly that one didn't think of them as changing at all. It seemed perfectly natural for artists to depict Alexander the Great wearing modern armor and using artillery. In the end, though, Dee had been the first to accept the concept, and Winslow had come to accept it too. But he had not yet taken the next logical step, for he could still not apply the same reasoning to the arts of the Grella. *That*, surely, must belong to the realm of the supernatural!

The tools of the Eilonwë, however, could at least be thought of as tools, and he now held one of them in his hands. The two cylinders, each about six inches long, were connected by a framework which allowed the distance between them to be adjusted to fit the spacing of human eyes. On his first try at looking through them, he had seen only a blur. Then, as instructed, he had turned a tiny wheel between the cylinders. All at once the world had come into focus—far closer to him than it ought to have been, bringing a startled oath to his lips. He'd been assured that it was only an application of the kind of magnifying glass lenses used in ordinary spectacles. Dee had coined the term "bi-oculars" in lieu of the device's unpronounceable Eilonwë name.

Now Winslow raised it to his eyes and gazed across at the slope where he had first set eyes on this world. There was nothing out of the ordinary to be seen. *But there wouldn't be, would there?* he reflected. There had seemed nothing out of the ordinary on Croatoan Island either.

"So it's there?" he heard from behind and to his right. It was the first thing he heard, as Virginia Dare slithered soundlessly up beside him in the tall grass just beyond the treeline.

"Yes. I can tell the general location from glimpses I had as we moved away from it. If I could actually get over there to that ridge, I could start looking for . . . well, the shape one ridgeline looks like when viewed at a certain angle, with another behind it. A pity that ridge is so open, with nothing in the way of concealment."

"But what good would it do us?" she asked in a voice that held the hurt of having had the fulfillment of a childhood hope held up before her, only to be instantly snatched away. "If all we can do is go from one Grella-ruled world to another—"

"They don't rule *ours* yet!" said Winslow, more harshly than he'd intended. "England may have fallen, but it won't be *conquered* as long as Englishmen are Englishmen, and know the rightful Queen escaped and may still live. I'm not yet ready to believe that there's nothing we can do. And if there is something . . . well, we may yet have reason to be glad to have our ability to pass through this portal opened by the Grella."

"I wonder about that, Mistress Dare." A rustling sound came from behind them as Shakespeare joined them. Winslow couldn't for the life of him remember how the young actor had prevailed upon them to let him come along on this outing. He wasn't moving through the undergrowth with Virginia Dare's noiselessness— Winslow feared he himself probably wasn't either—but he was making a surprisingly creditable effort. "Do the Grella really have to tear their way through the veil between the worlds before we humans can step through? Or is the portal open to us anyway?"

"What?" She looked puzzled that the question had even been asked. Actually, she had never quite known what to make of Shakespeare. Winslow could sympathize. "So Riahn has always told us. And what difference does it make? The Grella *have* forced this world's portals open. So why do you ask?"

"Oh . . . I was just wondering. I remember what Riahn said about the Near Void where we humans linger for a short time before passing into the Deep Void. I can't help wondering . . . " Shakespeare's eyes took on the far-away look Winslow had come to know. "Suppose that there are other portals in our world, and that people can unknowingly walk through them, finding themselves wandering in our world's Near Void, stranded there . . . doomed for a certain time to walk the night." He gave his quick filing-away nod. "Might it not go far toward explaining the stories one hears of ghosts?"

Winslow and Virginia Dare both stared at him for a moment.

"But," she finally broke the silence, "according to Riahn, people in the Near Void cannot be seen, as ghosts sometimes can."

"That does pose a problem," Shakespeare admitted.

"I can see why you have aspirations to be a playwright, Will," Winslow observed dryly. "You have an active imagination."

"So I've sometimes been told," Shakespeare acknowledged with a sigh. "Not least by my wife."

"But," Winslow continued, turning to Virginia Dare, "this raises a couple of questions about which I myself have wondered, Mistress Dare."

" 'Virginia.' Unless," she added with what he thought to perceive as a twinkle, "you'd prefer 'Alanthru.' "

" 'Virginia,' by all means. I'm English, not Eilonwë. And the name suits you." He paused a moment, watching for a reaction of which there was none, save for a brief eye contact before getting down to business. "You said, 'the Grella have forced this world's *portals* open.' When I think of it, it must be 'portals,' for they must have entered this world from somewhere."

"You're right. Thousands of years ago, they appeared at a place to the west of here, only about thirty miles as we English measure distance." She wore the look of someone considering questions that had never occurred to her before. "I don't know if there's any reason why the two portals should be so close together. Riahn has never said anything about it. I'm sure he doesn't know. Maybe it's just an accident. Or maybe something about these weak points in creation causes them to come into existence in the same area."

"If so," Winslow reflected, "then it must narrow the area the Grella have to search, after they enter a world, for the way into the next one. I can't understand why, in almost two thousand years, the ones here have never found the way to Crotoan, which their fellows once found."

"Riahn says they have to be practically on top of one of these points in space before they can perceive it with their mechanical devices. The ones who discovered the way into our world probably didn't want to share the secret with the others until they had forced the portal open and gone through. Perhaps this way they establish ownership of a world by right of discovery."

"A common enough way of doing things," Winslow nodded, recalling the Spaniards' practices in the Indies. He also noted, without comment, her reference to this world as *our* world. "The ones still here must have missed the ship, but they probably assumed it had come to grief somehow."

"As, indeed, it had," Shakespeare interjected.

"But I don't understand. How can the Grella run an empire across many worlds, when time moves differently in each?" Winslow struggled to express his meaning.

"How would it be if a soldier was sent from England to the garrisons in Ireland, stayed a year, and came back to find that in England *twenty* years had passed in his absence? His parents would be dead, his friends old, his children grown, his wife married to somebody else, and God knows what would have become of his property! Everything he had known would be gone. And what if it were *two hundred* years? His entire *world* would be gone!"

"The Grella don't think like us. Remember what Riahn said about them? He has explained it to us many times. They no longer have children; indeed they've given up the very ability to do so, and are all the same sex—or lack of sex. All of them are walking shells, reanimated over and over by their arts. They work together for mutual advantage, but they have no real attachments, no traditions, no families, no friends, no God. Maybe they did in the past, but if so they no longer even remember what it was like. All they have in common is their contempt for the rest of creation. Each of them is alone in the universe."

Both men stared at her, trying unsuccessfully to imagine such a hollow, meaningless existence.

"Likewise," she continued, "their mechanical arts reached finality ages ago, and no longer change. They are no more able to create than they are able to love."

"Perhaps the first ability cannot exist without the second," Shakespeare mused.

Winslow shook himself free of the chill that had touched his soul. "Well, be that as it may, there's something else—something Will's question started me wondering about."

"What? But I explained that the only two portals we know exist in this world had already been opened by the Grella."

"Yes. And we know that humans can pass through them. But once we do, and find ourselves in the Near Void, can we *stay* there?"

"But our parents, and now you, were only there a few moments before passing on into the Deep Void, to re-emerge—"

"Yes, yes. But they and we were caught by surprise, overwhelmed by strangeness. We could only . . . let the current carry us. But how would it be if we walked through that place purposely, knowing what we were in for, and *tried* to linger in the Near Void? Could we do it? Could we will ourselves not to pass on?"

"I have no way of knowing," Virginia Dare answered simply.

"Of course you don't." Winslow gazed hungrily across at the opposite hillside. "I have to try it." He turned to the other two, and thought to see in their faces the same curiosity he felt, tempered by alarm or at least prudence. "Are you with me?"

"But you said it yourself," Virginia Dare reminded him. "There's no concealment, except among the ruins. Once we emerged onto the slope, we'd be exposed to the view of any Grella flyer that happened along."

"Perhaps if we waited until nightfall . . ." Shakespeare suggested.

"I don't think I'd be able to find the exact location in the dark. Besides, how often do they fly over this area, now that the excitement over our little encounter with them has died down?"

"More often than you might think," Virginia Dare cautioned. "Remember, this is only thirty miles from the portal that admitted them to this world. They have a great fortress there, as you would expect. The area around it hums with activity."

"But that's thirty miles away." Winslow got up onto one knee before anyone could argue further. "Come on!"

Virginia Dare's eyes flashed with what Winslow interpreted as resentment at having her usual leadership role usurped. But Shakespeare, accustomed to regarding Winslow as his captain, followed. Rather than be left behind, she followed too. They slipped quietly along the edge of the woods, running in a half-crouch just under the covering foliage, then quickly descended into the valley of the ancient city.

At least, Winslow told himself, they were dressed inconspicuously. He and Shakespeare had donned the Eilonwë-style but human-proportioned garments of the ex-colonists, in colors designed to blend with those of nature. They had not brought any ranged weapons, because captured Grella weapons were too valuable to risk and guns were useless against the silvery suits which magically (as Winslow stubbornly continued to think of it) stiffened to steellike hardness where they were struck by any object moving above a certain speed. But blades—even blades wielded by Virginia Dare—were slower than that speed, and she had brought the beautifully designed curved sword that seemed an extension of herself. Winslow had stuck to his backsword; it might lack elegance, but he knew he could use it effectively. Shakespeare's usual boarding pike would have been too awkward to carry on this expedition, so he had brought a dagger which, he stubbornly insisted, an actor had to learn to convincingly use. Winslow only hoped the Grella would be convinced.

They scrambled down the slope and entered the haunted precincts of the dead city, flitting through the long-overgrown ruins like ghosts among the ghosts. The thought of ghosts reminded Winslow of his reason for insisting on coming here, and going on to the exposed slope beyond: a less than half-formed idea, a bare glimpse of a possibility that might be used.

It was a mistake to dwell on it, for it caused his attention to wander just before they emerged into the ancient courtyard, barely discernible as an unnaturally regular clearing in the forest, and came face to face with a Grella patrol.

Fixated on the threat of the Grella flyers, they had forgotten that the aliens might be stepping out of character and patrolling the region of the recent unpleasantness on foot. So Winslow was caught flat-footed when he saw the small aliens in the silvery one-piece garments, carrying the tubular weapons he remembered. The one closest to him—very close indeed—began to raise that weapon before he could react.

Virginia Dare sprang past him, bringing her curved sword around and down in the kind of blinding movement he recalled. He blinked, and therefore missed most of it. But then she had recovered and was again in fighting stance . . . and at appreciably the same instant, whatever the Grella used for blood shot out in a gushing jet from a slashed-open torso.

But that instant had been enough for the other Grella, further back, to raise their own weapons and fire them. Winslow barely had time to know himself a dead man.

But he wasn't. That might have been better.

Thomas Winslow was as familiar with pain, in its various forms, as any other sea dog. He knew what bone-jarring blows and slashing cuts felt like, and had long since taken their measure. But the various ways the flesh could be bruised or broken were *natural*. This was something else. It hurt in a way for which English held no word. He did not believe any other language of his world did either.

Where the weapon's faint beam of light touched him, it was a blistering burn. That, at least, he had felt before. But then his muscles knotted and his lungs and his heart seized up nightmarishly, ceasing to do their duty of pumping air and blood.

In the midst of his agony, what Riahn had told them flashed through his mind. The hand weapons of the Grella used mere light, but somehow directed it all in one direction, rather than spreading out to fill a space as the light from a candle or a lamp or a torch normally did. It had made no sense whatever to Winslow, but he had to accept the evidence of his eyes, and he had seen men's chests pierced and burst open by a pale line of light, and their bodies exploded into pink mist by larger weapons of the same kind.

But Riahn had also told them that those weapons could be set in a different way, so that a weaker beam of one-way light—too weak to kill or even inflict more than a small blister—carried with it a charge of . . . Riahn's English vocabulary had failed him. But whatever it was, it was what caused lightning to flash, and also caused whatever carried the commands of the human brain to the muscles of the body to turn traitor, and shock that body into unconsciousness.

All this ran through Winslow's mind in less than a second. Before he mercifully lost consciousness, he had time for one final thought. The Grella had set their weapons to stun their victims rather than kill them. They wanted him and his companions alive. They would live . . . for the time being.

— TEN —

WINSLOW WAS FAMILIAR WITH THE WAY HIS ARM FELT AFTER he had banged his elbow against a hard surface at exactly the wrong angle.

His whole body felt that way as he struggled unenthusiastically back into consciousness. His lungs and his heart were functioning again, but the voluntary muscles of his limbs were still undergoing feeble spasms.

But he didn't even notice any of that. What he noticed, before opening his eyes, was that he was suspended, hanging in some kind of bonds that held his limbs immobilized, and that a stiff wind was blowing.

Then he opened his eyes . . . and cried out in a kind of panic he had never felt before.

The valley floor was at least hundreds of feet below him, and nothing was keeping him from falling all that

153

distance but a line from the bottom of a Grella flyer. That flyer must have been full, for the Grella had trussed up him and Shakespeare and Virginia Dare like bundles and hung them from the gunwales of that magical boat. And now he was flying. *Flying!*

He must not have been unconscious for very long, for the valley was still below them. He looked around at his companions. Shakespeare was still dead to the world, but Virginia Dare, hanging beside him, was already conscious. She looked alarmed, but not panic-stricken; presumably the *idea* of flying was not novel to her, even if she'd never actually done it. The impossibility of showing fear before a woman steadied Winslow, and he looked downward with only a slight queasiness.

They were flying into the late-afternoon sun, and beneath them the ancient ruins fell behind. After a while Shakespeare regained consciousness, and stared below with a wonder that overpowered fear and even nausea. Presently the flyer turned to starboard to follow a bend in the valley. Ahead, Winslow glimpsed what had to be the Grella fortress.

He knew he had no right to be surprised at what the Grella could do—not now, after what had happened to England and after all he had seen here. But knowing that was one thing. What loomed up ahead was something else.

The first thing he saw was a metal arch that, at this distance, seemed to be of cobweb fragility—although an instant's thought told him that in reality it must be of incredible tonnage, given the manifestly impossible diameter it enclosed. As they approached more closely, that massiveness became more apparent—as did the fact that it wasn't really an arch, but rather a three-quarter circle with its base in the ground. The thought came to him that it must be the portal through which the Grella had entered this world, outlined in this way for reasons of their own . . . to make it easier to find, perhaps, or to make it more readily useable in some other way about which he could not even speculate.

Then his eyes began to take in what lay around the base of that incredible arch—the fortress, as Virginia Dare had called it, although it was more like a city. The closer they got, the more its scale was forced on his incredulous mind. So was the fact that its buildings were all of seamless metal, or what appeared to be seamless metal, like impossibly large castings. Only they were too smooth even for that. Had it not been totally insane, Winslow would have thought the fantastic structures he was seeing had been *grown* in metal.

And in the midst of all the mind-numbing, awe-inspiring strangeness, dwarfing all the rest, there rose a darkly gleaming dome, linked to a ring of outbuildings by soaring arches not unlike the flying buttresses of a Gothic cathedral. Their flyer proceeded on, past an outer ring of what Winslow could recognize as gun emplacements even though the guns were of a sort beyond his ken. As they drew closer, that sinister dome grew and grew, its size and complexity becoming ever more apparent, and the sense of timeless evil that suffused it becoming ever more horrifying.

A feeling Winslow had never experienced began to close over him. *So this is what despair feels like,* jibed a tiny voice within him.

The base of the dome was terraced, with machines of unguessable function alternating with wide openings flanked by obvious weapons. The flyer floated through one of those openings, and Winslow involuntarily closed his eyes, certain he was going to smash into the lower frame. But the three dangling human figures barely cleared it as they swept on through into the dome. They gazed about.

They were in an interior too vast for a word like *cavernous*. It was too vast to be indoors, and the mind-numbing complexity of what lay below them contributed to the impression that this was an enclosed city within a city rather than a building. The flyer swooped down toward that labyrinthine maze, with a speed that caused Winslow's eyes to squeeze shut again. But then it slowed to a halt and hovered. At some automatic signal, the cables holding them were released, and they were unceremoniously dumped into a kind of cul-de-sac, enclosed by featureless metal walls on three sides and open to the unnatural light panels that glowed from the dome's interior surface far above.

The flyer departed, its high-pitched hum rising to a whine, and they were left alone, groaning with the pain of their fall to the hard floor. At least, Winslow satisfied himself, nothing was broken. The same seemed true of his companions, for they seemed able to move normally.

Virginia Dare's disposition was another matter. She glared at him balefully. "You just had to try to reach that ridge in broad daylight, didn't you?"

"Nobody forced you to come!" Winslow retorted. His asperity was partially born of his guilty knowledge that she had a point. But even worse was the sheer oppressiveness of this unnatural place, created entirely by the Grella and utterly alien to anything wrought by God or man. He looked around at the three walled-in sides of their enclosure, which were too high and smooth to even consider climbing. Then he considered the wide-open fourth side.

Shakespeare read his thoughts. "Ah . . . Captain, even if they mean to leave us free to simply walk from here, I doubt if even your skill at navigation could find our way out of this place."

"Still, anything would be better than squatting here and awaiting their pleasure!" Winslow strode forward.

"No! Don't!" Virginia Dare cried urgently. Winslow ignored her and continued his advance.

It wasn't as bad as the weapon that had stunned them, for he didn't lose consciousness. But he cried out from the same burning pain, and his muscles contracted and his heart skipped a beat as before. Sparks flew until he fell to the floor, twitching, and lost contact with that invisible wall.

With a sigh whose theatricality Shakespeare must have envied, Virginia Dare rolled her eyes heavenward as though asking God to give her strength. Winslow slowly got to his feet, carefully avoiding her look. He glared up at the vast convex roof that shut out the sky, and the light panels that served in place of the sun. A flyer passed overhead, insultingly indifferent to them. The only sound was a distant murmur of unfamiliar machine noises. "Why have they left us here, ignoring us?" he demanded of no one in particular. "They must be trying to break our spirit."

"Not without success, at least in my case," Shakespeare muttered. He slumped down and sat in silence with his back to a wall. After a moment, Winslow followed suit, seeing nothing better to do and not wishing to voice the chilling thought that had suddenly entered his mind: the memory of those Eilonwë slaves, mindshackled beyond any ordinary conception of slavery. He wondered if the other two were thinking that was what lay in their own future, and if that was why no one spoke.

Time began to lose its meaning as they sat under those unchanging artificial lights, tormented by discomfort and anxiety . . . and, increasingly, by hunger and thirst. Finally, Winslow got stiffly to his feet and swallowed to lubricate his dry throat. "Hallo!" he cried out hoarsely. "Is anybody here?"

"For God's sake, be quiet!" hissed Virginia Dare. "Haven't you done enough already?"

"What the Devil have we got to lose?" Winslow took a deep breath and let out a bellow that could have been heard above a sea storm. "Bring us food and water, damn you!"

There was no response. Winslow, in a mood of sheer stubbornness, remained standing, hands on hips.

He was close to giving up and sinking back to the floor when three Grella finally appeared. While two of them stood with leveled weapons, the third did something with a small object in his hand. Then he spoke a few obviously inexpert syllables in the Eilonwë tongue, and beckoned to them to come.

"Is he crazy?" Winslow growled. "Or does he think we are?"

"He's caused the barrier to vanish," said Virginia Dare listlessly. She stood up and walked from the cul-de-sac unharmed. After a moment, Winslow and Shakespeare followed, the former with a hesitancy born of remembered pain.

They were conducted through oddly angled walkways and courts to a large central structure. The interior held the typically Grella lack of anything humans could recognize as ornamentation, but there was an unmistakable richness to the surfaces, and a spaciousness out of proportion to the building's diminutive masters. All of this was especially evident in the octagonal chamber to which their guards led them. Behind a long, low, gleaming-topped table, half a dozen Grella shared a couch rather than sitting on the individual chairs humans would have favored. They wore the usual silvery garments, but with complex gold chest insignia. The one with the most elaborate such insignia spoke. "I am Sett 44, Rank Orbassin 27." An instant passed before Winslow realized that the loathsome, sibilant voice had spoken in English. Virginia Dare wore a look of stark astonishment.

"We learned your language from individuals of your species whom we captured," came the hissing answer to their unspoken question. No mention was made of how the knowledge had been extracted, and Winslow decided he didn't really want to know. "I took the trouble to learn it because your species has recently become of more than usual interest." He paused, as though inviting comment. Virginia Dare merely glared in silence, and Shakespeare managed to restrain his usual loquacity. Winslow followed suit, and as he waited he had a moment to wonder why he continued to think of this sexless thing as *he*. Perhaps it was the fact that he had known them as monks in his own world. And there was certainly nothing suggestive of the feminine about them. Actually, there was nothing masculine about them either. But he found it impossible to think of something that talked as *it*.

"It is obvious," Sett 44 resumed, "that you human animals are not native to this world. That has been clear enough ever since you first appeared nineteen years ago. And you were first observed in the same general area where very old records indicate that a research vessel disappeared two thousand years ago. This led certain of my colleagues to theorize a connection between the two. I was a skeptic at the time. But since then, rigorous interrogation of the same captives from whom we learned your language has provided confirmation. They spoke in disjointed, meaningless terms of a transition from a different world, where your species lives in an appropriately primitive state. Furthermore, in that world they knew from hearsay of beings who resembled us, and who evidently were in the process of using their superior intelligence to secure control through the local tribal cult."

Winslow felt himself flush at hearing Christians—even papists—so referred to. But he held himself in check.

"Naturally, the animals in question died under interrogation," Sett 44 continued unfeelingly. "We brought them back to life . . . in fact we did so several times. But the rejuvenation process has odd effects on your species' rudimentary brains." A chill went through Winslow as he recalled the stories about old Juan Ponce de León. "Those effects proved to be cumulative, with repeated rejuvenations. In the end, the captives were useless and we discarded their mindless husks, which went to supplement the organic matter from which our artificial food is generated. By then they could do little but repeat their names: Ananias and Eleanor Dare."

It took some very small fraction of a second for the names to register on Winslow. At the instant they did, he turned to Virginia Dare, knowing what was going to happen and knowing that he had to prevent it.

He was too late. With a scream that raised his neck hairs, she sprang forward before he could grab her, and before the Grella guards could react. She was halfway over the table before a guard at the table's end raised his weapon. Too quickly for sight, she grasped the weapon by its muzzle and jerked it toward her, pulling it from the guard's grasp and throwing him off balance. Then she reversed the motion and punched the butt stock into his face with a crunch of whatever passed among the Grella for bone and cartilage. Then, without a pause, she threw away the weapon, grasping with her usual quickness that its effectiveness at such short range was too limited to justify the pause it would have taken her to bring it into action. Instead, she cleared the table with a leap and grasped the throat of a Grell who tried to interpose himself between her and Sett 44.

But by then the guards had recovered. Two of them leveled their weapons at Winslow and Shakespeare while the others' beams struck Virginia Dare. At least the weapons were still set to shock. Her back arched convulsively and she cried out once before collapsing. Even in unconsciousness, her hands had to be pried from the throat of the Grell, whose wheezing, gagging, rattling sounds were like the pealing of church bells to Winslow's soul. That Grell was led away, as was the guard with the smashed face. Other guards carried Virginia Dare off in response to a series of incomprehensible orders from Sett 44, who then turned his huge, empty, dark eyes back to the two men.

"The fault is mine. The female breeder who is the war leader of the human animals is notorious. I should have recognized her, and anticipated this sort of behavior." At the word *breeder*, the usual Grella emotionlessness seemed to waver, and Winslow could sense Sett 44's disgusted contempt. "Capturing her is a great coup. She should yield valuable information on the feral Eilonwë and their human allies before her mind is destroyed and she goes into the organic-matter vats. But at the moment, I am more interested in the recent loss of one of our patrols in the ancient city, under circumstances which seem to suggest the arrival of still more humans. This suggests a . . . permeability in the barrier between the human world and this one, of a sort for which there is no precedent. If you voluntarily give me useful information, you will merely be enslaved. I offer you this option because, as you have perhaps gathered, the more drastic forms of interrogation might render you useless prematurely."

Winslow forced his battered mind to concentrate on the implications of what he had just heard. The Grella—or, at least, Sett 44—had more knowledge, and more inferences from that knowledge, than anyone had credited them with. But there were still a great many things they didn't know. In particular, they were completely in the dark about the way in which humans—primitive animals in their eyes—traversed the barrier between the universes. In fact, Sett 44's choice of English words suggested that they didn't really understand it at all; they thought of it as a *barrier*, to be smashed through by extravagant application of physical energies at certain weak points. Nothing he had heard suggested that they were aware of the nature of the "Near Void" and the "Deep Void" as Riahn had explained it. At some point, ages in the past, they had by accident discovered their brute force way of bursting into the Deep Void and automatically bursting out of it at the nearest weak point in the nearest universe. And in all the millennia since then, in accordance with what Riahn had said about their lack of creativity, they had continued to make use of that lucky accident without even considering the possibility of reasoning from it and deducing what made it *work*.

For the first time, Winslow began to truly appreciate what the Grella had lost.

Which didn't happen to help him at the moment.

But perhaps it can. Perhaps it gives me something I can use. God knows I've used the Dons' blind arrogance against them often enough. Maybe I can do the same here.

"Yes, Lord!" he blurted. He saw Shakespeare's shocked look out of the corner of his eye, and in the guise of waving his arms gave the young actor a surreptitious jab in the ribs. "Yes, we can be useful! You are, of course, correct: we humans, for reasons beyond our poor powers of understanding, can somehow pass between the worlds. But it can only be done at those 'weak points' in the universal fabric where the Grella have applied their mighty powers, born of their superior wisdom." Winslow wondered if he might be laying it on too thick. But he saw no flicker of suspicion in Sett 44's bottomless eyes. The Grella were impervious to irony.

Sett 44 leaned forward greedily. "Can you show us where this place is?"

"Perhaps, Lord, the two of us together can. But," he added firmly, "only with the help of the woman . . . that is, the female breeder. She has indispensable knowledge. She must be kept alive at all costs."

"Very well. Water, and fodder suitable for your species, will be supplied. She should be fully recovered by morning. We will put your claims to the test then." Sett 44 gestured to the guards, and they were led back to their pen, as Winslow now thought of it. A large pail of water was there, as was another pail containing a tasteless gruel that Winslow and Shakespeare were too hungry to reject. Virginia Dare was also there, slowly returning to consciousness.

Winslow took her by the shoulders and shook her awake. For a blessed instant, her face wore a look of innocent blankness—before the recollection of what she now knew crashed visibly down. Winslow couldn't let it send her into either despair or berserk rage. He spoke quickly.

"Virginia, listen carefully," he whispered, lest the Grella have devices that could listen to their conversations from afar—although he doubted that they would be using such devices if they did have them, any more than humans would have used them to listen to the lowing of cattle. "Listen carefully, and don't reveal any reaction. I've told the Grella that I can find the portal."

Her disoriented eyes cleared, and their emptiness was instantly filled—with fury. "You *what*?" she gasped. "You damned traitor—!" And she reached for his throat.

Winslow had known exactly what to expect. So, in spite of her remarkable quickness, his hands were there a small fraction of a second before hers, gripping her wrists and twisting her body around so that he was grappling her from behind. It took all his strength to contain her twisting, writhing struggles. But he got one arm free for long enough to wrap it around her throat and apply a pressure just short of choking.

"Listen, damn you!" he rasped into her ear. "Can't you see that I'm tricking them?" She abruptly went motionless, although her muscles remained stiff. "Now," he continued, in a lower whisper, "I just want to know one thing. If you have to, can you pilot a Grella flyer?"

— ELEVEN —

THE DOME'S ARTIFICIAL LIGHTING DIMMED, DARKENED, AND awoke again in harmony with the natural rhythms of the sun. This made sleep possible. But they had nothing to sleep on except the hard floor, and they were abominably stiff and sore the following morning. And there were no sanitary provisions of any kind. Winslow and Shakespeare averted their eyes as Virginia Dare performed her necessities in a corner of their enclosure, and she did the same for them. The Grella, Winslow reflected queasily, had not thought of this subject, any more than humans would have thought of it in connection with livestock.

At least they were provided with more of the tasteless mush, and water to wash it down. Shortly thereafter, a procession of Grella arrived, with Sett 44 in the lead.

"We will put your boasts to the test," said Sett 44 to Winslow without inquiries into their welfare or any other

preliminaries. He indicated a Grell whose gold chest
insignia was less elaborate than his own. "Messuin 76,
Rank Orbassin 92, will take you aloft in a flyer. He speaks
and understands the Eilonwë language. You will commu-
nicate with him through the breeder, who is fluent in
that language . . . and for whose behavior you will be held
responsible. Do not attempt any surreptitious communi-
cations among yourselves in your own language. I will
be monitoring everything Messuin 76 hears." Winslow
had no idea what he was talking about, but Virginia Dare
seemed to understand, and take it seriously. And, he
reflected, it made sense that anyone with the ability to
cast voices across a great distance could listen across
equal distances. And he noted the implicit confirmation
of his supposition that Sett 44 was the only Grell who
understood English.

"You will give Messuin 76 directions to the location
you claim to know," Sett 77 continued. "A second flyer,
armed, will escort you closely. If there is any hint of
treachery on your part, you will die. If you fail to deliver
on your promises, you will die. If there is any further
violent behavior on the breeder's part, you will die. Do
you comprehend this sequence of events?"

"Perfectly, Lord," Winslow groveled.

"Good. One more thing: when you reach the portal
and land, you will be kept separate from your companions. If you yourself should somehow escape by passing
through the portal to your own world, as you humans
can evidently do, your companions will die. The breeder,
in particular, will die very slowly. Finally, as an added
precaution . . . " Sett 44 motioned forward a pair of
Grella who proceeded to affix to the humans' wrists
metallic bracelets connected by flexible foot-long cables

of the same metal—thin but, Winslow was certain,
unbreakable.

They were conducted through the maze of metal and
less familiar materials to a landing stage just inside one
of the wide openings in the base of the dome. A number
of the open-topped flyers rested there. They were prod-
ded aboard one of them, in the wake of Messuin 76, who
took up a position overseeing the open cockpit where
the pilot sat. Winslow felt no surprise that a potentially
risky assignment had been delegated to a flunky. He was
even less surprised that two guards followed them aboard
with weapons leveled at their backs. That was all there
was room for, besides the pilot. As soon as they all settled
in, the flyer rose up and swooped away.

It was Winslow's first experience of flight, aside from
being towed, dangling beneath one of these vessels. It
was certainly less unsettling than that had been—at least
he had a deck under his feet. Nevertheless, his stomach
lurched as the great dome and the other Grella structures fell away behind them and dropped below.

"Tell him to proceed back to where we were captured," he said to Virginia Dare, who translated into
Eilonwë. The flyer and its escort banked and followed
the valley eastward.

Soon the ancient ruins began to be visible among the
vegetation below. Messuin 76 hissed something to Virginia Dare, his testiness audible across the chasm of races
and languages. She glanced at Winslow.

"Tell him to bear two points to starboard," he said
without thinking. She gave him an exasperated look
"Uh . . . north-northeast," he amended, and pointed to
further clarify matters. Virginia Dare met his eyes for an
instant. In accordance with their whispered colloquy the

night before, he was directing the Grella away from the portal, toward the opposite side of the valley. She translated, and the flyer changed course. Their escort kept formation—rather sloppily, Winslow thought with a mental sniff—off the starboard beam.

Winslow then glanced at Shakespeare. He had no doubts about Virginia Dare's ability to cope with what was about to happen, but he couldn't be quite so certain of his other companion. Those large, luminous hazel eyes didn't hold the same kind of totally nerveless hair-trigger readiness he had seen in the woman warrior's green ones, nor would he have expected them to. But he did see a steadiness that, in its own way, was almost equally reassuring—a steadiness which, like so much else about the young actor, drew on depths he doubted his own capacity to ever fully understand.

He waited until he was certain they were at the most advantageous point. In fact, he waited long enough to draw a quick glance of concerned impatience from Virginia Dare. But he held himself in check for a second or two after that, before bellowing abruptly, "No! Hard a-starboard, you lubbers!" Virginia Dare, needing no translation this time, transmitted the command to Messuin 76 with a show of hysterical urgency.

The volume and suddenness of Winslow's shout had startled the Grella, and Virginia Dare's tone left them no leisure to wonder how serious the situation could really be. Messuin 76 emitted a kind of hissing rattle in the loathsome Grella speech. The pilot, conditioned to unthinking obedience, wrenched the flyer violently to the right. The escorting pilot, caught by surprise, tried to swerve out of the way. He almost succeeded. The two flyers struck each other glancingly, sending the escort skidding away across the sky, its pilot desperately trying to regain control.

The impact caused the two armed guards to lose their balance. Before they could react, Winslow whipped the length of flexible metal confining his wrists around Messuin 76's skinny throat. Lifting the Grell's feet off the deck, he swung him around between himself and the stunned guards.

At the same time, Virginia Dare brought her wrists together, gathered the metal cable together in a bunch and, lunging past Winslow into the cockpit, with all her strength brought her weighted double fist down on the pilot's right temple. Even above the whistling of the wind, Winslow could hear the sickening crunch. She shoved the limp Grell out of his seat and grasped the control levers, stretching her hands as far apart as possible, and jerked them to the left.

The guards, still trying to right themselves after the hard right turn, were thrown completely off balance. One of them flailed his arms for an instant and, with a quavering high-pitched hiss that Winslow decided must be a Grella scream, toppled over the gunwale and fell toward the ruins-strewn forest below. Winslow, who had been ready for the sudden turn, thrust Messuin 76's feebly struggling form before him like a shield—the Grell weighed no more than a ten-year-old child—and thrust it against the remaining guard. At the same time, Shakespeare moved in from the left and grasped the weapon the guard had hesitated to use, wrenching it free. With a final shove, Winslow sent the guard over the side. Then, with a convulsive backwards jerk, he broke Messuin 76's neck.

It had all taken only a few seconds. The escort flyer was visible in the distance, moving erratically; its pilot was evidently struggling to keep his damaged craft aloft. Winslow dropped the limp Grella corpse away and flung himself forward, where Virginia Dare was awkwardly fumbling at the controls with her confined hands. The flyer plunged sickeningly.

"Bring her up!" he yelled. "We're headed for the ground!"

"I'm trying!" she shouted back. She touched something gingerly, and the flyer lurched and turned its nose upward. Winslow hung on, ignoring Shakespeare's wail from aft.

"Let me take those controls if you don't know what you're doing!" he told Virginia Dare.

"I told you I've never piloted one of these things. All I know is what I've learned from watching the Eilonwë experiment with captured ones—which is a damned lot more than you know!"

But it soon became apparent that she could only control whatever magical rudder made the flyer turn to port or starboard. As for whatever unimaginable force kept the craft aloft, her efforts were as likely as not to achieve the opposite of what she intended. She gingerly touched a toggle. The flyer went into a series of skidding jerks, as if it were fighting itself, and from aft came a grinding sound culminating in a muffled explosion. The flyer shuddered, and began angling steeply downward.

Winslow forced himself to think calmly. The flyer obviously wasn't designed to glide like a bird; once the lifting force was gone, it wouldn't stay up long on the stubby down-turned wings that extended from its flanks. He looked below at the approaching ground, and tried to orient himself.

"Turn to port and bring her down as far as possible over there," he shouted into Virginia Dare's ear over the wind.

"Why?" she demanded.

For answer, he pointed to the north. The escort flyer was far in the distance, wobbling toward the ground, apparently crippled by damage from the collision.

"They'll probably land gently enough to live," he explained. "And even if they don't they'll have already summoned others from the fortress. They'll be all over this area, to cut us off. We have to lead them away from the Eilonwë refuge."

She turned and met his eyes for the bare second she could spare, and for the first time he thought he saw something like respect in her face. Then her attention was riveted on the control console as she followed his instructions.

"They won't even have to call," she said absently as she changed course while endeavoring to slow their loss of altitude. "Remember, Sett 44 was monitoring us—he knows something happened, and you can be sure more flyers are already on the way . . . We're going down. I'm going to try to land us in the woods, away from the ruins. Brace yourselves!"

The two men obeyed as best they could, as the ground rushed up to meet them. Winslow had a confused impression of treetops and crumbling buildings, just before the flyer smashed into the forest with a snapping of tree trunks and a grinding of crumpled metal. Winslow was thrown free and landed in the underbrush just in time to see the flyer plough into the ground and come to a shuddering halt, held up at a crazy angle by the splintered trees.

He got to his feet in the sudden silence, bruised and shaken but with nothing broken. Virginia Dare and Shakespeare were lowering themselves over the gunwale and dropping to the ground below. Shakespeare looked worse than Winslow felt, but he was still grasping the Grella weapon like a dog with a bone in its jaws.

"We've got to get away from here," said Winslow without preliminaries. "They'll find this wreck."

"One thing first," Virigian Dare demurred. "Give me that weapon," she told Shakespeare. She took hold of the thing, clumsily because of her confined wrists and because it was designed for the shorter arms and four-digited hands of the Grella. "Hold out your arms," she told Winslow, "with the wrists spread as far apart as possible." He obeyed, and she held the muzzle of the thing to the short metal cable and touched the trigger. The metal seemed to burn in the weapon's beam, and heat scorched his arms, but the cable parted. She then did the same for Shakespeare, and then instructed Winslow in freeing her own hands.

"Now let's move," he said. They struck out through the forest, shortly emerging atop a knoll which afforded a wide view. Ahead of them, beyond a short stretch of woodland, was the slope where they had first entered this world.

"Look!" cried Virginia Dare, pointing to the west.

Winslow swung around and squinted. Far in the distance, in the sky above the valley floor, the sun glinted off three approaching flyers.

"They'll land soldiers," Virgina Dare said in tones of grim fatalism, "and start combing the area. At the same time, the flyers will go back aloft and search for us from above."

"We'll never escape such a cordon," Winslow muttered. "We'd have to vanish into thin air."

Shakespeare diffidently cleared his throat. "Ah . . . perhaps, Captain, that is precisely what we should do."

They both stared at him.

"I recognize that ridge ahead," the young actor continued. "The one we've been calling 'Elf Hill.' You've told us you can find the portal. And I recall what you were saying before: that perhaps we humans can, by an effort of will, remain suspended in the Near Void instead of passing on as we have before."

"But I was just thinking aloud!" Winslow blurted. "We have no way of knowing."

"Perhaps it's time to find out," said Virginia Dare. "It seems to be the only hiding place we have."

"And," said Shakespeare, warming to his argument, "at worst, we pass on into the Deep Void and on to Croatoan—"

"—Where only a minute passes for every nineteen or twenty minutes here," Winslow finished for him. "So God knows what we'd emerge into when we came back here." He sighed. "You're mad, Will. But you're also right. I fear we're in a land where madness is wisdom." He took another breath, and put the tone of command into his voice. "Now let's move! We have to reach the portal and pass through it before they're close enough to have us in sight. If they watch us vanish, they'll know exactly where the portal is, and all will be lost for England and England's world."

They ran through the woods with reckless speed, accumulating scratches from lashing tree branches, and emerged onto open ground. "Stay close," Winslow admonished, "so we'll all pass through together. And hurry!" Looking over his shoulder, he saw that the three approaching flyers were visibly larger, shapes and not just points of reflected sun.

They sprinted up the slope. Shakespeare was gasping, but he kept up. Winslow looked around at the landscape, and summoned up the contours he had memorized. "This way!" he shouted, turning a little to the left.

"What will we have to do to remain in the Near Void?" Virginia Dare demanded.

"How the Devil should I know? I don't even know if we can do it at all."

"Perhaps," gasped Shakespeare, breathing heavily as he ran uphill, "if there's something in the human soul that allows us to pass through, then we're not just helplessly borne on the winds of the Void. Our souls are our own, and only God can command them! And surely, unworthy though we are, we do God's work here, seeking the liberation of our own world from the Grella. If we wish ourselves to remain here strongly enough—"

And as he spoke, it was as Winslow remembered. The sunlit late morning began to fade into a blurred, colorless, unnatural twilight against which his companions stood out in vivid contrast.

— TWELVE —

THIS TIME, WINSLOW WAS EXPECTING IT. AND HE KNEW
he had less than a minute before falling into the bottomless nothingness of the Deep Void.

He remembered what Shakespeare had said. Of
course, the actor had no real knowledge to go on. But
no one did, where these things were concerned. His
guesses were as good as anyone else's. So Winslow tried
emptying his mind of everything except his need to stay
here in this strange world where the fate of his own
world might be decided.

That need, he found to his dawning astonishment, was
inseparable from thoughts of Virginia Dare.

He looked at her and at Shakespeare, standing out
so weirdly in all their vivid, colorful solidity against the
nacreous world around them. He noted that they cast
no shadows.

175

"Can you hear me?" he called out to them.

"There's no need to shout," said Virginia Dare archly. Her voice—and his own, come to that—had an odd quality. It seemed to be coming from a great distance, but held a deep resonance and reverberation, as though the ordinary laws that governed the transmission of sound did not apply. But what was interesting was that he could hear their voices at all. In the Deep Void, he had not been able to hear his own scream, any more than he had been able to see his own body, or those of others.

It must, he decided, be as Riahn had told them. This was a realm that somehow coexisted with physical reality. Or, he mentally amended, remembering Riahn's solid circles surrounded by dashed ones, with *each* physical reality, each like a bubble afloat in the incomprehensible emptiness of the Deep Void.

The thought of the Deep Void reminded him that he had allowed his mind to wander. He wrenched his thoughts back to their previous state of concentration. From the looks on their faces, his companions were doing the same.

"I don't know how long we'll be able to keep this up," said Virginia Dare. Winslow didn't either. It was, he reflected, something he should have thought of before.

"Captain," Shakespeare said abruptly, "it's here at the portal that we passed on into the Deep Void before. So . . . how if we move away from it?"

"Move away from it?" Winslow repeated blankly. The possibility of moving while in this state of being had never crossed his mind. "How?"

"Why . . . by walking, I imagine." The actor suited the action to the word, putting one foot forward, then the other. He walked away from them at the same rate he would have in what had once been the only world Winslow had ever imagined could exist.

Winslow and Virginia Dare looked at each other, then walked toward Shakespeare. He noted that it wasn't really like ordinary walking. The pressure on the soles of the feet wasn't there. Come to think of it, the grass hadn't seemed to bend under Shakespeare's feet. He decided he'd worry about it later.

Tentatively, he stopped thinking about the need to stay in the Near Void. Nothing happened. He saw a relaxation on the others' faces that suggested they'd had the same thought.

"I think you were right, Will," he breathed. He took a moment to look around. Now, for the first time, he could observe the phenomena of the Near Void at leisure. He looked up into the sky. In these conditions, it was almost like looking up through clear water. The sun was a white disk that could be gazed at unblinking. He looked in the direction from which the Grella flyers had been approaching. They had landed, and were presumably in the process of offloading their soldiers.

"All very well," said Virginia Dare in tones of prim female practicality. "But if we can only get into this Near Void at the portal, then how do we get *out* of it and back into the solid world, now that we're away from the portal?"

"I never thought of that," Shakespeare admitted. "But . . . maybe we can only enter the Near Void at a portal because the Near Void is so unnatural for us. Shouldn't it be easier for us to return to where we belong—the good, solid creation that gave us birth?"

"You mean you think we may not need a portal to return to the world of nature?" Winslow wondered. "But . . . how?"

"I don't know," Shakespeare admitted with uncharacteristic brevity.

"We remained in this state by willing it strongly enough," Virginia Dare reminded them. "We may as well try the same way again."

"You may be right," Winslow nodded. "But I alone will try it. Don't you two even let yourselves think of it. And don't move."

"Why?" she demanded.

"Because I'm the only one I *know* can find the portal again, once back in the real world."

"All right," she said grudgingly. "But whatever you're going to do, do it quickly. The Grella flyers aren't going to sit on the ground forever. And remember what you yourself said about letting them watch us vanishing into the portal."

"Yes, yes," he said absently. Most of his attention was on the problem of how to do this thing, if indeed it could be done. Intense concentration on his need to remain in contact with the world of the Eilonwë had sufficed to keep him from falling headlong into the abysses of the Deep Void, but that was all it had done. Something more must be needed to actually return to that world, piercing the impermeable wall that separated it from the Near Void that was in some incomprehensible fashion superimposed on it.

Shakespeare had spoken of returning to where they belonged. Perhaps he should dismiss all his earlier urgent thoughts of the fate of worlds and concentrate on the essence of that very belongingness—small things rather than great ones. Memories of the meadows through which he had run as a boy, in a springtime that must surely last forever; of the smell of the salt air that blew

in off the sea marshes; of the feel of the sun-blessed chill
of a winter morning . . .

With an abruptness for which none of the previous
transitions had prepared him, the world was back in all
its sharp-focused primary colors and dazzling sunlight.

He blinked away the dazzlement of the sudden brightness and fought off his disorientation. He looked around
him. Shakespeare and Virginia Dare were nowhere to be
seen. And in the distance, the Grella flyers were rising
into the sky.

He forced calmness on himself. The crews of those
flyers surely weren't observing this hillside yet. He ran
in the opposite of the direction they'd walked in the
strange way of the Near Void. He cast his eyes about
him, watching the contours of the landscape. It all came
back into its remembered configurations . . .

And he was back in the twilight world of the Near
Void. Shakespeare and Virginia Dare had obeyed his
instructions; they were still standing where he had left
them.

"They didn't see you, did they?" Shakespeare asked
nervously.

"I'm sure they didn't." Winslow looked into the murky
distance. The flyers were moving slowly over the valley,
conducting a methodical search. "If they had, they'd be
speeding in this direction."

"I only hope you're right," said Virginia Dare. Her
tone wasn't as skeptical as her words. She took a deep
breath. "So now we know we can move about in the
Near Void, and need no portal to depart from it. For
now, though, we'd best remain in it."

"Yes. It's a perfect hiding place. And we're going to
need one. In fact, I see no reason why we can't walk all
the way back to the Eilonwë refuge while still in it."

"Will we be able to do what you just did, so far from the portal?" Shakespeare wondered.

"There's one way to find out," stated Virginia Dare, and she set out down the slope, striding through the indistinct twilight-that-was-not-twilight. The two men could only follow.

They reached the outskirts of the ancient city and began picking their way over crumbled walls and fallen, moss-overgrown pillars. As they progressed, and no dangers appeared, Shakespeare's attentiveness seemed to wander in the presence of those mute ruins and the forgotten memories they held.

"Leave not the mansion so long tenantless lest, growing ruinous, the building fall and leave no memory of what it was," he said to himself, and gave a satisfied nod and closed his eyes as he put the words into the filing system between his ears.

"Careful, Will!" Winslow called out as they turned a corner of a half-collapsed structure and a tree appeared, growing through the cracked remains of what had been a street.

But Shakespeare didn't come out of his reverie in time to notice. He continued on . . . and walked through the tree.

For a while, they all simply stood, unable to react—especially Shakespeare, who looked back at the tree and down at his own body, for once at a loss for words.

Virginia Dare finally found her voice. "Why can't we do that?" she asked Winslow.

"How do you know we can't?" he responded, surprised at his own words. "We haven't tried. Actually, Will didn't try either. Nobody would walk into a solid obstacle, unless his mind was elsewhere as Will's was and he didn't notice it. We've been avoiding bumping into things just as we would if we were out for a walk in the normal world. It's the natural thing to do." He took a breath, squared his shoulders, and strode unflinchingly toward a still-standing segment of an ancient wall—and through it.

There was a brief instant of darkness as he occupied the same space as the wall, as though a wing beat across the dim, pearly sun. But he felt nothing. And then he was on the far side of the wall.

"Well, well!" he said softly.

"Riahn is right," Virginia Dare nodded. "This is a . . . a state of being that somehow overlaps the real world. Even he doesn't understand why we can—more or less—see the real world from it, while we can't be seen."

"Or, it would seem, be heard," said Shakespeare, and pointed.

They all froze. A squad of armed Grella were advancing around a hillock that had once been a building but was now a mound with only a few projecting corners of angular stones to suggest that it was anything other than a natural formation.

They all froze instinctively. But the Grella continued their advance, oblivious. Overhead, Winslow saw a flyer slowly following its search pattern. But he couldn't hear it, any more than he had heard anything from their surroundings ever since they had entered the Near Void. He remembered how Manteo's final scream had faded into inaudibility.

A sudden wild mood took him. He advanced straight toward one of the Grella soldiers. He heard a sharp intake of breath from Virginia Dare, but ignored it. He walked straight toward the Grell as he had toward the ancient wall . . . and was beyond him. The Grella patrol moved on, oblivious.

"We are indeed like ghosts," Winslow heard Shakespeare say. "Except that ghosts can sometimes be glimpsed by mortals . . . or so we're told. In truth, I can't claim I've ever seen one."

"Besides," said Virginia Dare with the matter of factness she could be counted on to bring to bear on Shakespeare's observations, "we aren't dead. Not that I know of, at least."

"Well," Winslow declared, "if I'd died, I like to think I would have *noticed* it. And I don't think my spirit would feel as hungry as I do now. So I refuse to worry about it. Let's go. We'll be lucky to reach the Eilonwë refuge before nightfall."

As it turned out, they couldn't. Their pace increased markedly after walking through rather than around obstacles became second nature to them. Nevertheless, the dim white sun sank toward the west, and began to set.

But it turned out to make no difference. The indistinct grayness around them grew no dimmer or darker than before. Whatever it was they were seeing the real world by, it evidently wasn't ordinary light. Winslow simply accepted it as a fact, thankfully but without any attempt to understand it. He'd leave that to the likes of Riahn and Dr. Dee. For now, he filed it away as another mystery.

Shakespeare raised yet another mystery as they walked. "Ah, Captain, I can't help wondering about something."

"You never can," Virginia Dare muttered.

"The way we can pass through solid objects," Shakespeare continued, ignoring her. "Well, Aristotle explained that things fall down because it is their nature to fall. So why don't we fall down through the solid ground, and find ourselves beneath the earth?"

"You're asking *me*?" An incredulous laugh escaped Winslow. "I understand none of this. But I have noticed something." He told them what he had observed before, about the grass beneath their feet.

"We must be walking in some fashion beyond ordinary human ken," Shakespeare opined.

"Well," said Virginia Dare impatiently, "however we're walking, let's do some more of it. I'm hungry too."

"As am I," Shakespeare agreed. "Though the chameleon love can feed on the air, I am one that am nourished by my victuals, and would fain have meat." He gave a particularly satisfied blink and nod, but then took on a perplexed look. "Any yet, after all this walking I feel strangely little weariness in my limbs."

"Now that you mention it, so do I," Winslow acknowledged, and promptly forgot about it. Another mystery.

They pressed on. Even in this strange realm of shadows, Virginia Dare had no trouble guiding them into and out of the labyrinth of ancient tunnels. Presently the great old ruined building appeared ahead in the dimness.

"All right, Tom, tell us how you returned to the world of sound and feeling." It was, Winslow realized, the first time Virginia Dare had ever addressed him by his Christian name. He described to her and Shakespeare the thoughts and feelings he had allowed to take possession of his mind.

"But," he concluded, "don't try it yet. Let's continue on inside."

"Why?" Virginia Dare wanted to know. But Winslow hurried on up the curving old staircase, and his companions followed.

Inside, the artificial illumination gave neither more nor less light than the sun or the starlight had. But they were used to that by now, as they were to the ease with which they passed through the warren of partitions and cubicles. Finally, they came to the central chamber. It was largely empty, this late at night, but at the far end Walsingham and Dee were hunched over a table in conclave with Riahn and a pair of other Eilonwë. Their conversation was inaudible, of course, but worry etched their faces.

"*Now* will you tell us why we're still playing ghost?" demanded Virginia Dare, exasperated.

Winslow turned to her with a wide grin. "One thing I've never been able to do—in fact, I'm not sure anyone has ever been able to do it—is surprise Mr. Secretary Walsingham!"

The consternation that erupted when he appeared out of nowhere, a second or two before Shakespeare and Virginia Dare, was deeply satisfying.

— THIRTEEN —

WALSINGHAM FINALLY DROVE OFF THE SWARMS OF WELL-wishers, even putting his foot down with the Queen —and, what was rather more difficult, with John Dee and Riahn, both of whom were in a frenzy of curiosity. He insisted that the three returnees be allowed to sleep for what remained of the night.

Winslow was grateful; despite the odd lack of physical weariness they had noticed, they were mentally and emotionally exhausted. He knew, however, that as usual Mr. Secretary had an ulterior motive. He wanted them alert, refreshed, and able to respond to searching questions at a meeting the following morning.

That meeting turned out to be as small as Walsingham could arrange. It wasn't that he was worried about what a later era would call security leaks. It was impossible to imagine any of the Eilonwë spying for the Grella, and while only the naïve would doubt that there were humans capable of selling out their own kind, the Grella's arrogance rendered them incapable of exploiting that weakness. No, it was only that he wanted a gathering of manageable size.

Besides himself it consisted of the Queen (of course), Dee, Riahn, John White (limp with relief over the miraculous reappearance of his granddaughter), and Tyralair, an elderly female Eilonwë specialist in the theory of the Void. She, it turned out, was the only member of her race other than Riahn to have mastered English, driven by her desire to extract every possible crumb of information from the colonists about their transition to this world. Now she fidgeted with fascination as Winslow and the others related their adventures.

" . . . And so we returned," Winslow finished, rather anticlimactically. "Perhaps someone can answer a question Will raised: since we could pass through solid objects, why did we stay atop the ground instead of falling down through it?"

"First of all," said Tyralair, speaking as though most of her mind was elsewhere, "you were not so much 'passing through' objects as coexisting with them in the same volume of space but in another dimension—another phase of existence, if you will, wherein you could not physically interact with the material world. This last of course, answers your question. Your bodies were not physical objects at all, and therefore were not subject to the force of . . . " Tyralair sought unsuccessfully for an English word, then tried again. "To the mutual attraction between such objects which causes the lesser to seem to fall toward the greater."

"But Aristotle has clearly explained—" Dee began, before the Queen shushed him.

"In fact," Tyralair continued, ignoring him, "it is my belief that you moved in this state by sheer force of will. Your bodies went through the motions of walking as a matter of automatic, conditioned reflex, in response to commands from your minds to move from one place to another. This would account for the lack of apparent physical effort you noticed."

Shakespeare clearly hadn't been listening to this last part. He looked thoughtful, and a bit queasy. "What if we had returned to the solid world while our bodies—or *part* of our bodies—had been 'coexisting in the same volume of space' with, say, a wall . . . or a person?"

Winslow, to whom this rather gruesome thought had not occurred, now understood why the young actor looked queasy.

"The consequences would, of course, have been most regrettable," said Tyralair, still speaking in the same more-than-half-distracted way. "But I consider the possibility remote. The return requires a mental effort on your part, and I believe your minds would shy away from making the effort under such circumstances. Of course," she added in a tone altogether too detached for Winslow's taste, "it would be interesting to see if the mental barrier could be surmounted."

"Well," Winslow said hastily, before she could suggest making the experiment, "at any rate we're back. We thought that you, Dr. Dee, and you, Tyralair, would be interested in our experiences."

" 'Interested'!" blurted Tyralair. "I should say so! This opens up wholly new and unsuspected ramifications of your human ability to pass through portals. Of course, the question of whether you can do so at portals which the Grella have not yet opened up—'latent' portals, one might call them—remains unanswered."

"Even if we can," Walsingham observed, "the ability would have no usefulness. How could we know where such portals are?" He had initially been transfigured by the espionage possibilities, only to come down to earth with a bump as he remembered that nothing worth spying on was accessible to Croatoan Island. "Only by an incredibly unlikely chance would we stumble across one."

"Probably true," Tyralair admitted. "Although, given how difficult it is for the Grella to locate latent portals, they could be more common than we have assumed. Quite common, in fact."

"Yes!" said Dee eagerly. "Such unexpected transpositions in the distant past could be the source of any number of tales. And perhaps people who returned tried to mark the locations." He took on a faraway look. "All those circles of standing stones . . . "

"A fascinating possibility," said Riahn dryly. "But another question that remains unanswered—and one with somewhat more immediate practical significance —is whether we Eilonwë have the same ability as you humans to effortlessly pass through portals that the Grella *have* opened."

"And if so," Tyralair took his thought one step further, "can we also linger in the Near Void at will, and depart from it anywhere, as we now know humans can do?" She turned to Winslow. "Now that we know you can locate the portal reliably, perhaps we can finally answer these questions."

"Er . . . perhaps, my lady." He didn't know how else to address Tyralair. "But I caution you that there are hazards involved in reaching that hillside. Recall what happened to us when I insisted on trying it!"

"And after our escape," Virginia Dare added grimly, "the Grella will surely be patrolling the nearer fringes of the old city, although they still don't seem to suspect the hill slope itself."

"Yes," Walsingham sighed. "A pity." He had relinquished his visions of exploiting the Near Void's possibilities for spying—at least as far as Earth was concerned. Here, however . . . "You say, Mistress Dare, that it's about thirty miles from the portal to the Grella fortress at the other portal? Hmm . . . Only a two-day trek for the young and fit, especially considering that it would be less wearisome than it would normally be, from what you've told us."

"One moment, my Moor!" The Queen leaned forward, reading his thoughts. "Are you scheming to send your agents through this Faërie-like realm of the 'Near Void' to the Grella fortress to spy it out?" Riahn stared openmouthed; it was clearly a novel thought.

"Well, Your Majesty, the thought naturally crossed my mind. Invisibility . . . The ability to pass through walls . . . " The spymaster took on a dreamy look.

"We couldn't hear sounds from the real world, sir," Virginia Dare reminded him, "any more than we ourselves could be heard."

"The ability would scarcely be missed, as no one can understand the Grella tongue anyway." Walsingham looked for confirmation to Riahn, who nodded. "Yes . . . the possibilities . . . "

"Mr. Secretary," said Winslow, before he had fully worked out in his own mind what he was saying, "are you sure that's all you want to do?"

"Eh?" Walsingham blinked away his reverie. "What do you mean, Thomas?"

"You're forgetting that in addition to passing through the world in a ghostlike state, we can come *out* of that state wherever we wish."

"But then you'd no longer be invisible and invulnerable. And you'd be unable to resume that state, for you can only enter the Near Void at the portal. You'd be discovered."

For just an instant, before answering, Winslow let himself savor the undreamed-of sensation of being a step ahead of Walsingham. "All very true, Mr. Secretary, and a great disadvantage—*if all you're interested in is spying*. But everyone who's ever gone raiding has daydreamed of being able to appear out of thin air inside the enemy's stronghold—just as we appeared here last night." He grinned wolfishly. "Imagine if it had been armed enemies who'd suddenly been among you!"

"Sweet Jesu!" the Queen breathed. "You *are* a bold one, Captain Winslow!" Even more gratifying was the look on Virginia Dare's face he glimpsed out of the corner of his eye.

Riahn found his tongue. "So you would lead a raiding force through the Near Void to the Grella fortress, pass undetected into it, and emerge in their midst?" He shook his head. "Your Queen is right about you, Captain. And with such an advantage of surprise, I'm sure you could wreak fearful slaughter among the Grella. But there are too many of them, and their weapons are too devastating. Besides, Mr. Secretary Walsingham was right: once you left the Near Void, you could not reenter it, thirty miles from the portal. You would be trapped inside the fortress. The Grella would hunt you down like rats and kill you, and the sacrifice would have been for nothing."

"So it might well turn out, sir—and if we were fools enough to throw away an unsupported raiding party that way, we'd deserve it. But it's something else I have in mind. At the same predetermined time we attack them from within, you Eilonwë attack them from without."

For a moment, Riahn and Tyralair simply stared, as though not understanding what he was talking about. It came to Winslow that he had just blithely contradicted thousands of years of brutal experience.

"Attack them?" Riahn finally repeated. "You mean . . . attack them *directly*? *Openly*?" His face was a study in automatic rejection of a self-evidently suicidal suggestion. "But . . . but we *can't!*"

"I've seen you Eilonwë fight them," said Winslow.

"Oh, yes: furtive ambushes, pinprick raids. But an all-out frontal attack?" Riahn shuddered. "I think you still don't fully comprehend what their weapons can do. You should listen to those of us who have been fighting them for ages and are, if not wiser, at least more experienced than you."

"Having felt the heat of Saint Antony's Fire, I think we English have reason to know about their weapons," said Winslow quietly. "And as for your experience fighting them . . . you've never had us raising the Devil with them from within, distracting and disordering them for you. No weapon is any better than the skill and coolness with which it is wielded. The Grella will find it hard to summon up much of either in the midst of panic and chaos."

Elizabeth Tudor leaned forward in a way that could only be called predatory. "Yes, Sir Riahn! This is an opportunity you've never had before. Will you Eilonwë go on through all that remains of eternity, nipping at their heels like oft-whipped dogs, when now at last you have a chance to leap at their throats?"

Once again, Riahn's face was easy to read through its alienness. It was a battleground where tantalizing temptation warred with his blood's memory of a thousand ancestors who had lived long enough to beget children because they had been too cautious to throw themselves into the mouths of the Grella hell-weapons.

"But," he finally temporized, "my *sheuath* simply doesn't have the numbers to mount a mass attack. No *sheuath* does."

"Well, then," the Queen declared, "the answer would seem obvious: form a league with the other *sheuaths* and field an allied army."

Riahn blinked several times. "But it's unheard of! The *sheuaths* have never acted together. You have no idea of the eons of tradition behind their independence, nor of the jealousies that exist among the leaders. They would never agree."

Walsingham wore the look of a man who at long last found himself back in his own element. "If you will call a conclave of these leaders," he said smoothly, "I may perhaps be able to be of assistance in securing their agreement. I have some small experience in these matters. Ah . . . what was that, Thomas?"

"Nothing, Mr. Secretary," Winslow wheezed. "Only a cough."

"One point, Captain Winslow," said John White, speaking up for the first time. His voice held his usual diffidence, but underlying it was a determination none of them had heard before. "If you do essay this venture, I wish to be included in it. Indeed, I *will* be included in it."

"No offense, Master White," Winslow said carefully, "but you're no fighting man. You're not one of the sea dogs in my crew, nor one of the English who, like your granddaughter, have been hardened by twenty years' struggle against the Grella in this world."

"No. But I think I can truly say that I have more reason than most to want vengeance against the Grella. They owe me a blood debt. You are now offering me a chance to collect on it. You *must* let me come!"

Winslow exchanged a brief eye contact with Virginia Dare. Much passed between them in that split second. They had, by unspoken common consent, not told her grandfather what they now knew about how Ananias Dare and Eleanor White Dare had met their end. Now, without the necessity for words, they renewed their resolve that he need not know it. They likewise wordlessly resolved that he did, indeed, have the right to seek wergild from the Grella.

Something else Winslow read in Virginia Dare's eyes in that instant of silent communion. He had never felt the slightest desire to be a Grell, but now the desire was even further from his mind than ever. Indeed, he thought with a shiver, he was very, very thankful that he was not one.

"Very well," he told John White with a kind of gentle gruffness. "If you think you can keep up, you can come."

"This is all very well," said Dee in his most portentous voice, "but aren't we forgetting what Captain Winslow told us earlier about the danger of approaching the portal? It is dangerous even for an individual of a small group. How can a large raiding force hope to march up that naked hillside unseen?"

"That problem is even greater than you think," said Riahn, "for reasons I'll explain later. Nevertheless . . . I believe we can provide a device that will enable you to overcome it. This also I will elaborate upon in due course."

"You agree to the plan, then?" the Queen asked eagerly.

"I am at least willing to consider it. My agreement is conditional. I will commit my *sheuath* to an attack only if the other *sheuath* leaders agree to do so—an eventuality in which I do not share your confidence, Mr. Secretary."

"You are perhaps too pessimistic," said Walsingham mildly. "But if I am to provide help I will need for you to give me all available information about the individuals with whom we will be dealing: their ages, personal histories, beliefs, attitudes, habits, relationships . . . and, not least important, how they are regarded by their peers. I refer not just to the *sheuath* leaders, but to their key aides and advisors as well. And, of course, I will require the history, current status, capabilities and reputations of the *sheuaths* which they lead, with an emphasis on the positions they have traditionally taken on the overriding question of how best to deal with the Grella."

Riahn looked slightly dazed. "Ah . . . this involves a large volume of information."

"Indubitably. I suggest we confer on the matter tonight, unless you have other pressing business. Fortunately, I have a good memory . . . and at need I can largely dispense with sleep. Not as easily as in my youth, of course. But," Walsingham concluded with his favorite phrase, "knowledge is never too dear."

The Eilonwë, they discovered, did not personify their *sheuaths*, as humans did their nations, by giving them names. That kind of group identification was foreign to them. Their loyalties were personal, not to abstractions. The *sheuath* led by Riahn was referred to simply as Riahn's *sheuath*, for as long as he led it. And so it was with all the other leaders.

By devious routes, by night, through the labyrinths of ancient tunnels and ruins, those leaders came in response to Riahn's call. Not all of them that he had invited, of course. Some simply rejected out of hand anything so unprecedented. Others pleaded inability to make the journey in safety—perhaps truthfully. But enough arrived to fill the central chamber to capacity, and to require the removal of some of the surrounding partitions to make room for the overflow. Winslow didn't know the Eilonwë well enough to form an opinion as to whether the sheer novelty of the summons might have something to do with a turnout that exceeded Riahn's dour expectations.

It soon became obvious that there were no established procedures to govern a gathering like this, and certainly no rules of precedence among leaders who acknowledged no unity above the *sheuath* level. This wasn't entirely a bad thing, for it meant there were no procedural objections to allowing humans to sit in on the conclave. Some of the Eilonwë from other *sheuaths* had met the colonists before, and all knew of them. And by now, everyone had learned—with varying degrees of happiness —that new humans had arrived. So there were some stares of frank curiosity but no protests when Walsingham, Dee, Winslow and Virginia Dare took their places among the group that followed Riahn, as similar groups clustered behind the other leaders, in no particular order. ("Worse than Parliament," Walsingham was heard to mutter.) The Queen had not jeopardized the royal dignity by exposing herself to the disorder directly, but rather let her Principal Secretary represent her. He listened with a look of intense concentration as Virginia Dare provided a running translation.

"From time immemorial," declared Avaerahn, a *sheuath* leader from a region to the southeast, "the path of wisdom has been clear: avoid provoking the Grella into exerting the full extent of their powers against us. Some have indulged in petty displays of bravado"—a meaningful glance at Riahn—"but in the main we have all followed this prudent policy."

"And what has it gotten us?" grumbled the dour Imalfar, a nearer neighbor of Riahn.

"Survival! The Grella could exterminate us if we annoyed them enough to exhaust their patience. If driven to such an extreme, they could render our world lifeless!"

"Preposterous!" scoffed Imalfar. "This world is too valuable to them. What good would an uninhabitable ball of slag be?"

"How can we predict what they would do if sufficiently angered?" Avaerahn shot back. "They don't think like us."

"That's true," intoned Leeriven, a female as the Eilonwë leaders frequently were, and a consistent voice of indecision masquerading as prudence. "It would be unwise to rely on our ability to predict how aliens like the Grella would react to provocation."

"But," protested Riahn, "have you not been listening? If this works, we'll no longer have to worry about what they will do! If we capture their fortress, sitting there practically atop the portal to their other worlds, with their weapons in our hands—"

"Yes: if, if, if!" grumbled Avaerahn. "That's all we've heard from you, Riahn. Glittering schemes to free us from the grip of aliens, all of which require us to put our trust in *other* aliens." He gave the knot of humans behind Riahn a sour look.

Riahn bristled. "The humans have been among us for almost twenty years, and they've earned my trust!" Walsingham leaned forward, touched his shoulder, and whispered something in his ear. The Eilonwë nodded and resumed. "Furthermore, they have very good reason to aid us to the utmost. As long as the Grella rule our world, there is always the possibility that they will blunder onto the portal leading to the humans' world—as, indeed, they did long ago—and enslave it. But if we regain control here, those Grella now infesting the human world will be isolated, with no possibility of reinforcement."

"Riahn has a point, Avaerahn," said Leeriven, agreeing as was her wont with the last speaker.

"Yes, yes . . . But still, we simply *can't* attack the Grella directly. It's never been done before. It's without precedent. It's . . . "

Eventually the conclave broke up, having accomplished nothing as usual. Winslow got to his feet, stiff with weariness and discouragement. Out of the corner of his eye, he saw Walsingham in close conversation with Riahn. He strolled over.

"You want me to set up a meeting for you with *Avaerahn*?" the Eilonwë was saying incredulously. "But he's the leader of the faction most opposed to the plan. Why not Imalfar, who is inclined our way, or even Leeriven, who might be persuaded?"

"I thought I might be able to make our position, and the plan's advantages, clearer to Avaerahn," said Walsingham smoothly. "Incidentally, I think it would be best if

Tyralair could be there to translate. Avaerahn might be more comfortable with an Eilonwë interpreter."

"He might very well," said Riahn in a tone of studied understatement. "All right. I'll see what I can do."

"I think, Thomas," said Walsingham as Riahn walked off, "that you might want to be present. You may find it interesting. But please don't act surprised at anything I say."

"And so," Walsingham concluded through the medium of Tyralair's translation, "you can see why we humans are very much in earnest in this matter . . . and why your *sheuath* stands to benefit if the plan succeeds."

"Yes, yes," said Avaerahn with the ostentatious disinterest of one who had agreed to the meeting only as a courtesy to Riahn. "Although I hope you don't mean to imply that I, or any leader of any *sheuath,* would be motivated by any desire for competitive advantage over his fellows."

"Of *course* not," Walsingham assured. "Such a thought never crossed my mind—even when I heard the reasons why Leeriven is about to declare in favor of the plan."

Mindful of Walsingham's instructions, Winslow kept his face impassive. Not so Avaerahn, who practically sprang forward. *"What?"*

Walsingahm wore a flustered look that might have fooled some people. "Oh—you didn't know? Dear me! Perhaps I've said too much."

Avaerahn wasn't listening. "Preposterous! Everyone knows how cautious Leeriven is."

"Of course she is. That's why she isn't letting it become general knowledge yet." Walsingham gave a head-shake of bogus self-reproach for his careless tongue.

"But . . . but . . . what are her reasons?" demanded Avaerahn.

"Precisely the reasons I've been explaining to you: to improve the relative position of her *sheuath* in the world that follows the plan's successful conclusion. Think of the territorial concessions she could insist on—and, even more important, the share of captured Grella weapons. Whereas, on the other hand . . . those *sheuaths* which do *not* participate . . . " Walsingham left the thought dangling.

If Winslow hadn't known that the Eilonwë didn't go pale, he would have sworn that Avaerahn did so. "I can still hardly believe that she would . . . This must be investigated!"

"Most certainly," Walsingham nodded. "Permit me to suggest a possible avenue of investigation. There is a certain aide of Leeriven's. Here is his name." He slid a slip of paper across the table that separated them. Avaerahn took it. "I have happened to hear that he is, uh, friendly with one of your subordinates." Another silent transfer of paper took place. "You could have her sound him out, under circumstances where his tongue might be less guarded than it should."

"Hmm . . . your suggestion may well have merit." Avaerahn departed, looking very thoughtful. As soon as he was gone, Winslow turned to Walsingham.

"Is this true, Mr. Secretary? And if it is, will this aide of Leeriven's really reveal it to a paramour from another *sheuath*?"

"To both, the answer is, of course, no. The aide is one who, with Riahn's help, I identified early on as one of Leeriven's people who favored a bolder policy against the Grella. I have been working on him for some time, and have explained his role to him. He will, in an apparent heat of passion, repeat to Averahn's female subordinate the story I have just told Avaerahn. Shortly, everyone except Leeriven herself will know that she plans to declare in our favor." Walsingham stood up briskly. Winslow thought he hadn't looked so young in years. He was clearly enjoying himself more than a Puritan ought. "And now, let us proceed to our next meeting."

"Our *next* meeting, Mr. Secretary?"

"Yes—with Leeriven. There I will let her know that Avaerahn plans to join with us, and make sure she understands the implications of that for the future position of her own *sheuath*." Halfway out the door, Walsingham paused for an afterthought. "Oh, by the way, Thomas: I suggest you proceed to finalize your plans for the raid on the Grella fortress. With Avaerahn and Leeriven vying with each other to join Riahn and Imalfar, we'll have all four of the most important factions behind us and I anticipate no further trouble organizing the Eilonwë side of the operation." Then he was out the door, and Winslow could only follow in a daze.

It came to him, though, that he should feel no surprise. The Grella had made an enemy of Mr. Secretary Walsingham, and they were about to join a select company that included Anthony Babington and Mary Stuart. Only this time he, Winslow, was going to wield the headsman's axe.

On reflection, though, he decided he might well be persuaded to share the task with Virginia Dare.

— FOURTEEN —

WINSLOW STARED INCREDULOUSLY AT RIAHN. THEY WERE sitting in the elderly Eilonwë's private retreat: a small room cluttered with papers, books, maps, and a miscellany of objects most of which lay beyond Winslow's understanding. In one corner was a globe of this world to which Winslow's eyes kept straying, for the sense of familiarity that underlay its strange continental outlines was fascinating and somehow disturbing. But now he could think only of the incredible statement Riahn had just made.

"Are you saying the Grella have made *moons*?"

"Very small ones," Riahn assured him. "One of them could fit into this room. And not many of them—a few artificial moons, a hundred or so miles up. Their presence is one of the reasons we Eilonwë have to conceal ourselves and move about so stealthily. The Grella put them up there for the purpose of watching the world's surface. They circle the world every ninety minutes, traveling at eighteen thousand miles an hour." Seeing Winslow's incredulous look, Riahn tried to explain. "It is the speed at which an object keeps falling *around* the world rather than falling down to the surface. They mount devices which can instantly send images of what is below them, greatly magnified, to Grella observers in the fortress."

"But . . . but . . . " Winslow struggled to understand. "I can see how the images could be magnified, using lenses like those of ordinary eyeglasses—"

"Well, yes, you might say that," Riahn allowed.

"—but how can the Grella down here on the surface of the world see these images?"

"It is very difficult to explain. But you are, of course, aware of the way a magnet attracts iron. Dr. Dee has told me that the Queen's physician Dr. William Gilbert has performed experiments to see if that is somehow related to the way amber, when rubbed, attracts almost any very light matter. He has postulated a quality for which he has used the Greek word for amber: *electron.* In fact, the quality is not unique to amber. It is everywhere, and it can be used in innumerable ways. It is the basis for our devices for speaking across great distances. We had advanced that far before the Grella conquest. It can be used to send images as well as sound." Riahn spread his hands in one of the human gestures he had picked up. "I'm afraid that is the best I can do in your language. You must take my word for it."

"So," said Winslow thoughtfully, "if one of these . . . things is overhead every ninety minutes, we must make our move during one of those ninety-minute intervals."

"Just so. Fortunately, we have been ordering our lives around that interval for a very long time. We will have no difficulty timing the movement of your force to the portal."

"Well and good. But that still leaves the ordinary dangers: Grella on foot and in flyers. They may not be as thick in the area as they were, considering how much time has passed since our return." Winslow bit back his frustration at the length of time it was taking the Eilonwë alliance to get its forces into position. He knew the difficulties they labored under—it was more like an infiltration than a mobilization—but the waiting still gnawed at him. "Nevertheless, they're still patrolling."

"Yes—and you are contemplating moving a whole group of raiders up the open slope to the portal," Riahn nodded. "It would seem that your chances of success would be best if you moved under cover of a moonless night."

"Shakespeare suggested that. I'll tell you the same thing I told him: I doubt my ability to locate the portal in the dark. And a large group blundering about in search of it would have trouble staying together. I know from experience the dangers of trying to coordinate a night attack."

"Yes, Mr. Secretary Walsingham has indicated to me the nature of some of your experiences," said Riahn dryly. "Fortunately, I believe I can be of assistance." He rummaged in the clutter and emerged with what looked like a small pair of the bi-oculars with which Winslow was already familiar, except that they were set in a head-band of a flexible material that reminded Winslow of the rubber that the Portuguese had discovered in Brazil. Then he touched a tiny lever-like object in a wall, and the lights went out. Winslow didn't hope to understand, but now he wondered if the flameless lights might also be somehow related to Dr. Gilbert's experiments with amber. The room was now dark save for dim glows from a few instruments. "Put it on," said Riahn.

Winslow obeyed, slipping the flexible headband around his head and settling the lenses over his eyes. All at once he could see the room in all its detail, albeit in weird shades of green. A horrid oath escaped his lips. Riahn smiled.

"The device gathers light," he explained. "Even the tiny amount of light presently in this room. That's the only way I can explain it. It can do the same with the starlight. Seeing in this way, do you think you could find the portal at night?"

"I'll want to try using it outside, to see how well it works for distant objects. But . . . yes, I think I might. Is this one of the wonders from your great age, before the Grella conquest?"

"No. It was beyond our capabilities even then. We have copied it, with great difficulty, from a captured Grella device. Thus we have only a very limited supply of them, despite their great usefulness to us in evading the Grella. But we can supply one for you, and perhaps two others for your lieutenants—one of whom, I gather is going to be Alanthru . . . I mean Virginia."

"Good," said Winslow, not noticing the slip of the tongue. He took off the light-gatherer, and Riahn restored the room's light in the same incomprehensible way he had banished it. "I suppose this means," Winslow continued, "that we no longer need to worry about avoiding the passage of these . . . moons of the Grella. All we need do is proceed by cover of night."

"Unfortunately, this is not the case. The moons' devices also have means of seeing in darkness. You wouldn't be as visible to them as you would in daylight. But for safety's sake we must still plan to avoid them."

"They can do this from . . . there?" Winslow pointed upward. Riahn nodded. Winslow said no more. He was rapidly ceasing to worry about things he couldn't hope to understand. He understood that he could trust Riahn. That was enough.

One moonless night, Winslow made his lone, stealthy way to the portal. He needed to be certain he could find it using the light-gatherers. He also needed to perform an experiment, on whose results the practicality of the whole plan rested. He entered the Near Void, walked a short distance away from the portal, lay down, and went to sleep.

His often hazardous life had give him the ability to cat nap at need. He did so now, and awoke to find himself still in the indistinct gray world of the Near Void. Things looked the same there as they did in daytime, confirming Riahn's supposition that whatever he was seeing the solid world by was not ordinary light. But more importantly, Winslow had confirmed his own earlier impression that once one had made the conscious decision to stay in the Near Void, it took an equally conscious act of will to return to the material world. The raiders would be able to pause and sleep on their way to the Grella fortress —which, he thought, was very fortunate indeed. A forced march of thirty miles at a stretch was not impossible for young, fit, lightly laden people. But it would be for naught if they arrived too weary to fight a battle. And

John White would probably be lucky to make two fifteen-mile marches with a sleep period between. Relieved, Winslow made his way back.

That was the only transit of the portal they dared risk in the course of their preparations. Winslow would have liked to take his hand-picked raiders through for familiarization and training purposes, but it was out of the question. If they were caught entering or exiting the portal, thus revealing its location to the Grella, all would be lost. So the actual attack would be their first experience of the Near Void—a fact with which Winslow was far from happy.

Actually, it was even worse than that. Winslow had no way of being sure that all of them would be capable of the kind of mental effort required to remain in the Near Void rather than passing on into the Deep Void. All he could do was choose men—and a couple of women from among the colonists' children—who seemed to possess both intelligence and determination, explain to them carefully what was required, and hope for the best.

He also chose Shakespeare. The actor might seem somewhat out of place among a group—eleven sailors and soldiers from *Heron* and nine young English of this world—chosen as hard-bitten fighters, but at least he had proven his ability to negotiate the Near Void. He was also eager. Winslow only wished his eagerness had a little more warlike experience standing behind it.

Similar considerations caused Winslow to refuse to accept any Eilonwë for the raiding party, despite the passionate entreaties of some of the young bloods in Riahn's *sheuath*. In the absence of opportunities for experimentation, there was still no way to know for certain if the Eilonwë could pass through portals the way humans could, much less will themselves to remain in the Near Void. He could afford no stragglers on this raid.

Then there was the matter of equipment. Moving through the Near Void, a human could take with him as much as he could have carried in normal conditions. Tyralair was of the opinion that this was a limitation imposed by the mind, much like the walking motion the body underwent. Be that as it might, they were stuck with it. So Winslow wanted their weapons chosen with care.

Firearms, as they knew, were useless. The Grella hand weapons of focused light, and the small energy packs that powered them, were beyond the ability of the Eilonwë to reproduce. They were therefore limited to the precious, irreplaceable supply of captured ones, most of which must be used in the frontal assault if it were to have a prayer of success. But Eilonwë workshops could replace handles, stocks and triggers with ones suited to human hands. Winslow had five of these converted weapons, all of which he assigned to the local English, who were familiar with them.

Virginia Dare took one. She also had a new sword made, to the same design as the one which was now in the hands of the Grella. She loudly bemoaned the inferiority of the replacement. But Winslow, watching her practice with it, was reminded of tales he had heard from a Portuguese mariner who had been to the fabulous islands of Japan and seen warriors in fantastical lamellar armor wield the slightly curved two-handed swords he had sworn were the best in the world. He had also sworn that their ancestral fighting technique of *kendo* put a force behind those swords' supernally sharp edges that could cut a man in half—the *long* way—with a single stroke. Winslow had thought he was hearing typical sea stories. Now he wasn't so sure. *Not a man*, his mind still insisted. *But a Grell . . . ?*

Winslow's backsword was likewise lost. He looked over the slashing blades the Eilonwë had designed for humans, chose a two-handed one, and then asked the Eilonwë to shorten the hilt and add a lead-weighted pommel for balance. The result was a one-handed sword with authority. He wanted it one-handed so he could simultaneously wield a favorite knife of his: an old-fashioned but still very serviceable example of the ballock dagger, so called because of the suggestive shape of the guard.

Each of those who did not have one of the modifed Grella weapons carried a small but heavy bomb of Eilonwë make which could be set to explode at a desired instant. Winslow was skeptical of their utility. It would, of course, be wonderful to leave a trail of such things behind them as they advanced into the fortress. But they couldn't, unless the people carrying them reentered the material world—which, of course, meant that they'd be stranded there, in full view of the Grella. Still, he had agreed to take the things. One never knew what would prove useful.

Otherwise, everyone carried his or her usual weapon—including, in Shakespeare's case, his boarding pike. John White, about whose presence Winslow still had misgivings, would take the lightest sword he could borrow, and a stiletto.

Military amateurs like Walsingham and Dee, falling into the common fallacy of equating numbers with strength, wondered aloud why Winslow wasn't taking every able-bodied human fighter available. He did his best to explain it to them. In an infiltration raid like this, numbers were secondary. He preferred to appear inside the Grella fortress with a few raiders he felt he could be sure of. The other humans could do more good by stiffening the spine of the Eilonwë assault. He finally carried the point by citing the Biblical precedent of Gideon, who had overthrown the Midianites with three hundred reliable men winnowed from 32,000 volunteers. In the meantime, he put the enforced delay to good use by training his twenty-three people as thoroughly as circumstances permitted.

He also trained himself. He was exercising with his hybrid sword in his room beneath the great ruined building when he heard a sound at the door. Obeying battle-honed reflexes, he whirled in that direction, sword raised over and behind his head and dagger-armed left hand extending forward for balance. Then he saw who it was and relaxed, although it took a second before he recognized Virginia Dare. He had never seen her wavy dark-chestnut hair hanging free, unconfined by its usual thick braid.

"Interesting design for a handguard," she commented, indicating the two balls at the base of the dagger's blade.

"Uh, ahem, yes," he muttered, hastily putting the ballock dagger aside and lowering his sword. "Won't you come in?"

She entered but did not sit down. Instead she rested her back against the wall and stood with her hands behind her, in a posture Winslow had never seen her adopt. For a moment there was silence.

"Do you think this is going to work?" she asked without preamble.

"Of course!" He put heartiness in his voice. "Sett 44 and all his fellow vermin will befoul themselves, or whatever it is the Grella do, when we appear in their midst. And after thousands of years of bullying the Eilonwë, they won't know how to deal with a concerted attack on their stronghold."

"And afterwards? ... we'll be able to return to England?" She laughed unsteadily. "Will you listen to me? 'Return,' when I've never been there! But you know what I mean."

"Why, yes. We'll take a load of captured weapons back, whip the Dons out of England, and cleanse the world of the Gray Monks." He raised an eyebrow. "Why do you ask? Do you doubt it?"

"No, not really. I just wanted reassurance." Then, without the slightest change of tone or expression: "Do you have a wife or a sweetheart in England?"

"Wha—! Why, that is, no. I've never had the opportunity, you might say. And you? Among the young Englishmen here?"

"No." The negative was flat and emphatic. "We don't ... " Her face reddened. "We don't ... well, we only do things that ... can't cause children to be conceived."

"But children—quite a few of them—have been born to the colonists in this world. I'm going to be leading several of them on the raid."

"Oh, yes. The elders continued to have children here. For them it was ... habit, I suppose. They couldn't imagine *not* doing it. But their children—those born here and those of us who arrived here as babes—have not. Haven't you noticed the absence of small ones?"

Winslow hadn't, and now he wondered why he hadn't. In England, girls typically began childbearing in their mid teens. Even if half the infants died, as was also typical, there ought to be a gaggle of children under five or so here. But there were none.

"Why?" he asked.

"What right had we to bring children into the world—*this* world, that offered them nothing except inescapable doom? Life has held nothing for us except an endless, hopeless twilight struggle against the Grella. We would not force innocent children to join us in that trap. At first the elders thought we were being sinful, violating God's command to be fruitful and multiply. But they finally came to understand, and even to agree."

"Why are you telling me this?" asked Winslow after a lengthy silence.

"Because now things have changed." She advanced a step toward him. "We've been offered a way out of the trap. *You* have offered it to us. You've opened up possibilities we never dared dream of. The old reasoning no longer compels me, and I want to reject it." She drew a deep, unsteady breath. "I want to have a child."

All at once, Winslow became uncomfortably aware of how long it had been. And of how much he had wanted Virginia Dare since the moment he had first seen her.

But something within would not permit him to let this go any further without saying, "Our success isn't assured, you know."

She gave the same bold smile she had worn when their eyes had first met, and it was as if a bowstring twanged in his heart. "No, and I know well enough that thinking so is the shortest road to defeat. So let's give ourselves a reason why we *must* succeed." She stepped closer. She wore none of the perfumes of courtly ladies in England. But he could smell woman.

And it came to him that she was right. By risking a conception that would violate the tenets of her past life, she was throwing those tenets and that life to the winds and committing herself absolutely to the bold enterprise on which they were embarked.

But then she took another step forward, and all such thoughts fled his mind. There was only her. Their hands sought each other as if by a will of their own. Then they were in each other's arms.

"Do it!" she whispered harshly in his ear. Then, with sudden practicality: "And bear in mind that I'm a virgin."

He did so, with a gentleness he had never used before, and a depth of joy he had never experienced.

There were scattered clouds, but enough stars were out for the light gatherers to work their magic as twenty-four figures made their silent way through the predawn darkness, up the slope of Elf Hill.

The torturous process of getting the Eilonwë forces into position undetected was finally complete. There they would wait for two days, giving Winlsow's party time to march to the Grella fortress, enter it, and emerge fighting at the predetermined instant. Winslow would know when that instant had arrived because he wore strapped to his wrist a marvelously tiny timepiece of Eilonwë make. Naturally its markings bore no relation to honest English hours, but Riahn had shown him where the constantly moving little pointer would be at the time the frontal assault would commence. He had sworn to be in position by then, knowing full well that if he wasn't the outside attackers were doomed.

They continued uphill through the night, and Winslow looked around at the green-tinted world revealed by his light gatherer. Virginia Dare and Shakespeare wore the other two. A tightly grouped clump of seven followed closely behind each of the three of them, running through the dark in reliance on their guides.

"All right," Winslow called out in low tones, puffing for breath. "We're just about there. Remember what you've been told." He led the way over the last few steps.

"Captain!" yelled Shakespeare, shattering their rule of silence, "it's a Grella flyer!"

Winslow's head snapped around to follow the actor's pointing finger. The flyer was swooping in, its running lights glaring with unnatural brightness in the light gatherers. And of course, he thought with something close to panic, it would carry its own devices for seeing in the dark.

"Stop!" he shouted, jarring to a halt. "Turn back! We can't let them see—"

It was too late. Even as he spoke, the greenish world of the light gatherers faded into the even stranger grayish one of the Near Void.

He wrenched off the headband. Now they could all see equally well, and they all stood staring up at the flyer that could no longer see them. It hovered overhead, circling slowly, searching for the figures that had vanished. Finally, it turned west and flew away up the valley, toward the fortress, where its crew would report that the long-sought portal had been found.

Winslow took a quick roll call. Two men—a sailor named Foote from *Heron*, and John Prat, who had sailed to Virginia as a boy—were missing. They must have proven unable to remain in the Near Void, and passed on into the Deep Void, which meant that by now they were on Croatoan Island.

Winslow had given everyone strict instruction for such an eventuality: they were to remain on Croatoan, seeking out Manteo's people and making no attempt to return to the world of the Eilonwë, where their emergence at the portal would reveal its location.

Not, he thought bitterly, that it made any difference now.

"What do we do now, Captain?" asked John White.

"Do?" he snarled. "What do you think we're going to do? We're going to do what we planned to do. Only now it's not just a clever idea. It's something that *cannot* be allowed to fail. Don't you see?" He looked around. Shakespeare wore an expression of somber understanding that was beyond his years, but the others seemed bewildered. Winslow forced calmness on himself and explained. "The Grella aboard that flying boat watched as we disappeared. They know where the portal is. So now we *have* to crush them in this world and seal it off against others of their kind. Otherwise, they'll come pouring through into our world. Nothing there will be able to stand against them. The fate of England, and of all our God's creation, rests with us."

"Without intention, we showed them the way," said Shakespeare quietly. "It is up to us to put things right."

Winslow silently locked eyes with Virginia Dare. They had sought to commit themselves to the success of this raid in the most irrevocable way of which mortals were capable. It turned out they might as well have saved themselves the trouble.

Not, of course, that he regretted it.

"But Captain," someone asked, "won't the Grella in the fortress be on the alert for us?"

"No. They already know that we humans can pass through portals, but they don't know about our ability to linger in the Near Void at will. They'll think the figures they saw vanishing here tonight will have passed on into our world. That's our one advantage. Now let's use it!"

Without another word, and without looking back, he turned and strode west. He heard the others following behind him.

— FIFTEEN —

IT MIGHT WELL BE TRUE, AS TYRALAIR ASSERTED, THAT movement in the Near Void was purely ethereal, involving no actual physical effort, and that the apparent motion of walking was a figment of their minds. But weariness is, in the last analysis, a function of the mind, and it *felt* like they were marching.

Nevertheless, Winslow kept them at it for almost twenty miles, with only a couple of breaks for food and water, before calling a halt. He wanted to arrive at their destination early, with plenty of time for scouting and positioning. They all kept up, even John White, about whom Winslow had been worried. Perhaps it was simply that no one wanted to be left behind in this uncanny state. Afterwards, they all fell into a relieved sleep even though in this realm night and day were the same. One good thing: there was no need to post watches, in this realm that was in some incomprehensible fashion outside or beside the real world.

A buzzing sound somehow made by the wrist timepiece awoke Winslow at a predetermined time, and they resumed their march up the valley, through the strange shadowless luminescence. This time they only had to cover twelve or so miles before the vast arch loomed up in the distance against the pearl-colored westering sun. Near its base clustered the unnatural structures Winslow had seen before, seeming like toy houses from here, dominated by the grim dome off to one side. He had told all his people what to expect, so there weren't too many muttered oaths.

All at once, visible even at this distance, the arch began to flicker with lights around its edges, colorless white of course but as bright as anything ever looked as viewed from Near Void. That was all the warning they had before a Grella airship was suddenly present under the arch in all its massiveness, speeding in their direction and growing with impossible rapidity.

This time there were cries. Afterwards, Winslow wouldn't have sworn that his own wasn't among them. But then the airship slowed and swung off to port toward an open expanse that had to be a landing field. Winslow heard a collective whoosh of released breath behind him.

"Remember what Riahn has always told us?" Virginia Dare whispered. "About how the Grella force their way directly through the Inner Void from one world to another, ripping open a portal with the forces they can command?"

"Yes," Winslow nodded, watching the airship settle down to a landing.

"Well, I wonder if the arch is a way of avoiding having to do that."

"What do you mean?"

"Maybe, after opening a portal, they can build an arch like that and it provides the force. That way, a flying ship of theirs doesn't have to provide it."

"And therefore," Winslow took up the thought, "any ship of theirs can make the transit, not just specially outfitted ships like the one that burst through into our world a century ago as we measure time. Yes, that would pay for itself after a while, no matter how much the arch cost to build." He discovered that like all the others he had—involuntarily, absurdly—gone to his knees in the instant when that vessel had seemed to be shooting unerringly toward them. Slightly embarrassed, he rose to his feet. "Well, the point now is that they're going to be unloading a newly arrived vessel. Unless this place differs from all other ports I've ever seen, that's going to be engaging a lot of people's attention and causing a lot of confusion, which can only work to our benefit. Let's go. I want to see the inside of those gun emplacements."

They moved on, and soon they were among the outer structures. Winslow took the opportunity to lead them through walls, remembering how his own automatic rejection of such a manifest impossibility had needed to be overcome by experience. Even worse was the first time they saw the ghostly forms of Grella, and walked past and even *through* them. There was a general gasping and convulsive clutching of weapons before they all could accept the fact that they were invisible and impalpable.

They reached and entered one of the great weapon turrets that surrounded the dome. Winslow's plan was to leave a man inside each of those turrets facing the side from which the Eilonwë attack would come, to appear out of nowhere at the appointed time and slash the stunned Grella gun crew to pieces. But now . . .

"Where the Devil is the crew stationed?" he demanded of Virginia Dare as he looked around at a nearly solid mass of incomprehensible machinery.

"I don't think there *is* a crew," she said thoughtfully. "I think the weapon aims and fires itself in response to commands from afar. All the turrets are controlled from one central location, doubtless inside the dome."

"But—" Winslow clamped his jaw shut, reminding himself that the word *impossible* had a different meaning in this world, if indeed it had any meaning at all. He thought furiously. "We could leave one of our bombs here—"

"—but only if the man carrying it re-enters the material world," Shakespeare finished for him. *And is stranded there*, he didn't need to add.

The Welsh soldier Owain shouldered forward. "Captain, give me as many bombs as I can carry. I'll drop out of Dom-Daniel, leave one of them here, then move on to other turrets, leaving one in each."

"But Owain, you'll be unable to return to, uh, Dom-Daniel. You'll no longer be able to walk through the walls of the turrets. And the Grella will be able to see you."

"And kill or capture you," added Virginia Dare. "You're a brave man, Owain. But the instant you're caught they'll raise the alarm and our advantage of surprise will be gone."

"They'll have to catch me first!" A grin wreathed dark features which held the blood's memories of Romans and Phoenicians and Celts and nameless peoples far older than the Celts, who had raised the standing stones. "In my younger days, before entering Her Majesty's service, I had some small experience at, shall we say, moving about inconspicuously after dark."

"Poaching," Winslow stated shortly.

Owain gave him a hurt look. "That's a matter of definition, Captain. But be that as it may, if I could stay one step ahead of the damned English—no offense, Captain and milady!—I'll wager I can do the same with the Grella. Besides," he added with a wink, "there *is* one place hereabouts where I can duck out of the mundane world again." He smiled and sketched an arch with a forefinger.

"I never thought of that," Shakespeare breathed. "But yes, there *is* another portal here, isn't there?"

"One so obvious that none of us thought of it," Winslow nodded.

"But," protested Virginia Dare, "the arch is on the far side of this city. You'll never make it so far, Owain."

"It would hardly be ethical for me to place a bet on that," the Welshman grinned, "considering that if I lose I'll never have to worry about paying up!" Sobering, he turned to Winslow. "Let me try it, Captain. I'll find a way—a natural way—into the turrets, so I can plant the bombs. Then I'll work my way toward the arch. But I'll make it my first concern to stay out of their sight."

"Very well. Do it. But you'll only be the second string to our bow. The rest of us will continue on into the dome, try to find the place from which Virginia says they control their defenses, and appear there at the moment of the attack as we originally planned." Winslow smiled grimly. "We'll use their own powers against them. If they can command everything from one place, then they're vulnerable at that place. And if their subordinate officers are used to being able to report to their distant leaders and get instructions back in the blink of an eye, they've probably lost the ability to act on their own initiative. We'll paralyze them!"

Owain took four men's bombs, which were all he could carry besides his own. Virginia Dare, who knew the Eilonwë symbols and had been instructed in the relatively simple procedure, set the bombs' timers for the moment the attack was to begin. Then she gave Owain a quick, hard hug. All the others muttered their farewells. He gave a last jaunty wave and assumed a look of concentration.

All at once he was no longer sharply outlined and fully colored, but had taken his place in the indistinct grayness of the material world. They watched as he turned his back on the companions he could no longer see or hear and set about finding a crucial-seeming place in the machinery where a bomb could be hidden and, hopefully, explode with crippling effect. Finishing his task, he exited the turret through a hatchway.

"All right," Winslow told the others, "let's get inside the dome. We don't know how long it will take to locate this control center."

They set out through the walls and passageways of the outer city. Winslow had never traversed this labyrinth, only overflown it. He could never have found his way through the maze had it not been for the enormous, sinister dome that loomed over it, giving them an objective. They came to the dome's terraced, weapon-bristling base and passed through it in their incorporeal way. Once inside, the raiders stopped, awestruck and gazed about them. A couple of clandestine Catholics from *Heron's* crew forgot themselves and made the sign of the cross. Winslow, remembering his own initial reaction, couldn't blame them.

He decided his original impression of a city within a city had been accurate. The Grella they encountered here moved about with an air of disciplined purpose absent from those outside the dome. This was the citadel.

"Remember that large central building we were taken to for questioning?" he said to Virginia Dare. "Surely that's where the control chamber will be."

"We don't know that for certain," she cautioned.

"Still, it's the way to bet." He led the way, trying to remember landmarks he had sighted before.

The sun had settled behind a low-lying wrack of clouds, and the sky was dark gray with oncoming dusk, when Owain emerged from the weapon turret. He saw no Grella about, but flyers were drifting by overhead. He found a niche between two nearby buildings and settled in to await the fall of night.

As the stars came out, he discovered it was hardly worth the wait. The magic artificial lights—the Eilonwë insisted that they weren't magic, but Owain wasn't taken in by that for a moment—began to wink on, until the illumination exceeded that of a full moon. At least it wasn't as bright here as it was on the outskirts, where powerful beams of light turned the edges of the forest into day.

It made sense, Owain reflected with a nod. The Grella gunners who, according to Mistress Dare, were controlling the weapon turrets from afar in some sorcerous way, would be able to clearly see any attackers who emerged from the woods . . . as the Eilonwë would soon be doing.

The thought reminded him of the urgency of his mission. Hefting his load of bombs, he emerged cautiously from his bolt hole and looked around. Off to his right, he sighted another of the turrets—they were tall, to give them a clear field of fire over the low buildings, and reflected the unnatural light. He began moving stealthily in that direction, keeping as much as possible in the shadows cast by the buildings.

Very few Grella seemed to be out. Owain was congratulating himself on his good fortune in that regard when he turned a corner and a figure appeared ahead. He flattened himself against a shadowed wall and held his breath, but there was no commotion. Easing himself away from the wall with great caution, he saw the figure shuffling away, and as it passed under the lights he saw it for what it was: one of the soul-robbed Eilonwë slaves. It continued on into an area where low huts clustered among sparse-foliaged trees. The area was dimly lit, but Owain could make out other figures, all moving in the same listless way toward the huts. Evidently this was their curfew time—and their subjugation was so complete that the Grella need not even herd them into the kind of pens Owain had imagined. A shudder of loathing ran through him, for he now knew there were worse things than death—worse even than ordinary slavery.

He rejected his half-formed thought of seeking the slaves' aid. These ensorcelled creatures couldn't even *wish* to help him free their race. But at least they wouldn't be very alert. He hurried past, flitting from one shadow to another, and made his way to the turret.

Remembering how he had gotten out of the first one, he turned a wheel on the hatchway and swung it open. Apparently there was no need for locks here, where there

was—or was supposed to be—no one but the Grella
themselves and their mindless servitors. As expected, the
interior was identical to the one he had seen previously.
He placed a bomb in the same critical-seeming place,
hoping as before that he was right about its criticality,
and moved on.

He had placed another bomb in another turret, not
far from the arch, before old habits caught up with him.
His previous experience with elusiveness had taught him
to keep a sharp eye in all directions—except *upward*. So
he had no warning when a beam of dazzling light from
a Grella flyer speared him from overhead.

An ululating wail from the flyer brought him out of
his momentary paralysis, and he saw Grella figures
approaching at a run, their hand-held light piercing the
darkness. He sprinted into the shadows, dropping his
bombs and letting them roll. It was too bad he couldn't
detonate them, but at least they would provide confusing
distraction when they roared to life at the time Mistress
Dare had set them for. And without their weight, he was
able to dart among the buildings. The flyer was easy to
evade, but he knew with cold certainty that the foot
patrol would find him.

His half-joking boast was suddenly no longer a joke.
Darting from shadow to shadow, he made his way toward
the arch.

The raiders reached the central structure and passed
through its walls. Winslow recognized some of the corridors through which he had been led as a prisoner.

"What is this control center going to look like?" he
demanded of Virginia Dare.

"How should I know? Although," she amended, "I'm
sure it will have lots of the . . . desks with buttons and

lights where the Grella sit when they're controlling
things at a distance. Oh, and it will probably have screens
of glass, or something like glass, on which you can see
distant images as though you were there."

*Something else to do with Dr. Gilbert's experiments
with amber*, Winslow thought, and left off any attempt
to understand it beyond that. Instead, he led them from
one room to another with increasing haste and anxiety,
looking for what Virigina Dare had described.

He was glad he had pushed them so hard on the previous march, so as to arrive here ahead of schedule. But
his self-congratulation was tempered by his gnawing fear
that they still might not have allowed themselves enough
time to find what they sought, in this oppressive labyrinth.

They found themselves in a kind of foyer, with a double doorway to one side. All at once, the doors slid aside
to reveal what looked like an empty closet—empty save
for two Grella, who emerged and walked away. The
doors slid shut behind them. Winslow wondered what
they could possibly have been doing inside that tiny,
bare chamber.

Virginia Dare grabbed him by the arm. "I have it! That
little room—it goes up and down. The Eilonwë had them
in their great age, using some kind of pulleys. They're
for getting from one floor to another without having to
climb stairs. There must be levels below this. And that's
where the Grella will have their control center. It would
be the most secure place."

"But how do we make this . . . moving closet take us
down?"

"We don't have to. They must have stairs—or ramps,
which the Grella prefer—in case the power fails."

Winslow looked around, and pointed to a door off to the side. "Let's try that."

They descended the ramp, past several switchbacks. Finally there was no further to go. They emerged through a wide doorway into a vast circular chamber whose walls were lined with what Virginia Dare had tried to describe: large windows that looked out on scenes far away—on the outskirts of the city, or so it seemed to Winslow, for the artificially lit landscape they revealed looked like the weapon turrets' fields of fire. The floor was largely covered by concentric, outward-facing rings of the instrument-bearing desks, most of which seemed to have their own smaller versions of the glasslike screens on the walls. Grella sat at most of these desks, but by no means all, and the scene held an unmistakable quality of humdrum routine.

At the center of the chamber, like the hub of a wheel, was what looked unmistakably like a citadel within the citadel: an octagonal space completely enclosed by armored walls that rose to the ceiling.

Winslow, ignoring the nervous mutterings of his followers as they gazed at those sorcerous-seeming windows, turned to Virginia Dare and indicated the Grella in the chamber. "These must be the watch—the ones who're now on duty."

"Yes. They have no reason to suspect that this is anything but an ordinary day. When the alarm is sounded, they'll bring in a full crew to man all these desks." She gazed intently at the central stronghold. "Unless I miss my guess, the leaders direct things from in there, where they'll be even safer and where they can see their underlings without being seen. They'll enter it directly from the upper floors, by way of the moving closets."

Winslow glanced at his timepiece—and bit back a startled oath. Finding this place had taken them longer than he'd planned, and there was little time left before the Eilonwë would launch their assault. He thought furiously.

"Virginia, set two of our remaining bombs to explode five minutes *after* the time for the attack." She gave him a sharp look, but knew this was no time for arguments or questions. As she set to work, he turned to Shakespeare. "Will, I want you to take these two bombs, go back up the ramp we just came down, and wait at the first landing. When the attack begins, reenter the normal world and leave the bombs on the landing, one to each side of the passageway. Then come back down here and rejoin us."

"Uh . . . how will I know when the set time is, Captain?" Shakespeare indicated the timepiece which Winslow wore and he did not.

"Trust me: you'll hear a lot of noise down here. That will be your signal." Winslow grasped Shakespeare by the shoulders. "This is important, Will. I'm entrusting it to you because I need a man I can rely on." There was also the fact that the actor was less likely than anyone else, with the possible exception of John White, to be useful once the fighting broke out, but Winslow saw no pressing need to mention that. Shakespeare swelled a bit with a young man's pride in being given a responsible charge, took the bombs, and scurried off.

"Now," said Winslow, indicating the armored command center, "let's scout that out."

The enclosed chamber held only one Grell, wearing the chest insignia of rank, although there were chairs and desks for several others in an outward-facing semi-circle from which an array of glass screens showed various views, including the large room outside. In the very center of the chamber, on a kind of raised dais, was a circular desk overlooking everything. Directly above it, set into the ceiling, was a dome of obscure purpose.

"So there's just one officer of the watch," Winslow stated, not even needing confirmation from Virginia Dare. As she had predicted, there was one of the double doors of the little moving rooms. Another, very secure-looking door gave egress to the main space beyond.

Winslow reached a decision, and turned to a sailor who was, if not precisely brilliant, utterly reliable. "Grimson, remain in here. When we appear in the outer room and start killing, you'll see us in that . . . window. At that moment, return to the real world in the way I've explained to you and kill this Grell. Then open the door to admit the rest of us, and stand guard here, at this double door, and kill any Grella that come through." He grinned. "While you're waiting for them, you can amuse yourself by smashing as many of these instruments as you can."

"Aye, Captain," Grimson acknowledged, knuckling his forelock.

The rest of them passed through the armored walls—the last time they'd be able to do that, Winslow reflected—and spread out, drawing their weapons and taking up whatever positions suited them. He himself stood to the side of a desk behind which sat a Grell who couldn't yet see him. He had no compunctions about killing a Grell from behind, any more than he would have in the case of any other vermin. But he wanted this one to see him first. To his amusement, he was able to carefully line up his stroke against the neck of the oblivious Grell. Even more amusingly, he brought the blade *through* the unfeeling neck before resuming his stance.

He stole a glance at his timepiece. It was time.

Abruptly, the instrument panels flashed into activity. On the large glass screens around the outer walls, captured weapons in Eilonwë hands began to flash in the darkness. The Grella at the desks jerked to attention and began shouting soundlessly at each other.

"NOW!" shouted Winslow.

He himself was the first to resume physical actuality. The world around him snapped into solidity and color and noise, assaulting his senses with a suddenness that would have been startling if he hadn't been prepared for it.

The Grell in front of him certainly wasn't prepared for his abrupt appearance out of nowhere. The alien mouth opened, and was still opening when Winslow's sword flashed around in a glittering three-quarter circle, and his head flew from his body in a spray of whatever the Grella used for blood.

Then the other English began to pop into existence, and all Hell broke loose.

— SIXTEEN —

IT WAS A SLAUGHTER. NONE OF THE GRELLA WAS ARMED, here where no enemy could possibly reach them. And even if they had carried weapons, they would have been too stunned to use them as the humans inexplicably popped into existence and began slashing, stabbing and hacking the life from them. The quavering high-pitched hissing sounds of Grella screams were lost in the shrill alarm that must be summoning the rest of the command center's crew.

That thought made Winslow pause in the killing and look toward the ramp. *Where is Shakespeare?* he wondered anxiously. Much depended on the placement of the two bombs in the passageway.

At that instant the young actor sprinted through the entryway. "Captain," he gasped, "they're close behind me!"

"Did you leave the bombs as I told you?" Winslow demanded. He didn't know how much time had passed since the attack had begun, but he was sure it was less than it seemed, as was always the case in battle.

"Yes, but—"

The first of the Grella emerged . . . only they weren't Grella. A wave of the Eilonwë slaves came through first, advancing in their nightmarish mind-controlled way.

"Weapons on stun!" cried Virginia Dare to those of her fellow English colonists who bore the modified Grella weapons. The flickering beams shot out, and the slaves tumbled in unconsciousness. Nothing more could be done for them now. If this battle was won, the Eilonwë mind-doctors would go to work. If it was lost . . . but that didn't bear thinking about.

Then the Grella themselves appeared. Some of them were technicians like those the English had just finished killing, but others were soldiers, trained to react coolly in unanticipated situations and armed with the light-weapons. Those weapons were *not* set to stun. With every barely visible beam, an Englishman died.

Then, with a concussion that caused the floor to jump beneath Winslow's feet, Shakespeare's bombs went off. The blast, funneled through the entryway, blew the just-emerged Grella off their feet. Behind them, the roof of the ramp's passageway collapsed, as Winslow had rather hoped it would when he'd told Shakespeare to place his bombs on opposite sides of it. The command center was now sealed off.

The Grella stumbled to their feet only to face a berserk charge by Englishmen and Englishwomen whose fury had been stroked to white heat by the sight of those soul-robbed slaves—the fate that awaited them in the event

of defeat. They didn't even bother with the bloodless
light-weapons.

Winslow struck a Grell's weapon aside with his sword
before the alien could bring it to bear. With his left hand
he plunged his dagger in, then withdrew it with a twist
he hoped would be as disemboweling as it would have
been with a human belly. The results did not disappoint
him. Off to one side he saw Virginia Dare bring her two-
handed sword down in a diagonal slash that sliced into
a Grell's right shoulder and exited below the left armpit.
The Grell fell to the floor with two distinct thuds.

Maybe, Winslow reflected, awestruck, *that Portuguese
wasn't such a liar after all.*

"All right," he called out to the remaining English,
now alone. "Let's take care of that central chamber!" He
pointed with his sword toward the door . . . which he now
saw was still closed.

Before he could say more, a pale death beam lashed
out from a weapon set on the outside of that armored
wall in a flexible mount just under the ceiling above the
door. A *Heron* crewman screamed as it impaled him and
his body fluids exploded outward in a burst of steam.

"Take cover!" Winslow yelled. They all scrambled
behind the control desks, which proved capable of stop-
ping the beams—at least for now. He crouched behind
one with Virginia Dare, Shakespeare and John White as
the beams tore at it.

"What happened to Grimson?" demanded Virginia
Dare.

"He must be dead," Winslow grated. "The Grella must
have some kind of death trap in there."

"In their own inner sanctum?" gasped John White.

"We've seen that their overlords don't even trust their
own underlings, and are prepared to kill them," said

Winslow as another light beam attempted to drill through the barrier that sheltered them. "Who else would that weapon be aimed at?"

He looked around at the still-functioning vision screens that lined the chamber's walls. The battle was raging at the city's perimeter. As he watched, a formation of Grella flyers swooped out, their weapons seeking the Eilonwë in the forest. But the beams of captured and long-hoarded Grella heavy weapons stabbed out—blindingly, for these were the kind of weapons that had been used against the English fleet, destroying matter by bringing it into contact with its intolerable negation —and one by one the flyers exploded in a blinding effulgence of light. An involuntary cheer burst from Winslow's throat as he watched St. Antony's fire turned on its creators.

But his cheer died in his throat, for some of the Grella weapon turrets were still in action, and they mounted far heavier versions of the Hell weapons. They burned fiery trails through the darkened forest, and Winslow's stomach clenched at the thought of how many Eilonwë must be dying.

"Owain didn't disable all the turrets," he thought out loud. "And they can still control them from in there." He indicated the armored central citadel.

"The Eilonwë will never be able to break through with those things in action," said Virginia Dare in a bleak voice. Winslow didn't like that voice, for in it he could hear the long-term hopelessness that was her birthright creeping back.

"We've got to get in there!" he declared. He grabbed Virginia Dare's light-weapon and fired it. The beam barely even scratched that door, as heavily armored as the wall in which it was set.

Then he remembered the gunpowder-filled iron buckets that, when all else failed in an assault on a fortress, a pair of men would carry forward and hang from a nail driven into a gate. The French called it a *petard*.

He looked to his right and left, at the English crouching behind other control desks. "Martin! Jonas!" he called out to two sailors who hadn't given up their bombs to Owain or Shakespeare. "Roll your bombs over here!"

They obeyed, and the deadly spherical objects rolled across the floor, unnoticed by the Grella observers. Winslow caught them. "Virginia, set these things for two minutes from now."

"What?" Her eyes widened as understanding dawned. "You're going to try to . . . No! They'll kill you before you can get there."

"Even if they don't," Shakespeare added, "there's a saying about being 'hoist with your own petard.'" Characteristically, he had instantly grasped what was afoot.

"What else can we do?" Winslow demanded. "Squat here and watch them grind the Eilonwë down?"

John White spoke up in a voice which, though mild, got their attention, "At least, Captain, don't try to carry both bombs yourself. If you fall, then all is lost. Give me one. If we give them two targets, the chances are double that one will get through."

Virginia Dare's eyes grew even wider. "Grandfather, no! Don't do this. You're not a young man anymore!"

"All the more reason to do it. I have less life left to lose than the rest of you. And in any case, my life is completed." He smiled at her. "God has granted me something that has been given to no other man: to see my own grandchild turn from a babe in arms to an adult in a pair of years. I missed your childhood, and that I regret. But having known, if only for a little while, the woman you've grown into is enough for any man." He turned back to Winslow and his eyes held his need.

"All right," said Winslow, not meeting Virginia Dare's eyes. "But listen carefully and obey orders! Here's what we're going to do. We'll run for the door, well apart from each other and taking advantage of as much cover as we can. Once we get up against the door, we'll be safe; I've been watching that weapon, and it can't swivel but so far. We'll leave the bombs against the base of the door. Then we'll get away fast—Master Shakepeare is right about what often happens to *petardiers*!—moving along the base of the wall so we'll still be inside the weapon's field of fire. Understand?"

White nodded jerkily.

"Set the bombs, Virginia," Winslow said quietly.

Her eyes darted from one man to the other. Then she swallowed and set to work, deftly despite the tears that misted her vision.

"Martin!" Winslow called out while she worked. "Pass the word to the men that when I say 'Now,' everyone is to create a ruckus. Throw things, shoot with the light-weapons, anything to draw their attention."

"Aye, Captain."

Virginia Dare handed her grandfather and him each one of the hefty bombs and performed one last adjustment on them. "You now have two minutes," she said levelly.

"Now!" shouted Winslow.

From around the concentric circles of control desks the English yelled, waved their swords, took futile pot shots with the light-weapons. Whoever was remotely controlling the swivel weapon was clearly startled, for a rapid fusillade of crackling beams lashed out in various directions.

"Go!" Winslow snapped at John White. Without waiting to see if he was being obeyed, he sprang out from behind the right-hand end of their shelter and ran, zigzagging, toward the door.

A crucial pair of seconds passed before the hidden controller grasped what was happening. The weapon mount swiveled and a beam sought him, searing the floor, just as he dived behind a control desk, hitting the floor and rolling. It was the last shelter he would have. Between him and the door was only open space.

Then, to the left, he heard a commotion as John White lunged forward. With insectlike swiftness, the weapon mount swung in that direction, spitting beams. One of them caught him.

From a distance, Winslow could hear Virginia Dare's stricken scream.

Without pausing to think or feel, Winslow sprang to his feet and sprinted the last few yards. Not daring to slow down enough to go into a roll, he crashed into the door and crouched against its base.

The weapon mount swiveled downward, seeking him with insensate fury. But it could only burn sizzling holes in the floor a few feet away from him. He was inside its turning radius.

He paused for a look backwards. John White was still alive, sprawled on the floor. Their eyes met. White actually managed to smile. Then, with a weak motion, he sent his bomb rolling across the floor. Winslow reached out and caught it, risking the beams. But the weapon had turned back to John White, finishing its work.

Winslow continued to deny himself feeling or thought. Instead, he placed both bombs against the door's base.

Then, not knowing how much time he had left, he scurried away along the wall, staying out of the swivel weapon's reach and putting as much distance as possible between himself and the door. When he had gotten to the opposite side of the stronghold, he went to the floor and crouched into something like the position he had assumed in his mother's womb.

Eternal seconds passed. He wondered if something had gone wrong.

When it came, it wasn't two separate explosions, because Virginia Dare had set the bombs for the same instant. It was a single concussion that deafened him and might well have snapped his spine if he had been standing with his back to the wall. As it was, an instant passed before he could stagger to his feet and run back along the wall in the direction he had come.

The door hung askew, blasted from its frame. The swivel-mounted weapon above it drooped lifelessly.

Out of the left corner of his eye, he saw Shakespeare and Virginia Dare running toward the entry that now lay open.

"Attack!" he yelled at the room in general. He drew his two blades, kicked the ruined door aside and plunged through choking, reeking smoke into the innermost Grella citadel, stepping over a dead Grell.

As he emerged from the smoke he took in the entire scene with a glance.

Off to the side he saw Grimson's charred body. In the screens, the weapon turrets had obviously fallen silent in the absence of commands. Around the control desks, the surviving Grella milled about in their cold natures' closest approximation of panic. And behind the circular desk on the raised dais stood a Grell in whose features and chest insignia Winslow recognized Sett 44.

But mostly he saw the Grell directly in front of him—the only one in the room with a weapon, which he had just raised. Winslow looked directly down the orifice of that weapon, and with cold certainty he knew himself to be a dead man.

Then Shakespeare, charging in behind him, tripped over the dead Grell and, arms flailing, blundered into the Grell, throwing the weapon off just as it was fired. The beam barely missed Winslow's head, and he caught a whiff reminiscent of summer thunderstorms. Before the Grell could regain his footing and snap off another shot, Winslow rushed him. With his sword arm he shoved Shakespeare out of the way. With his other hand he plunged the ballock dagger in and then up with a force that lifted the diminutive alien off his feet. Winslow threw him aside and plunged forward.

The English were crowding in, butchering the Grella and smashing at the instruments they didn't understand. Vision screens and banks of lights began to flicker out.

Winslow left all that to the others. He pressed on through the chaos toward the dais where Sett 44 stood behind his control desk. Their eyes locked in a split second of mutual recognition—a communion of sorts.

Yes, it's me, you maggot, Winslow thought savagely. *And I've come to kill you!*

But then there was a loud humming and an incomprehensible flashing of lights, and the dome above that central command dais began to lower itself down. It settled over the dais and clamped itself onto the top of the wraparound desk, enclosing Sett 44 in an openwork cage. Looking upward at the ceiling where it had been, Winslow saw what it had concealed: a circular tunnel leading upward.

An escape hatch, he realized. Even as the thought flashed through him, the now-enclosed dais—whose base evidently held the same mysterious engines as the Grella flyers—began to rise upward toward the tunnel.

Winslow had no time for thought. He dropped his sword, clenched his ballock dagger in his teeth, and ran the rest of the way as fast as pumping legs and tortured lungs could take him. Then, just before Sett 44's escape capsule could rise beyond reach, he jumped and caught the edge of its lower platform with both hands.

A split second later, a wobble in the rising capsule told him that another human body had added its weight. He looked to his right and met the eyes of Virginia Dare, likewise hanging by both hands. She had dropped her light-weapon, but her two-handed sword was still strapped to her back.

Then they were rising more rapidly, and entered the tunnel.

There was barely room for the two dangling human bodies in that enclosed space. Feeling his back slamming against the tunnel walls, Winslow suspected that Sett 44 was deliberately swinging his vehicle from side to side, trying to dislodge his two unwanted passengers. He held on grimly in the darkness. Above, he could glimpse a faint glow of light, growing steadily stronger.

Abruptly, they burst from the tunnel into the great artificially lit dome above. Below was the small city. Directly below, about fifteen feet underneath, was what looked like a landing field for the flyers, which were desperately streaming toward the great openings in the dome. Sett 44 swung his escape capsule onto a course to follow them.

Through the whistling of the wind, he heard Virginia Dare's shout. "He's going to get out and head for the arch! He'll be able to go through and warn the Grella in the next world beyond to counterattack in full array with ships that can force their own way through the portal, without the aid of the arch."

Even as Winslow was considering the consequences of that, Sett 44 made a series of side-to-side swinging motions. Winslow barely managed to hang on. Virginia Dare wasn't so lucky. Winslow heard her scream, and caught sight of her falling toward the landing field below.

As before, when he had watched John White die, Winslow denied himself all emotion. That could come later, if he was alive. For now, he concentrated every fiber of his being on climbing, hand over hand, up the undercarriage of the escape pod. He occasionally allowed himself glances ahead, where the great opening in the base of the dome was growing and growing, the night outside riven with the flashes of battle.

Finally, lifting himself up with a last, agonizing one-handed heave, he glimpsed Sett 44's head above the control panel.

Hanging on grimly with his left hand, he took the ballock dagger from between his clenched teeth with his right hand, drew it back, and hurled it.

It was not a throwing knife, and lacked the proper balance. It clanged off the edge of the control desk and, deflected from its course, struck Sett 44 a glancing blow on the cheek before falling into the abyss below.

Startled by the blow, Sett 44 briefly lost control of his vehicle before righting it and bringing it to a hovering position just inside the wide exit portal toward which he had been steering. He raised a hand to his cheek, brought it away covered with the unnatural Grella body fluid, and looked around. He soon saw Winslow, weapon-less, hanging by both hands.

He stood up, leaving the escape pod to hover, and looked down at Winslow. His tiny lipless mouth opened slightly in what Winslow imagined was a smile. He reached into a pocket and withdrew an object which was obviously a weapon—too small to be of any military use, but doubtless adequate for its present intended purpose.

There was a deafening clang, and a concussion that sent the escape pod staggering sideways. Sett 44 was thrown off his feet, and Winslow barely held on. Then the damaged pod began slanting drunkenly downward and to the side. As it did, Winslow glimpsed the flyer that had glancingly collided with it, even more damaged and likewise on its way down.

His eyes met Virginia Dare's.

She must, he had time to think, *have hit the ground in that landing area beneath us and survived the fall. We weren't very high or moving very fast when she fell—and she's nothing if not tough. And she knows just enough about those flying boats to get one aloft, and pilot it to a collision.*

But then she was out of his field of vision—and Sett 44 was back into it, rising unsteadily to his feet. He took aim again with the weapon he had managed not to drop.

The pod smashed into the side of the vast exit door with a force that finally broke Winslow's grip. He fell ten or twelve feet, instinctively twisting to the side and hitting the floor with a roll. He went on rolling, out of the way of the falling escape pod, just before it crashed.

Sett 44 crawled from the wreckage, toward the weapon he had dropped. It lay on the floor about twelve feet from him and a good deal further from Winslow, who heaved his battered body up and tried to force it to walk.

Then the crippled flyer hit the floor and skidded over with a scream of tortured metal, smashing into the grounded escape pod and recoiling several yards before lying still only a short distance from Sett 44's hand-weapon. Virginia Dare stood up and lowered herself to the floor with obvious pain. She must have hurt her ankles in her fall. But they were not broken, for she slowly walked toward the weapon.

Sett 44 crawled faster, pulling his broken body along in a grotesquerie of haste, emitting what had to be wordless sounds of pain.

Virginia Dare, limping though she was, reached the weapon first. With the hardest kick she could manage, she sent it spinning across the floor into the shadows.

A few fleeing Grella were starting to run through the wide door. Eilonwë appeared behind them, shooting them and cutting them down, pursuing them into the dome. Virginia Dare ignored them all. She drew her sword from behind her left shoulder and, moving even more slowly than before, advanced on Sett 44.

"Captain!" Winslow heard a familiar voice.

"Owain!" he shouted back as the Welshman emerged from among a crowd of Eilonwë. "You're alive!"

"Indeed, Captain. I was only able to plant bombs in two more of the turrets before a patrol spotted me. I eluded them, but then I had nowhere to go but the arch. There, I returned to the Near Void and hid until the excitement began. Before returning to the real world I got to watch some of their flyers coming through the arch as they made good their escape. You should have seen it! They flickered for an instant in the Near Void, like something revealed in the dark by flash of lightning, before vanishing into the Deep Void." He looked around as the Eilonwë poured on into the dome in pursuit of the fleeing Grella. "It looks like you did for the rest of the turrets."

Winslow allowed his abused body to slump back down to the floor. "Yes. Well, the Grella did for some of us, too." The memory of John White would no longer be held at bay. *At least,* he thought, remembering the fate of White's daughter and son-in-law, *he only died once.*

Owain was silent for a moment, then sank to the floor beside Winslow. "I'm sorry I didn't do better, Captain."

"Don't talk foolishness. There are quite a few Eilonwë alive now who would have been consumed by Saint Antony's fire if you hadn't done what you did."

They watched as Virginia Dare reached Sett 44. She winced with pain as, with one foot, she rolled him over onto his back. She planted her foot on his midriff where the solar plexus would have been on a human and held her sword with the point resting, ever so gently, on the scrawny throat. The huge empty dark eyes stared up at her.

"Look at my face," she said quietly. "It is the last thing you'll ever see. And someday—maybe a thousand years from now, but someday—a face that looks like mine will be the last thing that the last Grell in all creation ever sees, just before a human kills him."

With a quick, economical flick of her wrist, she tore out his throat.

— SEVENTEEN —

CONSIDERING WHAT THEY HAD COME TO WITNESS, IT WAS a curiously subdued group that stood on a landing of the vast Grella dome, looking out over the half-ruined cityscape and the arch beyond it.

The Queen stood at the head of a small group of humans that included Walsingham, Dee, Winslow, Virginia Dare and the few remaining elders among the Roanoke colonists. Elizabeth had long since been without the elaborate cosmetics and wardrobe that had almost defined her, holding at bay the signs of aging she had always loathed. Her hair was conspicuously gray at the roots, and was rapidly losing its artificial crinkly curliness. All her wrinkles were exposed, without the mask of white makeup that had concealed them. She wore the utilitarian Eilonwë garment, little different for male or female. All was stripped away.

She had never looked more regal.

Beside the human group stood the Eilonwë, with Riahn at their head. The other *sheuath* leaders stood behind him: Imalfar (as was fitting), Avaerahn (insisting to everyone who would listen that the attack had been his idea all along), Leeriven (finally with a consensus to follow, thus lending her the illusion of consistency), and the various others. But Tyralair stood beside Riahn. Like all of them, she stared at the soaring arch that loomed over all the Grella works that clustered at its feet. But her face wore an expression that was strangely ambivalent, considering that she was present at the moment of her people's final, definitive awakening from a nightmare that had lasted thousands of years.

Those Grella flyers that had managed to escape had flashed through that arch and vanished, thus confirming Virginia Dare's inspired guess as to its function —although Tyralair was of the opinion that it probably required a pair of arches, one at each of the two portals in the two linked worlds. If any further confirmation had been needed, Owain's observations from his vantage point in the Near Void would have provided it. So what was about to happen now was necessary. Of course, after suppressing the last resistance and establishing firm control over the city, the Eilonwë had cut off all power to the arch. (They didn't pretend to understand all the principles involved, but they could sever connections.) But no one could be sure about the full extent of what the Grella could do, even from an alternate world beyond. And there was no time to be lost, for given the differentials in time rates between the worlds there was absolutely no way to know how long or how short a time it would take the Grella to mount a counterattack.

So this had to be done, without further delay. Everyone agreed on that. And yet there was no disguising the wistful look in Tyralair's eyes as she gazed at that soaring arch, gleaming in the sun.

An Eilonwë technician approached Riahn and muttered something in their tongue.

"It is time," said Riahn.

At first, it was barely noticeable. There were merely a couple of puffs of smoke, close to the arch's two bases. Then there were a series of other puffs, up the arch's curve.

The sound didn't arrive until a moment later. Riahn had said something about the speed of sound being incomparably less than the speed of light. Like so much of what Riahn said, it made absolutely no sense to Winslow. But it seemed to hold up, explaining, for example, why one always saw lightning before hearing thunder. And when this sound arrived, it was rather like distant thunder, even though the sky was cloudless—not a shattering blast, across this distance. But the rumbling grew and grew, always lagging behind what they were seeing.

The arch's collapse began at the base, where the first explosive charges had cut it off. As it began to slide down, it also began to break apart as the other charges did their work. The great curve, in all its unimaginable tonnage, dissolved into segments before they all crashed to the ground with a sound that reached their ears shortly thereafter in a roaring crescendo. Soon the breeze blew away the dust cloud to reveal the rubble.

Dee broke the silence. "You realize, of course," he said to Riahn, "that this does not absolutely seal your world off. The portal itself still exists, and Grella can still come through it in vessels specially designed for the purpose."

"Of course. But we have reason to believe that such ships are expensive and therefore relatively rare. This, no doubt, is why they built the arch in the first place, so their ordinary flyers could make the transit. Now they can no longer do so, and we don't have to fear a sudden swarm of invaders. And any ships that do emerge will have to face . . . that." Riahn gestured at the nearest of the weapon turrets. Like all the others that could be brought to bear on the portal, it was a-swarm with Eilonwë, working like Trojans to change its orientation and adapt its controls. Fortunately, the turrets Owain had disabled had been on the other side of the city.

"Any ships that appear in the portal will fly into their fields of fire," Riahn continued. "We won't even have to rely on the Grella aiming devices, for the weapons will already be pointed at the only place from which a threat can appear. And remember, these are the heavy Grella weapons—larger and more powerful versions of the small ones that, according to your description, destroyed your nation's fleet."

"So any Grella invaders of your world will be consumed by Saint Antony's fire," Dee nodded. "How fitting."

"And," said the Queen, "by keeping them out of your world you will also be keeping them out of ours. We will not forget our debt to you."

"I observe that you have not begun adapting any of the turrets that face in the opposite direction," Walsingham observed. "Are you not concerned with the Grella still remaining in other parts of this world? Of course, they can no longer escape through the portal." He indicated the wreckage that had been the arch. "But what if they organize themselves and mount a counterattack against you here?"

"We are aware of the danger, but so far they have been too stunned to take any action. Not that they have any great capability to do so. They are scattered thinly around the world—mangers of plantations and mines and factories staffed by Eilonwë slaves, for the most part. And they are unarmed except for small and lightly equipped military detachments scattered among them."

"Why haven't the Eilonwë of those other lands risen up against them, over the course of the centuries?" Walsingahm wanted to know.

"Sometimes they have—and been savagely punished by expeditions from this fortress. This has always been the center of their power. Fear of reprisals from it has kept the Eilonwë submissive across most of the world. But now we have been spreading the word that it has fallen, and that the remaining Grella are trapped in our world and cut off from any hope of reinforcement. Uprisings are breaking out all over this continent, and have begun to spread to others. The Grella are leaderless and on the defensive . . . and, by all accounts, completely demoralized. Nothing like this has ever happened to them before. They can scarcely believe it." Riahn looked like he still scarcely believed it himself.

"Still," Walsingham cautioned, "those military detachments—even if, as it seems, they're more like sheriffs than soldiers, and have only the light-weapons —can do much hurt."

"No doubt. But we can help. We've already begun to send out captured flyers loaded with weapons and experienced fighters . . . and, more importantly, representatives to bring the *sheuaths* of the other regions into our alliance."

"That may be a delicate matter," said Walsingham with an air of studied understatement, as he contemplated the altered political dynamics of an expanded league.

"Indeed." Riahn's glance slid aside, in the direction of his fellow *sheuath* leaders. Winslow tried to imagine what was going through his mind, and the not necessarily identical things going through theirs. "But only if we are united can we hunt the Grella to extinction throughout our world and secure ourselves against their return. We've learned that now—thanks in part to you."

"Yes, undoubtedly," said Dee in tones of somewhat perfunctory interest. "But for now, we have an experiment yet to perform."

Tyralair visibly perked up.

"Now remember what I told you," said Winslow to his two companions. "When we enter the area of the portal, it will be exactly as it was when we did the same thing on Croatoan Island, Doctor Dee—"

"Yes, yes," puffed Dee as he struggled to keep up.

"—but you must both follow the instructions I gave you in order to remain in this world's Near Void."

Even as he spoke, the world faded in the now-familiar way. He automatically invoked the patterns of thought that enabled him to linger in the Near Void. And, he saw, Dee had done the same, for the magus was there in sharply defined color, walking about as Winslow had told him he could do, looking around him in wonder at the blurred grayness of the material world.

But Tyralair was still part of that world, standing forlorn amid its dimness and staring in the direction where her human companions had vanished.

The two men willed themselves back from the Near Void and walked back to face Tyralair. "I'm sorry," said Winslow in a voice turned gruff by feelings of inadequacy.

"Oh, don't be," said Tyralair with an airiness which would not have deceived a child. "It was never more than a possibility. Now we know for certain that the quality that permits effortless entry in to the void through an opened portal is unique to humans. Knowledge is always to be sought . . . even when it disappoints our hopes."

"And now that you Eilonwë possess the records and devices of the Grella for study," said Dee, trying to be encouraging, "you can doubtless discover their secret of forcing a vessel through a portal to another world."

"That's right," said Winslow heartily. "We'll welcome you as visitors to our world yet."

"I would like nothing better. And I do not doubt the possibility. But any such visits would have to be brief ones, given the difference in time rates. If, for example, I were to spend a year in your world, I would return to find that almost twenty years had passed in mine."

"I once said something of the sort to Virginia Dare," Winslow recalled. "She explained why it was not an insurmountable obstacle for the Grella. But for you . . . "

"Yes," Tyralair sighed. "Perhaps it is just as well that we cannot pass through unaided."

Dee cleared his throat. "We, however, can. And the time has come for making preparations to do so, and return to our own world."

"Which means," Winslow said thoughtfully, "that the humans who have lived here so long have a decision to make."

The hall filled almost all of one of the buildings under the great over-arching dome. No one knew what the

Grella had used it for, but it held all the survivors of Raleigh's Roanoke colony who had blundered into this world nineteen years before, and their offspring, sitting on improvised benches. And it had the look of a meeting hall, for there was a dais at one end. There, John Dee stood and addressed the assemblage, with Walsingham, Winslow and Virginia Dare behind him.

"By now," Dee was saying in his well-trained voice, "you are all aware of the difference in the rates at which time passes in the different world. If you don't understand it, do not be troubled; neither does anyone else. Nor do we need to understand it. All we need to know is that, by God's grace, it works in our favor. While a day passes here, only a little more than an hour passes in our own world.

"Nevertheless, each such hour is another hour in which the Gray Monks, through their Spanish puppets, rule over England—which is an hour too many. So, now that the Grella can no longer prevent it, Her Majesty and those of us who came here with her must return without further delay, bearing with us the captured Grella weapons that can turn the scales in our world.

"Any of you who wish to come with us can, of course, do so. I must tell you, however, that we have only two ships—which we last saw just before they were blown away in a storm—and even those two were crowded. If you come with us, we will have to leave most of you on Croatoan Island, to await later transportation back to England."

"With Manteo's people," Ambrose Viccars nodded. Then his thick gray beard broke in a smile. "But of course! I forgot. Good old Manteo himself is very little older than we remember him!"

"Little older than *you* remember him," a young-sounding voice from the crowd corrected. It was like a release, for an ambivalent muttering now filled the room.

A man in his twenties stood up and spoke hesitantly. "Your lordships, I'm Robert Ellis. My father Thomas Ellis is long dead . . ."

"Yes, Robert," Winslow prompted. "You fought well in the raid on the Grella fortress. Say your say—you've earned the right."

"Well, Captain, what I meant to say is . . . I can dimly remember the world we came from, for I was a boy then. But only dimly . . . and many of us were born here and can't remember it at all." Ellis stretched a hand behind him as though for support. A teenaged girl took it. His voice firmed up. "We've lived among the Eilonwë, we have friends among them. We speak their tongue. And now we . . . well, we've begun to give ourselves a real link with this world." He drew the teenaged girl to his side, put an arm around her shoulders, and took on a look of quiet defiance.

So, thought Winslow with an inner chuckle, *now there's a* second *generation of native-born humans on its way into this world. Evidently Virginia wasn't the only one among them to decide that the reasons for their reluctance to have children no longer obtain, now that there is a possibility of going home. Only some of them have begun to wonder just exactly where "home" is, now that they have the luxury of wondering.*

Walsingham stepped forward, and Dee yielded place to him. "Her Majesty and I have spoken to Riahn and the other *sheuath* leaders. There will be a place here for any of you who wish to remain. And remember, such a decision is not irrevocable. Captain Winslow will show you how to locate the portal, and now that the Grella danger is removed you can pass through it whenever you choose. And no matter how long you take to make up your minds, only a twentieth of that time will have passed in our world."

"By the same token," Dee cautioned, "the decision to depart with us *will* be somewhat irrevocable. If you should decide after, say, a year to return to this world, you will find it—and everyone in it you knew—twenty years older."

The murmuring in the room sank an octave. They hadn't thought of this.

Virginia Dare stepped forward and stood beside Winslow. "The struggle against the Grella has bound our lives together all these years. Now those bounds are loosened, and each of us must decide as an individual what is best for himself or herself—and for our loved ones." For an instant her eyes wavered in Winslow's direction. "All I can say is that I myself am returning. We've freed one world from the Grella. Now there's another to be freed."

In the end, the majority of them—especially the youngest, and those with the strongest attachments among themselves—decided to remain, a decision they could tell themselves was only provisional. But the few remaining older ones, and a larger number of the younger ones than Winslow would have expected followed Virginia Dare into the effectively one-way journey back.

Evidently, freeing worlds from the Grella was a hard habit to break.

They stood on the lower slopes of Elf Hill, in a tightly packed group—those who remained of the party from

Heron, and those of the Roanoke colonists, led by Ambrose Viccars, who had elected to return. All were laden with all they could carry of parts of captured Grella weapons—they could be disassembled, and Dee was confident he had learned how to reassemble them—and the even more important cylinders that held, by some unfathomable means, the energies that powered those weapons. They were limited to what they could carry, so they had eschewed the handheld light-weapons, for they didn't expect to have to face Grella so armed. It was more important to carry as many of the surprisingly heavy cylinders as possible, for once those star-born energies were exhausted the anti-matter weapons would be useless. Even the Queen had scoffed at Walsingham's scandalized protests and gamely hefted a weapon component of something that was translucent but was not glass. Held by her, it looked like a large scepter out of some realm of faërie.

By unspoken common consent, none of the English who had chosen to cast their lot with this world were present. Any necessary farewells had already been spoken.

But Riahn and Tyralair were there. All the pompous official ceremonies of leave-taking were past. This was something else.

"I feel diminished by our inability to aid you as you have aided us," said Riahn.

"You should not, for it is no fault of yours," Walsingham assured him.

"No," Dee agreed. "It is the work of the Fates, or the Norns, as our pagan ancestors would have said." Winslow expected the Puritan Walsingham to bridle, but he didn't.

Virginia Dare stood before Riahn. "If there's one thing I've learned here, I've learned not to deceive myself. I'll never see you again."

"Probably not. Or, if you do, I'll be so old you'll hardly recognize me. So perhaps it is best that you leave now, before all our memories overcome your resolve."

From behind him, among the *Heron*'s company, Winslow heard Shakespeare say, "If it were done when 'tis done, then 'twere well it were done quickly."

Riahn bowed deeply to the Queen. She inclined her head in turn. Then she walked up the hill. All the others followed, except Virginia Dare. She paused for a last look. Then she took Winslow's hand and followed as well.

The world that now belonged to the Eilonwë again faded away. Then it vanished altogether, and for the second time Winslow found himself in the empty, silent, immaterial aloneness of the Deep Void. But he somehow knew that he was still holding Virginia Dare's hand.

He found he was holding it when Croatoan Island began to emerge in shades of gray.

— EIGHTEEN —

IT WAS DUSK ON CROATOAN, SO THE CHANGE WHEN THEY emerged from the Near Void wasn't as startling as it would have been in broad daylight. They were in the same unnaturally regular area of thin second-growth vegetation from which they had departed.

Looking around him at the thicker forest that surrounded them, Winslow saw almost at once a dozing figure sitting propped against a tree trunk. And his features broke into a grin, for he recognized the *Heron* crewman who had inadvertently passed through the Deep Void.

"Morris!" he called out. "I'd know you anywhere —asleep as usual!"

Amid the laughter of his shipmates, Morris jerked awake and scrambled upright, only to fall immediately

on his knees at the sight of the Queen, who motioned
him to his feet.

"Your Majesty! Captain! You're back already! But of
course—I keep forgetting about the time magic. What
happened? How went the battle?"

"We won, and the power of the Grella in that world
is broken. They're little more than a handful of fugitives
now, and the Eilonwë are hunting them down like
trapped rats."

"God be praised! If only I'd been there . . . " Morris
came to an abrupt halt, and his exultant expression dissolved into a mask of embarrassment. "As God is my
witness, Captain, I never sought to—"

"Of course you didn't," Winslow assured him, clapping
him on the back. "You were as eager as any of us to
come to grips with the Grella. No one thinks ill of you.
We expected to lose some of our number to the Deep
Void. All taken with all, we were lucky to lose only the
two of you. And you did exactly as you were told, letting
the tides of the Deep Void carry you back here and
waiting for our return."

"Aye, Captain. It's only been a couple of days here, you
understand, and the two of us have spent them standing
watches here."

" 'Standing watches'?" queried Shakespeare archly,
occasioning a fresh gale of laughter.

"Well, we're back now," said Winslow, rescuing Morris. "And we've brought a rare booty of hell weapons."
He indicated the components of alien technology that
festooned them all. "We'll return to England and see
how the Gray Monks like being roasted in their own
unholy fire!"

Once again, Morris' face fell. "Well, Captain, as to
that . . . The fact of the matter is, there's been no sign

of *Heron* or *Greyhound* here. Manteo has mounted watch on the coast, but nary a sail has been sighted."

Winslow's eyes met Virginia Dare's for an instant. Then he turned to face the Queen and Walsingham. No one could think of anything to say.

Manteo had a great deal to absorb all at once—joy at the return of *Weroanza* Elizabeth, and sorrow at the death of his old friend John White, along with much else. But he dealt surprisingly well with the sight of Ambrose Viccars as a graybeard and Virginia Dare as a young woman. His capacity for bewilderment simply shut down from overload, and after listening to Dee's attempt to explain he simply filed it away under the heading of *Beyond understanding; to be accepted on faith.* Since the day—not long ago to him—when he had watched the English party fade from sight, he had been inured to the uncanny. And the rest of his people were more than willing to adopt the same practical philosophy. So was Dick Taverner, who had once seen his fellow colonists vanish into nothingness.

Besides, everyone could appreciate a good story. So after the welcoming feast, they all sat around the fire in the village's central pit and listened avidly, far into the night, to the tale of the returnees' adventures in a world so remote that, as Dee put it, one could walk until Judgment Day and not reach it.

"And so," Dee concluded, "the Gray Monks are without hope of aid from their fellow Grella in other worlds, although they don't know it yet. And we've brought back the means to deal with them. Only," he concluded anticlimactically, "we have to get at them."

"Yes," Manteo nodded. "We have watched the horizon every day, but your ships have not appeared. I fear that when we do see sails, they will be those of the Spaniards. I am surprised they are not here already."

"I'm not," Winslow declared. "First of all, they'd cross the Atlantic in their old, slow, lubberly way of letting the winds and currents carry them, swinging far to the south. Then they'd stop in Florida where the Grella flying ship crashed, so the Gray Monks can pick up the instruments that enable them to find portals. And then they'd work their way slowly up the coast, beating past Cape Fear the way we did. And they'd proceed very cautiously all the while—we're even further into hurricane season now."

"Nevertheless," said the Queen, "we know they're coming, sooner rather than later. Dr. Dee, we must be ready to receive them."

"Indeed, Your Majesty. I will begin without delay to assemble the anti-matter weapons. I promise you the Spaniards and the Gray Monks will have a surprise in store."

Dee set to work the next day, with the help of the assistants he had trained before departing the world of the Eilonwë. He understood the *why* of what he was doing little if any more than they did. But he had committed to his formidable memory the details of connecting *this* to *that*, with the aid of the picture diagrams Riahn had supplied. And so the partially translucent, strangely harmless-seeming assemblages began to take shape.

In the meantime, everyone debated the best way to employ them. Walsingham was the voice of caution, arguing that they should be emplaced ashore to surprise Spanish landing parties. Winslow disagreed; he wanted to make catamarans out of the Indian canoes and carry the weapons out to attack the Spanish ships directly, which was precisely the way the Gray Monks had used them off Calais. To use weapons of such fearsome destructive power against individual enemy soldiers would be, as he put it, like "swatting flies with a sledge-hammer." And after that power had been demonstrated, he hoped to use the threat of further such demonstrations to force the surrender of ships in which they could return to England.

They were still debating when, one day, one of Manteo's lookouts ran into the village shouting and gesticulating frantically. "Ships," Manteo translated.

"The Spaniards—already?" gasped Dee.

Manteo put a series of questions to the tribesman, who drew a rectangle in the dirt with his finger. Then he walked over to a framework where the village women had hung fruit they had gathered. He crushed a red berry, rubbed his finger in the juice, and drew the red cross of St. George on the rectangle.

The whoops of joy from the English startled him.

Little time could be spent bringing Jonas Halleck, Martin Gorham and the others who had been at sea up to date on all that had befallen the shore party. The tidings the ships brought back were of more immediate urgency.

"The hurricane carried us less far than I'd feared," Halleck told the gathering in Manteo's longhouse. "But when it was over, we found ourselves well to the east, and a fairly stiff south-wester was still blowing. So we had to swing well east and south working our way back to the coast before turning to starboard and coming back

around. We raised the coast south of Cape Fear. Closer
inshore than we, and further south, we spotted the Spanish sails."

"How many?" Walsingham demanded.

"We were too far and too hurried to count them, your
lordship. But it's a fair-sized fleet."

Dee looked pale. "So they must be following close
behind you."

"I think not. Just after we sighted them, a fresh gale
came up. We ran before it, and it carried us past Cape
Fear."

It was Winslow's turn to blanch, as he tried to imagine
the risk Halleck had taken, riding a gale past that treacherous cape.

"But before we lost sight of them," Halleck continued,
"we could see that the Spaniards were scattering. They
were close-hauled off a lee shore, and their admiral probably ordered each ship to claw off as best it could. Now
they're probably reassembling, and will have to work
their way around the Cape Fear shoals the way we did
when we first arrived."

"Except, of course, that it will take them far longer,"
Winslow finished for him. "That gives us time."

"Why will it take them longer, Captain?" inquired
the Queen.

"Because their ships are high-charged, Your Majesty,
while ours are race-built." Seeing a blank look, Winslow
explained. "To the Dons, the purpose of warships is to
carry soldiers into battle and put them in the best position to board the enemy. So their ships are built the old
way, with fighting castles fore and aft, to give their soldiers the advantage of height. This doesn't matter with
the wind astern—which is why they always make their

voyages that way—but to windward, the size and windage of the castles causes the ship to blow down to leeward, even when they're as close-hauled as they can go." Warming to his theme, Winslow failed to notice that his listeners' eyes were beginning to glaze over. "In the meantime, we English have designed our ships for fighting at a distance with long-range guns rather than for boarding. So we've stripped the castles off, and our ships are long and low, lying snug to the water. We've also begun to cut our sails flatter, so they can be set closer to the wind. Why, *Heron* can make a good two point to windward! At the same time—"

"Thomas," Dee interrupted gently, "why don't you just say that our ships can sail into the wind better than theirs?"

"I did," Winslow said, puzzled. From Virginia Dare's direction came a sigh of exasperated resignation.

"At any rate," said Walsingham, taking charge with his usual understated firmness, "we now know for certain that the Spaniards are coming. So we must settle our earlier debate on how best to receive them, and set about the preparations for which God has granted us time. Thomas, I could always appreciate your argument that our captured Grella weapons are best employed against ships—large, flammable targets—as we English learned to our sorrow earlier this year. My reason for rejecting your proposal was that, given the conditions in these waters, the Spanish ships would not approach the shore to within the weapons' range. And I feared to entrust those weapons to flimsy craft improvised from the local canoes. I mean no offense, Lord Manteo," he added hastily. "But any misfortune to those craft would leave our only advantage lying at the bottom of the sea."

"Yes, Mr. Secretary," Winslow admitted. "That was always a danger."

"Now, however, your sturdy ships have returned and we can mount the weapons on them. So my one objection no longer obtains. I therefore say: go out and meet them!"

A general noise of agreement arose.

"So be it." The Queen's voice brought the hubbub to a sudden silence. "Captain Winslow, on the advice of our Principal Secretary and Privy Counselor, we command you to seek out the Spanish fleet and engage it." It had been a while since Winslow had heard her use the royal *we*, so the impact was all the greater. Then, with the sudden shift back to the first person singular that she had always used to such good effect: "And I will accompany the fleet."

At first, Winslow was without the power of speech. "Your Majesty," he finally managed, "I must point out that were are going into battle, against unforeseeable dangers. I cannot permit—"

"*By the bowels of almighty God!*" The daughter of King Hal surged to her feet, and everyone else must perforce rise with her—except Winslow, who went to one knee. "*Permit?* Do you forget, sirrah, that you once told me your claim to authority over your ship was 'only under God and Your Majesty'? Will you next be setting yourself above God, Captain?"

"But Your Majesty—" Winslow began, only to be overridden.

"We *will* sail with you, Captain, in this venture on which the future of our realm depends! And besides," she continued with a disconcerting shift from imperiousness to matter of factness, "if you lose, what will become of me, waiting here on this island for the Spaniards to arrive? I would rather go down with your ship than be taken alive and paraded before my people as the final proof of their subjugation."

"I believe, Thomas," said Walsingham, "that I, too, would rather take my chances with the sharks than with the Inquisition."

"And I, of course, must come," Dee interjected. "I believe I can, without fear of contradiction, claim a better understanding of the anti-matter weapons than anyone else." He naturally failed to add that that was saying very little. "But Thomas, since we *do*, after all, have those weapons, aren't you exaggerating the danger to Her Majesty and the rest of us?"

"Perhaps I am, Doctor—assuming that the Spaniards, and the Gray Monks who surely accompany them, haven't brought similar weapons of their own. But what if they have?"

Dee paled a shade or two. He wasn't the only one.

"Surely, Thomas," ventured Walsingham, "they'd feel no need for such power, to deal with nothing more than Raleigh's colonists and perhaps some fugitives such as ourselves." There was a general, relieved nodding of heads.

"I devoutly hope that's true, Mr. Secretary. If they don't have the weapons, then our prospects are very good. If they do, then our only advantage will be their surprise at our also having them."

"Not our only advantage, Captain," said the Queen. "We also have England's ships—and the men who sail them."

"I hope you're right, Your Majesty. And whatever I can do to make you right, I will do." Winslow looked around and saw Halleck and Martin Gorham swelling with pride. And out of the corner of his eye he noticed Virginia Dare. Her face wore an odd expression, as though she wanted to speak but was uncharacteristically hesitant.

The Queen, following Winslow's gaze, saw it too. "Have you anything to add, Mistress Dare?" she prompted.

Still Virginia Dare hesitated. Growing up in the exile society of the lost colonists, an infinity away from the fixed social hierarchies of England, she had never had the reticence to speak out in any kind of company that would have otherwise been expected of someone of her origins. But now something else seemed to be constraining her. "Your Majesty won't be offended?"

"I'll be offended if you deny us the benefit of your counsel," said the Queen briskly. "After all, you have more experience fighting the Grella than any of us here."

"That's true, Your Majesty: I've spent my life fighting them, and I know what they are. So all the talk of English and Spanish means little to me, for the Grella are the enemies of *all* humans—of all life besides themselves, in fact."

There was a general silence of blank incomprehension.

"But," Winslow finally protested, "the Spaniards are their puppets, manipulated by them through the Church of Rome!"

"My parents, while they were alive, tried to teach me to be a proper daughter of the Church of England. And I do try to be a good Christian. But I have to say that the talk of Catholic and Protestant doesn't mean much to me either." Before the incomprehension around her could solidify into shock, she hurried on. "Your Majesty, as little as I know of these matters, I *do* know the Grella. The Spaniards may be their unknowing servitors, but it will win them no gratitude—the Grella have none to give. To them, the universe holds only themselves and slaves. Slavery will be the Spaniards' fate in the end, as soon as they've lost their usefulness. Which means the Spaniards are natural allies of ours—they just don't know it yet. So maybe our aim should be to let them know it, and wean them away from their allegiance to the Grella."

There are ideas so outlandish that they cannot even arouse indignation. That seemed to be the general reaction, as the silence continued. But Winslow, looking around the array of faces, noticed two that were thoughtful rather than blank.

One was the face of Elizabeth Tudor, whose policy of tacit toleration of law-abiding Catholics among her subjects had always scandalized her Puritan supporters. The other was that of one of those Puritans' leaders, and Winslow would have expected him to be having a stroke. But this was a Puritan who was a student of Machiavelli as well as of Calvin. And Mr. Secretary Walsingham looked very thoughtful indeed.

— NINETEEN —

USING EASY SAIL FOR BEATING AGAINST THE SOUTHWEST wind, *Heron* and *Greyhound*, race-built ships both, needed only five tacks to clear the sound and gain the open sea. Four hours after departing, they were a dozen miles south. Winslow, expecting compliments on the ships' ability to windward, was crestfallen at the Queen's and Walsingham's obvious impatience at what they considered a tedious back-and-forth process. Virginia Dare, who had never seen an ocean or set foot on a sailing vessel in her life, was too fascinated by it all to notice.

"Now," Winslow told his passengers, "we'll make more sail and stand further out to sea, close-hauled on the starboard tack—" Seeing the familiar glazed look, he cleared his throat. "Ahem! I meant to say that we'll proceed southward, still beating against the wind, further from the coast than I guess the Dons will be, but just barely within sight of it. When we sight them, we'll come around and be in perfect position to win the weather gauge."

"I've heard you speak of 'the weather gauge' before, Captain," said the Queen. "I used to hear Drake speak of it. What, exactly, does it mean?"

Winslow opened his mouth, then closed it. After a second or two he opened it again . . . and closed it again. Some things are so obvious they are difficult to adequately put into words.

"It means to be upwind of the enemy, Your Majesty," he finally managed.

"Is that all?" she frowned.

"*All?* But . . . but Your Majesty, a captain in that position has the initiative. He can choose his moment to bear down. He can force engagement, and maneuver with the wind, which is easier than against it. Furthermore, the smoke of the guns drifts downwind into the enemy's face. And in this case, the Dons will be between us and a lee shore, so they'll have the added worry of running aground. And—"

"Yes. Of course. Thank you, Captain. I see that I can safely leave matters in your capable hands." The Queen gave a gesture of gracious dismissal and turned to peer at the coastline that was little more than a dark line on the horizon. Aboard *Heron* she had been reunited with her ladies-in-waiting and her wardrobe. Now she was restored to a semblance of the Virgin Queen of memory, complete with farthingale, white makeup, and dyed and crimped hair with a fringe of pearls. Winslow, who had seen her without all that dross, preferred her that way. But he was forced to admit that not everyone had so seen her, and that without it they might have difficulty recognizing her for who and what she was.

Presently, she departed to discuss something with John Dee. Winslow, who on this voyage had long since given up trying to uphold traditional restrictions on access to the quarterdeck, found himself sharing it with Walsingham and Virginia Dare. For a time, they shared it in silence, as Virginia Dare gazed intently at the distant coast. Then Walsingham cleared his throat.

"Mistress Dare," he began, in a voice so unlike him that Winslow worried for his always problematical health.

"Yes, your Lordship?"

"I'm no lord. Call me 'Mr. Secretary,' please. It's what everyone calls me."

"Very well, Mr. Secretary. But in that case, please call me 'Virginia.' I imagine people in England would be scandalized, but we're a long way from there."

"So we are. We are far away indeed, and about to go into a battle in which we may die. I will not run the risk of going before my Maker without having first unburdened myself to you, Mistress—Virginia."

"To *me*, Mr. Secretary?"

"Yes." Walsingham drew a deep breath. "It was I, working through my cat's-paw Simon Fernandez, who arranged for your parents, and all the others, to be stranded on Roanoke Island. Thomas, here, already knows why: I was playing a game of chess with the King of Spain, and Raleigh's colony was a piece that had to be sacrificed. Only . . . I had been playing chess too long. I had forgotten that my pieces were not unfeeling bits of carved ivory, but human beings and God's children." For an instant, Walsingham hardened into sternness. "Make no mistake: I have sent many to the rack and the scaffold—and some, like Anthony Babington, to be cut open and disemboweled while still alive and conscious —and I have no regrets. They were traitors who sought the death of Her Majesty and the rape of England, and I feel no pity for them. But in this instance, I knowingly condemned innocent people, including women and children, to their doom. And by so doing I exposed them to a fate never imagined even in our worst visualizations of Hell—the kind of unnatural repeated deaths your parents suffered."

For a long moment the only sounds were the wind in the rigging and the unending creaking of a wooden ship under sail. Both seemed unnaturally loud. Winslow held his breath, not knowing what to expect from Virginia Dare—and not knowing how he should or would behave in response. For now, he merely kept a wary eye on the sword strapped to her back.

When she finally spoke, her voice could barely be heard. "You could not possibly have known of the shadow-Earth of the Eilonwë or of the dangers it held, Mr. Secretary."

"That, Virginia, is a lawyer's quibble. As a lawyer myself, I need have no respect for it. A robber may not intend to commit murder, but if the master of the house he robs dies defending it—or merely breaks his neck coming down the stairs to investigate the commotion —he will hang for murder. Likewise, my lack of intent cannot alter my responsibility for all that has befallen you and your people for the past twenty years, as you have experienced time. I know I cannot expect your forgiveness. I ask only that you believe this: what I did was done not out of malice or self-interest but only out of duty to England."

"If you hadn't done as you did, Mr. Secretary, the colony probably would have been founded as Sir Walter intended. A toddler named Virginia Dare would this day be living by the shores of the Chesapeake Bay . . . and facing a life that held nothing except death or enslavement at the hands of the Spaniards, in a world ruled by the Grella from behind the curtains of the Vatican and the Escorial, in their role as 'Gray Monks.' Instead, we passed through the veil between worlds that is the Deep Void, and you followed us. For that reason, mankind now has a fighting chance to free itself." She flashed a crooked smile. "That, too, was not what you intended. But intentionally or not, that is what you have given us. And for that, I like to think my parents would have forgiven you. I may do no less."

Sir Francis Walsingham, Privy Counselor and Principal Secretary, bowed his head to the common-born young woman in plain Eilonwë garb. "Thank you, madam," he barely whispered, and waved aside her demurral at the honorific. "I had no right to expect the absolution you have granted me. But now I can face that which lies before us with a blithe heart and a clear mind."

"For which," Winslow told her dryly, "you've done us all a favor."

At that moment, a lookout's cry of "Sail ho!" shattered the stillness.

In fact, it was almost twenty sails. That became appallingly apparent as they drew closer and the Spanish fleet came into focus against the backdrop of the coastline of Wococon Island, still further to westward.

"You know what this is, don't you?" Winslow asked no one in particular. "It's the core of the Armada—the twenty or so galleons that were built from the keel up as fighting ships. They must have come here from England as quickly as they could be refitted and reprovisioned, before hurricane season was even further advanced. I see none of the forty 'great ships'—lumbering Mediterranean cargo carriers that had been loaded down with guns too heavy for them to fire without shaking themselves apart. And none of the merchant ships they were using as troop carriers. And none of the galleys and galleasses that could never have survived an Atlantic crossing. No, they don't need any of that when they're not mounting a full-scale invasion. There's no fat here—only muscle."

"Why would they have thought it necessary to bring so much . . . muscle?" wondered Walsingham. "As you said, they must have thought they would only have to deal with a few colonists and fugitives."

"I imagine the Gray Monks insisted on it, Mr. Secretary," Winslow replied absently, never taking his eyes off that array of sails. "They weren't about to risk this venture without the full fighting force of their human servitors arrayed around them."

The Queen peered at the ships, whose hulls were growing more distinct. "They do appear rather . . . formidable, don't they, Captain?"

Winslow grinned wolfishly. "The more I hear you say that, Your Majesty, the less I'm worried about them." He turned to her and explained the seeming paradox. "Remember what I explained earlier about the towering fore—and after-castles the Spaniards still build on their ships? It makes them look bigger than they are—and so, I suppose, serves a purpose by frightening their enemies. But it also ruins the ship's sailing qualities. *Heron* can sail circles around them. And even *Greyhound*, old as she is, has been cut down so she has almost as low a freeboard as a newer race-built ship. Our ships never could take full advantage of this when fighting the Armada in the Channel. They weren't dealing with individual ships, but with a rigid, closely spaced formation which they didn't dare penetrate lest they be boarded from both sides." He gazed westward again. "Here, they're not trying to maintain any such defensive mass of ships. They never thought to need it off this desolate coast. That's another advantage for us."

"One advantage you forgot to mention, Thomas," said Dee with a kind of nervous levity. "Their sheer, dumbfounded surprise at two ships daring to challenge them. But of course our *real* advantage is our possession of the Grella anti-matter weapons."

"Actually, Doctor, I plan to withhold those as long as possible." Winslow's eyes never left the Spanish fleet. "Ah, yes. I see they're detaching three ships to deal with the impudent intruders." He could barely keep from his voice his disdain at the sluggishness with which the Spanish galleons changed course to windward.

"Ah . . . what was that about *withholding* the Grella weapons, Thomas?" inquired Walsingham. He didn't exactly sound nervous—imagination failed at the idea of him sounding that way—but he kept casting glances at the converging Spanish ships.

"That's right, Mr. Secretary. I don't want to use them until I can use them decisively. I want to penetrate to the core of the Spanish fleet—what our ships were never given the chance to do in the Channel." Winslow had no idea how chilling his expression seemed to the others. "I want to get within range of their flagship and shove one of those weapons up their—" At the last instant, he remembered the Queen's presence and concluded by clearing his throat.

"But, er, Thomas," said Dee, "what about . . . ?" He indicated the approaching Spanish ships, and unlike Walsingham he sounded indisputably jittery.

"Besides," Winslow continued as though he hadn't heard, "I don't think those weapons will be needed just yet. You see, we have a couple of other advantages which I haven't mentioned yet." As he spoke, his eyes remained fixed on the pattern of ships. *Greyhound* was ahead and off the starboard bow; she would encounter the leading galleon, slightly later than *Heron* would meet the other two, which were more or less abeam of each other as they struggled to windward.

Winslow shouted a series of commands, and *Heron* swooped in from upwind, drawing alongside her closer opponent—a twenty-gun galleon, he saw. Her gunwales and castles were agleam with the sun's reflection off breastplates, morions and burganets.

"Overcrowded with soldiers, as usual," he remarked disdainfully. "They still think we're going to let them board us." He turned to his companions, who looked uneasy at their unexpected closeness to the enemy. But the English had learned in the Channel fighting that the long-range gunnery on which they had originally pinned their hopes was a waste of powder and shot; they must close practically to within pistol range for their guns to be effective. He considered suggesting that the Queen seek the relative safety of the cabin, where the ladies-in-waiting now cowered, but then thought better of it. "Prepare yourselves," was all he said.

"What 'other advantages,' are these, Captain?" asked the Queen in a steady voice.

At that moment, the Spaniard's guns fired with a deafening series of crashes. The three landlubbers involuntarily ducked as cannonballs screamed overhead. One of those balls punched a hole in *Heron's* mainsail, and a few lines were cut, but the broadside had no other effect.

"That's one, Your Majesty," Winslow explained. "It, too, results from our having the weather gauge. The cannons of the lee ship—that's them—are tilted upward, and are apt to completely miss a race-built ship like ours, with its low freeboard. For the same reason, ours are angled down, so . . ." He paused with unconscious drama, studied angles and distances, and bellowed, "*Fire!*"

Heron shuddered as her port battery belched forth an ear-bruising broadside that crashed into the Spaniard's hull, smashing timbers and visibly rocking her back. Winslow roared another series of orders, sails were luffed, and the shaken Spaniard glided on past.

"Hard a-port!" Winslow shouted to the steersman. With a suddenness that almost threw the Queen and the two elderly landsmen off their feet, *Heron* swung to port. Her bowsprit barely missed scraping the Spaniard's poop as she crossed her opponent's vulnerable stern.

Heron only had enough gun crews to man one side's battery at a time—the usual case. Now they ran across the decks to the unfired starboard battery.

"Fire as your guns bear!" Winslow called out. As the first gun belched fire and thunder, the Spanish captain's cabin seemed to explode outward in a shower of wood and glass. Then ball after ball smashed home, and Winslow visualized them roaring down the Spaniard's length from stern to stem, smashing everything and everyone in their path. One of them brought the mizzenmast down, and it fell slowly over the starboard side, fouling the mainmast's rigging. Then they were past, and as the wind blew the rotten eggs-smelling clouds of smoke downwind they could see that the galleon was adrift, seemingly out of control.

"We got their rudder, or I'm a Turkish pimp!" exulted Martin Gorham.

"Now hard a-starboard!" Winslow ordered, and the steersman hauled the whipstaff in the opposite direction with all his strength. As *Heron* came about and began to draw down on the second galleon, the gun crews crossed the deck again and began to reload the port guns.

"Another advantage," Winslow resumed conversationally, ignoring his listeners' stunned looks, "is our gun carriages, which roll back with the guns' recoil until their cables halt them, allowing the crews to reload. The Spaniards, who think only in terms of a single broadside to soften their enemy up before boarding, can't do this. Actually, we couldn't have done it if we'd had to fight a battle on our voyage from England to Virginia, because all the clutter on the gun deck left no room for recoil. But now I've had that cleared away. And this Spaniard—who thinks our port battery has shot its bolt—is about to get a surprise."

As they drew alongside, the wind picked up a bit and both ships heeled more sharply. So this time the Spanish cannonballs flew even further overhead, while *Heron*'s smashed home at or below the waterline. They left their second opponent listing alarmingly to starboard as they turned to port, crossing her bow—unfortunately, there was no time to reload the port battery for another broadside —and leaving her behind, taking on water.

The Queen, Walsingham, Dee and Virginia Dare gazed aft, where the wrecks of two larger ships lay wallowing helplessly in *Heron*'s wake. Then they turned to Winslow and simply stared, openmouthed.

He barely noticed, as he scanned the scene revealed by the dissipating smoke. Ahead, *Greyhound* was pulling away from the Spanish ship she had raked across the bows, and was converging on the main Spanish body. She would close with that main body slightly sooner than *Heron*, even though the Spanish were now much closer. Only one of them was in a position to interpose herself between *Heron* and what Winslow was certain was the flagship.

"Yes," Walsingham nodded when asked for confirmation. "That is the *San Martín*, the great Portuguese galleon that was the Armada's flagship. I see she is still flying the flag King Phillip had presented to his admiral, the Duke of Medina Sidonia, before he sailed from Lisbon—I received a report of the ceremony." He gazed through squinted eyes at the huge flag. "Yes: the royal Spanish arms with the Virgin Mary on one side and the crucified Christ on the other, over a scroll with the words *Exurge Domine et Vindica Causam Tuam*—'Arise O Lord and Vindicate Thy Cause.'" Walsingham looked like he wanted to spit.

"Well," said Winslow, "we'll make for her although *Greyhound* will be in range first. And I think it's time to reveal our Grella weapons by using one of them on that galleon that's moving to protect the flagship." *Heron* mounted two of the anti-matter weapons, one forward and one aft. Winslow looked at the fragile, harmless-seeming object that was so obviously out of place on the poop. "Dr. Dee, you'll oblige me by telling me when, in your judgment, we're in range of her."

"I believe, Thomas, that we will be close enough soon . . . soon . . . *now!*"

Winslow signaled to the crew on the poop, and a tracery of evil energies wavered up and down that translucent tube. In the sunlight the beam it projected was barely visible or audible—nothing more than a flickering, crackling line. But it speared the approaching galleon like a needle, and at its touch her side simply exploded into white-hot flame with a noise like the crack of doom, followed by a shock wave that caused *Heron*'s timbers to shudder.

But at appreciably the same instant another narrow line of unnatural light shot out from *San Martín*'s forecastle, and *Greyhound*'s entire waist boiled into seething flame, breaking her in two. Her mainmast flew cartwheeling through the air, trailing flame, until it splashed into the sea.

"Steersman!" Winslow bellowed while everyone else stood marbled in shock. "Make for their flagship—two points to port."

Heron, with every inch of canvas laid on, sailed past the flaming wreck of the screening galleon, and approached the Spanish flagship. Winslow could see figures on her quarterdeck, including one very richly dressed one and another that was tiny and gray-robed. He also saw the Grella weapon on the forecastle swinging toward him.

Impulsively, he grabbed a megaphone of stiff leather. "Hold!" he called out in Spanish, his amplified voice crossing the intervening water. "We have weapons like yours—you just saw us use one. Fire on us, and we will reply in kind."

A hurried colloquy ensued on *San Martín*'s quarterdeck, with the small gray-clad figure expostulating to the splendidly cloaked man, who hesitated, shook his head, and turned to speak to someone else—the flagship's captain, probably. The latter took up a megaphone like Winslow's. "Surrender now and we will spare your worthless heretic lives. Otherwise, Saint Antony's holy fire will consume you before you can 'reply in kind,' Lutheran pig!"

Winslow laughed scornfully. "We have two of the antimatter weapons—and yes, we know all about them. If you fire first, you'll probably get one of them. But before the ship goes down, the other one will send you to your own papist Hell!"

What followed was a moment, not of silence—there were too many survivors clinging to flotsam and crying for rescue for that—but of expectancy that was almost unbearable in its tenseness.

Walsingham stepped to the rail and took the megaphone from Winslow's hands. "In the name of Her Majesty, I propose that we meet to settle this impasse."

There was another hasty consultation aboard *San Martín* before the same man responded. "You lie! The heretic bastard you call your Queen is dead!"

With an oath, Elizabeth snatched the megaphone and spoke in a voice that barely required it. "We are Elizabeth, by grace of God Queen of England, Wales, Ireland and France, and Defender of the Faith . . . and," she concluded without the slightest hint of irony, "*Weroanza* of Virginia—off whose coasts you are cruising without permission. And you, sirrah, will keep a civil tongue in your head! You will also turn the megaphone over to your admiral. I do not deal with underlings!"

Even at this moment, it was all Winslow could do not to laugh at the flabbergasted commotion that arose

aboard *San Martín*. The Gray Monk seemed even more
agitated than before. But the grandee turned away from
him and took the megaphone.

"I am Don Alonzo Pérez de Guzmán el Bueno, Duke
of Medina Sidonia and Captain General of the High
Seas. If you wish a meeting, I grant permission to come
aboard my flagship under safe conduct."

Winslow didn't even bother to reclaim the megaphone. "What kind of simpletons do you take us for?"
he shouted across the water with cupped hands. " 'Safe
conduct!' The same kind of safe conduct Jan Hus had
from you papists, I suppose, before you burned him
alive!"

"You have the word of honor of a Spanish nobleman!"

Walsingham shushed Winslow before he could make
a rude noise, then conferred in undertones with the
Queen and took the megaphone. "To avoid any mistrust
or misunderstandings, Your Grace, we propose that we
meet at a neutral site. Wococon Island lies just to our
left—I mean, to port. It is dangerous to try to pass the
sandbars into the sound. But given the fineness of the
weather, let us anchor just outside the inlet and take
small boats to the beach—say, not more than ten people
on each side. In the meantime, our flagships can continue to hold each other hostage."

There was a long pause. Winslow could not interpret
what he saw of the activity on *San Martín*'s quarterdeck.
But presently Medina Sidonia took up the megaphone
again. "Very well. I agree. Come ahead."

— TWENTY —

THE ENGLISH PARTY WAS ASHORE ON WOCOCON FIRST, TO Winslow's smug lack of surprise. Besides himself, it consisted of the Queen, Walsingham, Dee, Virginia Dare, a pair of the soldiers of the Queen's guard, and four crewmen who, with the soldiers, manned the oars of the longboat that brought them. Winslow couldn't recall what had made him decide to include Shakespeare among those crewmen, but the young actor pulled his oar gamely enough. They waited on the narrow sandy beach, against the backdrop of the loblolly pine forest, and watched as the Spanish party rowed ashore. Wococon's Indian inhabitants, if any, were not in evidence.

The Spaniards also had six rowers: four sailors, and two men in cowled gray robes. Likewise gray-robed was a diminutive figure at the sight of whom Winslow's hackles rose. The remaining three were obvious Spanish noblemen, led by the one who had spoken from *San Martín's* quarterdeck. As he stepped ashore, Winslow saw that he was in his late thirties, of only medium height but neatly made and rather broad-shouldered. He had the look of a horseman rather than a seaman, which was consistent with what Winslow had heard of the Duke of Medina Sidonia. His neatly bearded face, with its dark, intelligent eyes, was obviously that of a sensitive and thoughtful man. Not quite equally obvious, at first glance, was that it was also the face of a courageous one.

He ran his eyes over the eleven members of the English party. "I was under the impression," he said mildly, "that our agreement stipulated not more than ten persons for each side."

Walsingham stepped forward and spoke with equal smoothness. "Naturally *persons* cannot be construed as including Her Majesty." He made a leg and indicated the Queen with a sweeping gesture.

"Ah." Medina Sidonia looked perplexed—as well he might, Winslow thought with grim amusement. How does one behave toward an anointed Queen whom one's own Church has declared a usurper, her subjects released from obedience to her and absolved from guilt for assassinating her? It was a difficult question, especially when one had agreed to treat with her. The Duke resolved it by inclining his head fractionally lower than he would have for a lady of equal social rank and murmuring, "Madam."

For an instant, Elizabeth's eyes flashed fire at the pointed omission of *"Your Majesty."* But she smoothed her expression out and gave a small, quick nod and a frostily correct "Your Grace" in return.

"And I," Walsingham resumed, "have the honor to be Her Majesty's Principal Secretary." He ignored the startled glares he got from the Spaniards, to whom his name was all too well known. "And these two gentlemen are Dr. John Dee, a learned adviser to Her Majesty, and Captain Thomas Winslow of Her Majesty's ship *Heron*."

"Ah, yes," nodded Medina Sidonia. "The noted charlatan and the equally noted pirate."

"Privateer," Winslow corrected with a wince of wronged innocence. Dee, at his loftiest, did not deign to respond.

"I have already introduced myself," said Medina Sidonia, ignoring them. He turned to one of his fellow nobles, distinguished-looking but elderly and walking like a man who suffered from sciatica. "This is Don Juan Martínez de Recalde, Captain General of the Squadron of Biscay." Winslow looked up sharply at a man whose name was known and respected by every fighting seaman. "And this is Don Diego Flores de Valdés, Captain General of the Squadron of Castile. And this," Medina Sidonia concluded, indicating the small gray-robed figure, "is Father Jerónimo of the Order of St. Antony of Padua."

Winslow stared at the Grell, barely recognizable as such save for his size because his cowl hid most of the alien face. His two human acolytes, however, had their cowls down, and Winslow, looking at those ordinary Spanish faces, saw a look he had seen before on the faces of enslaved Eilonwë. For all the difference in race, it was the same look: a look too empty even to hold hopelessness, for hopelessness implies the ability to hope. These young men lacked that, because their souls had been stolen. At the sight of them—humans this time, not Eilonwë—Winslow's gorge rose.

"Ah . . . Father Jerónimo," said Walsingham with a perceptible pause before the name. "I am glad the Duke included you in his party, for our business concerns you."

"There could be nothing concerning me to interest heretics," came the sibilant voice from within the cowl. The Spaniards muttered in agreement.

"Oh, but there could . . . Father Jerónimo." Walsingham's pause was now openly ironic. "Many things—and the answers to many questions. For example, how we English happen to know about the anti-matter weapons, and have them in our possession." As he spoke, Walsingham's head turned toward Medina Sidonia, and their eyes met.

The Duke's expressive face was a battleground of emotions, as automatic denial warred with doubts and curiosity. "We *had* wondered about that," he conceded.

"The answer is simple enough, Your Grace. I doubt if . . . Father Jerónimo has explained to you the purpose of your voyage here, save in generalities." Medina Sidonia's expression made it clear that Walsingham had guessed correctly. "The purpose is to find the way back into the world from which the inhuman abominations whom we know as the 'Gray Monks' came to infest ours."

"Silence, heretic!" hissed Father Jerónimo.

Walsingham swung away from the dumbfounded Spaniards and faced the Gray Monk. "You are too late. We have visited that world. There, we helped the Eilonwë free themselves from their servitude to your fellow Grella!"

"What babbling is this?" spluttered Diego Flores de Valdés. But he quickly fell silent and, along with the other Spaniards, stared at Father Jerónimo. The Gray

Monk had staggered back as though from a physical blow, and his cowl had slipped partially back, exposing more of his lipless, almost noseless face with its huge empty eyes. He had never looked more alien.

"What do these unfamiliar words mean, Father?" asked Medina Sidonia in a level voice.

"Yes!" said Walsingham mockingly. "Tell them what it all means, if you dare. Tell them what you are, Grell!"

"Be silent!" Instead of the usual hiss, it was a ragged rasp that, Winslow decided, must be a Grella shout. The Gray Monk turned to the Spaniards. "What are you waiting for, you cowards? In addition to these lesser scoundrels, we have in our hands the arch-fiend Walsingham —Satan in human form! Have you forgotten that he sent the martyred Mary Stuart to the scaffold with his forged letters?"

"If memory serves," Walsingham interjected mildly, "even the so-called Queen of Scots herself abandoned that line of defense at her trial."

"And better still," Father Jerónimo went on, ignoring him, "we have the bastard whelp of the whore Anne Boleyn—probably sired on her by her own brother!" The Queen flushed beneath her makeup at being reminded of the most scurrilous of the trumped-up charges against her mother, whose real crime had been her failure to give Henry VIII a male heir.

"Father," said Medina Sidonia coolly, "leaving aside the practical matter that there are no more of us than of them on this beach, I promised them safe conduct."

"A promise to a heretic means nothing! I absolve you from it."

"The word of honor of a Guzmán el Bueno means a great deal, no matter to whom it is given. Furthermore, their ship and *San Martín* still hold each other under threat of—how to put it?—mutually assured destruction."

"Your ridiculous, primitive ship does not matter!" Father Jerónimo brought himself under control with a visible effort. "What I meant to say, my son, is that we, unlike they, have ships to spare. The important thing is that you convey me onward to complete my holy quest."

Winslow barked laughter. "We can help you with your 'quest.' What you seek is on Croatoan Island, just north-east of here. And you won't need your instruments to find it. Oh, no! We'll be glad to show you the way! And once you use your flying ship to go through the portal, you'll be just one more bit of vermin for the Eilonwë to eradicate, along with all the other Grella still defiling their world."

Virginia Dare stepped forward. She hadn't understood the exchange, for they had all been speaking in Spanish. But she grasped what was happening. And now she stood before the Spaniards and the Grell. Walsingham hadn't included her in the introductions, and it had never occurred to the Spaniards to ask to have her introduced. In their world, a plainly dressed young woman in these circumstances could only be a servant to the Queen. So they had never noticed her. Now they noticed—and stared at the sword strapped to her back. Their stares grew even more round-eyed as she faced Father Jeró-nimo and spoke in the Eilonwë language.

Again, the Grell recoiled backward in shock. Then he rallied and hissed furiously at her in the same language. She laughed and spoke a few more Eilonwë phrases, which reduced the Grell to a state of glaring speech-lessness.

"Father," said Medina Sidonia in a voice that was now quite hard, "I do not know this tongue. But you evidently do. Perhaps you can explain."

Dee chuckled. "I picked up a smattering of the Eilonwë language while we were among them. I believe she just reiterated what Captain Winslow had already told him, but phrased a trifle more strongly."

"I require an explanation, Father," Medina Sidonia said, more firmly than before.

A quivering ran through Father Jerónimo, and something seemed to awaken in his strange eyes. Winslow had thought those eyes to be holes through which nothing was to be glimpsed but an infinity of emptiness. Now he saw that there was something there after all: a contempt so utter and abysmal that it passed beyond contempt and became an emotion for which no human language had a name.

"You 'require,' do you, you filthy breeding animal?" Before anyone could react, the Grell reached within his gray robe and whipped out a pistol-shaped object. Winslow recognized it as a small hand-held version of the weapons which shaped and intensified light into a deadly immaterial rapier. At a hissed command in the loathsome Grella tongue, the two acolytes, moving like the automata they in fact were, drew similar weapons with grips modified for human hands. One of them pointed it to cover the English party, including Virginia Dare, who froze into immobility at the sight of a weapon she knew only too well. The other did the same for the Spanish sailors who stood, mouths agape, by their longboat. Father Jerónimo himself leveled his weapon at the group of Spanish nobles, aimed directly at the Duke's chest.

He made no move to fire it. But Recalde, who happened to be in the best position the interpose himself, shouted "No!" and, moving as quickly as his age and infirmity permitted, threw himself between his captain-general and what his half-century of warlike experience told him was a weapon of some kind.

The crackling, searing line of light that Winslow remembered speared Recalde through the chest. He fell backwards in a burst of superheated pink steam.

With a cry, Medina Sidonia went to his knees in the sand beside the man who had been his mentor in the lore of the sea. But the gallant old admiral was already dead.

With cold deliberation, the Grell fired his weapon again. Diego Flores de Valdés died.

"Any usefulness they may have had to the expedition," said Father Jerónimo, still holding his weapon steady, "was outweighed by the value of their deaths, in demonstrating to you how little any of your lives mean, except to the extent that you are useful to us, your natural masters."

Medina Sidonia looked up from where he knelt, and his face wore a look obviously foreign to it: a look of cold, murderous hate. But he, like everyone else, remained motionless under the sights of those unnatural weapons.

"And now," the Grell continued, "to my inexpressible relief, I need no longer pretend to take your tribal superstitions and absurd metaphysical hairsplitting seriously —except, of course, to your subordinates, who will be told that the heretic Elizabeth has seen the error of her ways and joined our expedition. Thus we will avoid the destruction of the useful weapons aboard the two flagships. And she can be held as a hostage for the good behavior of the rest of the English as we proceed to this Croatoan Island."

"Are you insane?" Dee blurted, heedless of the light-weapons. "There's nothing left for you on the other side of that portal. Your dominion over the Eilonwë is over. The great arch that allowed easy passage to your other worlds beyond is a pile of wreckage. Haven't you been listening?"

"Yes, I have been listening to your pathetic attempt to deceive me. It is, of course, all nonsense. The Eilonwë, while somewhat more knowledgeable than your humans, are equally products of random natural processes. As such, they could not possibly have overcome a higher, consciously self-created form of life. However, your lies contain one element of obvious truth, which requires further investigation. Your knowledge of the Eilonwë language proves that you humans did indeed blunder onto the portal—and passed through it, in some fashion that does not require artificial aid. This must be studied. Perhaps we can make use of it."

Winslow smiled tightly. "You're welcome to try."

"It is of no particular importance if we do not. We will simply complete the repair of our scout craft, for which we have been awaiting the rediscovery of the portal. In the meantime, your Queen will be a hostage against any foolish attempt by you to use your ability to pass through the portal when you show me its location."

Through all this, Virginia Dare had stood in uncomprehending silence, remaining absolutely still. Perhaps it was for that reason that the Grell seemed to have forgotten her presence—or perhaps because he had absorbed the attitudes of the Spaniards among whom he had lived. It was probably the latter, for when she slumped down in an apparent swoon his alienness could not disguise his attitude of exasperated but unsurprised contempt. He spoke a command to the acolyte who was covering the English party. The latter stepped forward in the machine-like way of his kind, still holding his weapon level while reaching down with his other hand to haul her out of the way.

With explosive suddenness, she lashed out with a kick from her crouching position, connecting with the acolyte's right knee and causing him to stagger. At the same instant, she surged to her feet, grasping the wrist of his gun hand and forcing it down. He reflexively got off a shot, searing the sand into a steaming puddle of molten silica. Then she wrenched the arm up while grasping him around the neck from behind with her other arm. While he was still off balance and unable to bring his weight and strength to bear, she swung him around to face the being who had been known as Father Jerónimo.

The Grell unhesitatingly swung his weapon toward his minion and fired a bolt that would effortlessly burn its way through both the struggling bodies. But Virginia Dare shoved the acolyte forward, and he took the light-ray through the head while she herself fell to the sand. The top of the acolyte's head came off as his instantly superheated brain exploded. His lifeless body fell over backwards across Virginia Dare's prone form.

Medina Sidonia jumped to his feet and drew his rapier. The Grell swung his weapon back toward him.

Acting before he had time to think, Winslow sprang forward with a roar, sweeping out his sword. Lunging, he just barely struck the weapon from the Grell's hand with the sword's point. As the Grell staggered back with a high-pitched hiss, Winslow had a split second to meet the eyes of the man whose life he had—to their mutual astonishment—just saved.

A rapid-fire crackling was heard as the remaining acolyte fired repeatedly at the Spanish sailors, who had begun an enraged rush, drawing their knives. He killed two of them before the other two bowled him over and set about their knife work. His weapon went flying and landed in the sand.

With a kind of quavering, wailing hiss, the Grell scrambled toward that weapon, his gray robe half falling off in his frantic scramble and revealing his hairless, inhuman head. Before anyone had time to react, he had reached it and scooped it up. The human-adapted grip was awkward for him, but he took it in both hands and raised it.

No one had noticed Virginia Dare pushing the dead weight of the acolyte off her and springing to her feet. But now, at the last instant, Winslow caught sight of her as she rushed in from the side, reached behind her left shoulder, and swept out the curved Eilonwë sword. There was the blinding motion Winslow remembered, and the Grell was watching his weapon, with the two hands holding it, falling to the sand.

His hiss had no time to rise to a full, high-pitched Grella scream. For she brought her sword around in a smooth two-handed recovery and whipped downward, laying him open from forehead to crotch.

Silence fell, shuddering, on the beach. The English sailors, who had taken no part up to now, came running up . . . only to stop and stare, as did their Spanish fellows. Then they all looked away. Shakespeare turned aside and was sick. Several others looked as though they might do the same. Winslow himself nearly gagged. For what bulged out through the Grell's slashed-open robe was nothing like the guts of men or even of beasts. And the blood that soaked into the sand was not the proper color or consistency of blood.

These were hard men, born into hard times—times when executions by hanging, drawing and quartering were considered public spectacles, and bear baitings were a favorite form of entertainment. Butchery in itself had no power to shock or disgust them. What nauseated them was a sense of filthy and obscene wrongness.

"Your Grace," Walsingham finally said after swallowing hard, "Captain Winslow spoke truth. If you wish, we will convey you to Croatoan Island and show you the portal through which the flying ship now lying crippled in Florida entered our world. If it is your further wish, we will convey you, or a trusty deputy, through the portal, where the beings known as the Eilonwë—lately enslaved by the Grella, as they mean to enslave mankind—will confirm what we have said."

Medina Sidonia drew a deep breath and released it, as though to cleanse his lungs. "I would be fascinated to do so. But I don't believe it will be necessary. Not now." He gestured to indicate that at which none of them wanted to look. Then his features firmed into a mask of determination. "Besides, we have more urgent matters in hand—a cleansing that must be done. The only question is whether we deal first with the Gray . . . that is, the Grella in Florida, or return to Europe at once."

"Setting a course for Florida would mean beating against the prevailing winds all the way," said Winslow, relieved to be back in the world of practical seamanship. He restrained himself from remarking condescendingly on the difficulty the Spanish ships would have sailing into the wind. "Also, no seaman in his right mind wants to linger in these waters in hurricane season."

"Agreed." Medina Sidonia's emphatic nod suggested that he was only too willing to be persuaded to let the winds and currents carry them easily back across the Atlantic. "Furthermore, the Grella in Florida can do no

harm, stranded there with their ruined craft. They
be dealt with later. It is more urgent to free Europe
—beginning with England."

"England?" Dee exclaimed, clearly surprised that
Medina Sidonia would want to start there. "Its liberation
may not be easy, even with our anti-matter weapons. I'm
sure the Grella there have others."

"So they do. But I have reason to believe we won't
have to face them." Medina Sidonia looked grave. "It is
my devout hope that King Phillip will see what needs to
be done, once he knows the truth about how we have all
been deceived. But just in case there are . . . difficulties,
we will need allies. And we have a natural one in the
Duke of Parma."

"Parma!" Walsingham exclaimed, for once taken
aback.

"Yes. He is still in command in England as governor-
general, until all resistance is put down and it is safe for
King Phillip's daughter Isabella to arrive and assume the
throne, with Dr. William Allen as papal legate to
advise her."

"Allen!" Walsingham's jaw clenched at the mention of
the Catholic exile, founder of the English College at
Rome, who had tirelessly advocated the overthrow of
Elizabeth. "That foul traitor! And Parma, who ravaged
London, and before that played a deceitful game of pre-
tending to negotiate with our commissioners in the Netherlands, all the while knowing that Phillip had no
intention of making peace. Oh, yes, I've read their correspondence."

"As regards London . . . " Medina Sidonia spread his
hands as though to say that war was war. "And I happen
to know that Parma was under the King's orders to

be . . . less than candid with your commissioners. Those orders never sat particularly well with him. Lying does not come naturally to him; he is a soldier, not a lawyer." Walsingham flushed darkly at the jibe. "I also know—as even you may not—that back in March he tactfully advised the King that our ends might well be gained with less expense by making an honorable peace with England."

Walsingham, who in fact hadn't known it, blinked once.

"And," the Duke continued, "I have reason to believe that he would be amenable to our cause. You must understand, he is a prince by birth, and has for some time felt that he deserves, as a reward for his services, a kingdom of his own. Or rather a kingdom for his line, for his wife is a royal princess of Portugal and so his children have a better claim to the Portuguese throne than does King Phillip, who kept it for himself. Likewise, he was disappointed in his hopes for a kingdom in the Netherlands. Some of the wits in the Armada were saying that we'd have to fight a second war, over who would be King of England after we conquered it." Seeing that his listeners didn't appreciate the humor, the Duke hurried on. "At any rate, I believe he would join us if England agrees to support his claim as King of the Netherlands."

"But," Dee wondered, "will the Dutch accept him?"

The Queen answered him. "I believe they very well might, as long as he is willing to respect their traditional liberties, about which they feel very strongly. I have always tried to convince Phillip of Spain that if he would only do so, the Dutch were perfectly willing to be his loyal subjects. Is that no so, my Moor?"

"Indeed, Your Majesty," said Walsingham sourly. "But he of course sought to impose the popish religion on them, persecuting them for their faith."

"As Catholics are persecuted in England for not conforming to your heretical church?" queried Medina Sidonia pointedly.

"They most certainly are not! Her Majesty is perfectly willing to allow her law-abiding Catholic subjects the free exercise of their faith." *More willing than some of us would prefer*, Walsingham loudly did not add.

"Subject to a fine for not attending your heretical 'Church of England.' And you yourself have subjected priests of the true Catholic faith to the rack and other tortures, and even to death!"

"They were spies and secret agents, seeking to incite rebellion and procure the assassination of Her Majesty! It was for that, and not for their deluded faith, that they fell afoul of the law!"

"And you have suppressed the Mass!"

"Mummery of the Devil!"

"Heretic!"

"Papist!"

"*Oh, for the love of God, will you two have done?*" The Queen's voice silenced the Duke as thoroughly as it did her own Principal Secretary. She drew a deep, exasperated breath. "Can you think of nothing but your bickering? How much do our differences mean, in the face of *that?*" She swept an arm toward that which had been Father Jerónimo. "We must stand together against the enemies of all Christendom—no, of all mankind. Afterwards, we'll have plenty of time to decide how we should best worship the God we all share—or maybe even allow each of God's children to decide it for himself.

But if we fall to fighting among ourselves, it may be that no one will be left to worship Him at all."

For a few heartbeats, Medina Sidonia and Walsingham —the hidalgo and the Puritan—continued to glare at each other with jaws outthrust. To Winslow, who was not generally troubled by an overabundance of imagination, it was as though History held its breath. Then one of them—afterwards, Winslow was never quite sure which— extended his hand. The other took it.

With a smile, the Queen laid a hand atop the two men's clasped ones.

"Your Grace," she said, "you have the words *El Bueno*, 'the Good,' after your name. I believe they suit you."

The Duke smiled wryly. "Honesty compels me to relate the tale of how my branch of the Guzmáns won the right to add that to the family name. One of my ancestors stood by and impassively allowed his son to be murdered by enemies who had captured him, rather than letting the boy to be used as a hostage to the disadvantage of the king he served. That is the sense in which 'good' is meant."

The Queen bestowed her most dazzling smile. "Perhaps you will now add a new meaning to it."

Medina Sidonia bowed. "Perhaps . . . Your Majesty."

— TWENTY-ONE —

"THE TRUTH OF THE MATTER IS," SAID ALEXANDER FARNESE, Duke of Parma, in his Italian-accented Spanish, "I was never particularly enthusiastic about invading England. Admittedly, I once considered the idea of a surprise raid by my own forces, crossing in barges under cover of darkness."

"Did you indeed?" The Queen sounded slightly nettled by the wistful tone that had crept into Parma's voice.

The most feared general of the age had proved to be a rather small, wiry man of forty-two whose dark brown beard was trimmed and trained into a dapper point which he couldn't possibly have sustained in the field. Around his neck, beneath his ruff, he wore the chain of the Order of the Golden Fleece. Winslow couldn't overcome a sense of unreality at the thought of sitting across a table from this man, here in the Red Lion Inn at Plymouth, in the very room where it had all begun.

Now that room was crowded nearly to bursting. Its windows overlooked a harbor where *Heron* was lost among Medina Sidonia's galleons and the scattered, surviving English ships that had begun to trickle in.

"Yes, but the moment when that was possible passed," Parma continued imperturbably. "Afterwards, I was always skeptical of the King's plan for the Armada. It violated a basic principle of generalship by attempting a rendezvous in the presence of the enemy—quite aside from the fact that the rendezvous was in itself impractical. But beyond all that, I disagreed with the advice my uncle the King was receiving from people—especially English exiles with axes to grind—who assured him that conquering England was necessary if the Dutch rebels were to be subdued. In fact, it was precisely the other way around." He smiled. "In a world without the Gray Monks, Your Majesty could have lost your fleet and England still would have been defended by the Dutch."

"Not that she would have been likely to lose it," Medina Sidonia admitted ruefully from where he sat at Parma's right.

"Still and all," the Queen observed, "your lack of enthusiasm did not prevent you from invading this realm."

"No, Your Majesty," Parma acknowledged forthrightly. "After the Gray Monks produced their 'miracle,' my duty did not permit me to do otherwise." His features hardened. "But then, after we landed in England and I finally met His Grace here face to face, he delivered to me the sealed orders he had brought from Spain."

"And which I had never read," Medina Sidonia interjected. "Had we never landed here, I was under instructions to return them to the King unopened."

"Yes," nodded Parma. "They might have gathered dust in the royal archives for years or centuries before someone read them and saw, as I did, the pointlessness of the whole enterprise."

"This is the first I have heard of these orders, Your Grace," said Walsingham, perking up with interest at the mention of an official Spanish correspondence which, for once, he had not read.

"In essence, they authorized me to negotiate a peace if the military situation in England proved difficult, and set forth the terms the King insisted on. One of these was a monetary recompense for the depredations of English pirates—" Parma gave Winslow a sidelong glance "—but this was understood to be a mere bargaining point. The real demands were surrender of the Dutch towns currently under English occupation, and freedom of worship for Catholics in England, including Catholic exiles, who must be allowed to return home."

Silence stretched as Walsingham and the Queen waited for Parma to continue.

"Is that *all*?" Walsingham finally managed.

"But," the Queen spluttered, "those Dutch towns were already under negotiation—the negotiations *you* were under instructions not to allow to succeed!" Parma made a delicate gesture that could have meant any number of things. "I would have been perfectly willing to wash my hands of the Netherlands altogether, if Phillip would only have granted the Dutch the same kind of tolerance you say he wanted for the English Catholics. And as for those English Catholics, they're already free to worship as their consciences dictate, as I'm forever telling anyone who'll listen. The exiles are in exile not because they're Catholic but because they're guilty of treason, rebellion and conspiracy to assassinate me."

"Your Majesty has summed the matter up admirably." Parma's expressive face wore a look compounded of grimness and sadness. "So much for the holy crusade to deliver England from heresy and liberate it from the . . . ah, ahem, from Your Majesty. If necessary, my uncle was willing to settle for things that could be won by negotiation. His only real reason for invading England was to try to put himself, through his daughter, on the throne. Had I known all this—the contents of those orders, and the fact that my uncle was keeping me in the dark about them until after I had committed myself by landing in England—then I would have responded to Your Majesty's indirect and subtle overtures, and sought a separate peace based on English support for my claim as King of the Netherlands. I would have done this even without knowing that the Gray Monks had attached themselves to the King's ambitions and made puppets of us all."

"But now that you *do* know this . . . " Walsingham let the sentence linger.

"Yes, of course." Parma nodded emphatically. "I agree to Her Majesty's stipulations. Under my reign, the Dutch will enjoy their ancient liberties as they always did under my grandfather, the Emperor Charles V."

Grandfather on the mother's side, and on the wrong side of the blanket, Winslow thought, but prudently held his tongue. There was, after all, no reason to doubt Parma's sincerity. He was receiving from Elizabeth the kind of reward to which he had long believed himself entitled, and which Phillip had denied him. He had also heard Medina Sidonia's account of what had happened on Wococon Island, and seen the unnatural remains that had been brought back across the Atlantic, preserved in a vat of wine from which Winslow wished King Phillip could be forced to drink.

"On that understanding," said Walsingham smoothly, "we have received assurances that the Dutch will joyfully give Your Grace their true allegiance as their rightful king."

And if they don't they'll no longer have the English support that has enabled them to hold out against Phillip. That might have something to do with it. Winslow chided himself for the cynical thought, for here again everyone was perfectly sincere. The Dutch really *would* be joyful to bring the war to an end and get back to the serious business of making money, in which field they were the acknowledged masters. ("Jesus Christ is good," their saying ran, "but trade is better.") And once that commercial powerhouse was up and running, Parma's revenues from only moderate taxes would shortly make him one of the richest princes in Europe. Winslow wasn't sure how he felt about the justice of that, as applied to the man who had led his army in the sack of London. But he reminded himself that they were all allies now. Walsingham's next words underscored that.

"In the meantime, Your Grace, what news of the response to your secret couriers?"

"All reports from our garrisons are favorable. Fortunately, there were never more than a very few Gray Monks in England. Once the couriers informed the local commanders of the true facts, those few and their acolytes were taken by surprise and dispatched with relatively small loss, despite the weapons which—by means beyond my understanding, although you assure me that they do not involve sorcery—turn light into an instrument of death."

Dee looked troubled. "I wish it were possible to spare those acolytes. As I have explained, they are not responsible for what they do, for their wills are not their own. And, with the help of the Eilonwë, it might someday be possible to win their souls back from darkness."

Parma made a gesture indicating small interest in the matter. "At any rate, Dr. Dee, we have captured more of those weapons—of which, I am told, you have some understanding which you can impart to us. We will have still more of them when my other couriers—the ones I have dispatched to the Netherlands—have also done their work."

"Have you also sent word to Spain?" Walsingham inquired.

"Not yet. I feel I should make sure of my position in the Netherlands before presenting the King with the facts. I hope those facts will speak for themselves. So should the fact that his fleet is with us. And arguably I have won his minimum demands! But he can be . . . difficult." Parma turned to Dee, clearly disturbed. "Is it possible that the Gray Monks have made him . . . as their acolytes are?"

If they had, would anyone have noticed the change? Winslow wanted to say.

"It is possible," Dee said judiciously. "But I would be inclined to doubt it. That kind of enslavement destroys the mind in the end, and an obvious madman would be of no use to them. They probably preferred to do as you yourself suggested earlier: encourage the ambitions he already harbored, and make themselves indispensable for the attainment of those ambitions."

"Yes," said Parma grimly. "They probably had no difficulty doing the same in France with the Duke of Guise. As you probably know, they've been effectively in control of the Holy League for some time." His tone was eloquent of a professional soldier's disdain for religious zealots, even those ostensibly on his side, with their uncontrollable and unpredictable enthusiasms.

"At the same time," Dee continued, "I think it not impossible that they may have made such a slave of the Pope, keeping him in isolation save for occasional, tightly controlled public appearances and issuing commands in his name to his underlings."

Parma, Medina Sidonia and all the other Spaniards shuddered and crossed themselves. "Well," Parma finally said briskly, "be that as it may, there must be a housecleaning, of the Church as well as of Spain. And we ourselves must set our own house in order."

"Of course," acknowledged Walsingham. "However, at the same time, the Grella in Florida must also be dealt with. And the hurricane season in those seas is now drawing to a close, so the voyage can be safely attempted."

Medina Sidonia spoke up. "When we stopped there on our way to Virginia, I saw relatively few of them—they must be spread thin, here in Europe. Also, I had the impression that their capacity for mischief-making is limited, at least for now. As the one we knew as Father Jerónimo said, they have never repaired their flying ship. Partly this is for the reason he gave: they have been awaiting the rediscovery of the portal through which it can take them. But in addition, it is evidently a daunting task even for them."

"Still," Dee cautioned, "remember what we told you of the devices by which they can send their voices winging across great distances. We dare not assume they will remain unaware of what is happening to their fellows in Europe."

"I know," Parma nodded. "But consolidating the Netherlands and Spain must come first. And yet who knows what devilment they may hatch in Florida if we give them time?"

"May I propose a solution, Your Grace?" offered Walsingham. "We English can deal with this problem while you are, as you put it, setting your own house in order." He hastily held up a hand. "Be assured that we have no designs on Florida. As regards those lands, we recognize the claim of Spain . . . whoever is speaking for Spain at the time." He and Parma exchanged a meaningful look. "But, as we are now agreed, the Grella are the enemies of us all. We will soon be in a position to mount an expedition while you are attending to the Grella in Catholic Europe. And," he added, turning to Winslow, "we have just the man to command it—a man with some experience in fighting the Grella."

"So, Will, I understand they're already rebuilding the theaters in Southwark. I imagine you'll be resuming your career as an actor."

"Or perhaps," Virginia Dare added, "pursuing your ambition to be a playwright."

"Perhaps so, Mistress Dare. I've even received some new inspiration in that field. Before the Spaniards departed, I met a young ensign of my own age—a certain Lope de Vega. He also has aspirations in that field. We had some stimulating conversations."

They stood on *Heron's* quarterdeck, amid the squadron that stood ready to depart Plymouth for Florida, awaiting the Queen's arrival amid the captains and various dignitaries—including John Dee, whom the Queen and Winslow had granted leave to accompany the expedition to Florida. Winslow was beginning to fidget, because the tide would soon be out and the wind was favorable. He wasn't quite sure how Shakespeare had worked his way into the group, but he wasn't particularly surprised.

"Yes," Shakepeare continued, "London is an exciting place to be, with all the rebuilding. And yet . . . Captain, do you remember when I saved your life, during the attack on the Grella fortress?"

"Of course, Will. How can I forget?" Shakespeare, it seemed, *had* forgotten that the feat had consisted of tripping and falling.

"When I think back on all we've been through and done, I wonder if I've mistaken my true calling. Perhaps I should make my way in the world as an adventurer rather than as a playwright."

Winslow placed his hands on Shakespeare's shoulders, looked into his eyes, and spoke with quiet but intense earnestness. "Will . . . be a playwright!"

Shakespeare brightened, as though hearing what he'd more than half wanted to hear. "Do you really think I'd make a better playwright than a sea dog?"

"I think you'll make a *great* playwright!" Winslow diplomatically left it at that.

"You think so?" Shakespeare brightened still further. "Well, if you're sure you won't need me . . . Devise, wit! Write, pen! For I am for whole volumes in folio!" He gave a more than usually satisfied nod.

He's himself again, Winslow thought, with ambivalent feelings.

At that moment, a fanfare of trumpets sounded and a line of carriages began to turn onto the pier. The array of luminaries who alighted from them was wondrous to behold. Sir Walter Raleigh was resplendent in silvery parade armor, especially in contrast to Walsingham's Puritan black. White-bearded William Cecil, Lord Burghley, had managed the journey despite his age. A multitude of lesser courtiers followed. But they all fell to their knees when the last carriage halted and the first foot that descended from it touched the pier. So did all the crowds. So did Winslow. But he raised his head and peered at the apparition—all farthingale and pearl fringes and red hair dye and white makeup—that descended from the carriage to the lowly cringing earth. And he remembered the weathered, determined queen who had braved an alien world. He missed that queen. But this was what England expected. This was what England needed. This was what England required of her. And she could not withhold it, for she and England were one—now more than ever.

On Raleigh's arm, she came aboard, proceeded through the mass of kneeling sailors in the waist, and ascended the stair to the quarterdeck. "Arise," she said, and looked around. "So, Captain, have you acquainted yourself with your Spanish counterpart?"

"Indeed, Your Majesty," said Winslow, relieved to find himself in the world of practicalities. The Spaniards had insisted on being represented in this expedition, claiming that honor required them to have a hand in purging their Floridian possessions of the Grella. Winslow suspected that a desire to share in any captured weapons and equipment might also have influenced them. At least the captain they had assigned seemed a good man, and his galleon, the *San Pedro*, seemed a well-found ship. "Allow me to present Captain Francisco de Cuellar."

"Your Majesty!" Cuellar, a handsome man of considerable Latin charm, bowed with the kind of almost languid courtliness that often caused the English to dismiss Spanish gentlemen as fops. But Winslow had sensed the toughness underneath. This man, he felt sure, would survive in almost any imaginable situation.

The Queen looked around at the familiar sights of *Heron* and drew a deep breath of salt air. "At times I almost miss this ship. I see, Captain, that you have elected to stay aboard her, even though you now have larger ships to chose from."

"Aye, Your Majesty. Size in a warship is no particular advantage in itself. As long as she can carry a useful outfit of guns, the smaller the better, because she'll be handier."

"Drake used to say much the same thing." The Queen's eyes took on a faraway look at the thought of Drake. "Captain, I recall when I stood on another quarterdeck—that of Drake's *Golden Hind*, after he had returned from his voyage around the world and put 160,000 pounds into my treasury, and King Phillip wanted his head for piracy. You'll have heard the tale."

"Of course, Your Majesty. Who hasn't?"

"But you've probably heard it wrong. Everyone thinks I said I'd take his head with a gilded sword, and then knighted him. In fact, I handed the sword to the Sieur de Marchaumont, envoy from the Duc d'Alençon, with whom I was then engaged in certain negotiations." *Marriage negotiations,* Winslow recalled, part of the endless diplomatic game she'd played while childbearing had still been a possibility for her. "I asked him to do it, because it is for a knight to bestow knighthood." She paused. "I have no gilded sword here, Captain. But that's a rare one strapped to your back. Give it to me."

Wonderingly, Winslow drew the slightly curved Eilonwë sword and handed it to her hilt-first. She held his eyes. "Kneel!" she commanded.

As though in a trance, he did as he was bidden.

"Sir Walter," the Queen said to Raleigh, "will you do the office?"

Raleigh examined the strange sword fastidiously. "It is hardly a knightly blade, Your Majesty."

Elizabeth glared. "Is it not, sirrah? Deeds have been done with it that are knightly beyond common conception. But if you're disinclined . . . well, perhaps this time I'll actually do it as everyone merely *thinks* I did it with Drake." And she turned to the kneeling Winslow who could barely hear her for the roaring in his head. But the words *in the name of God, St. Michael and St. George* penetrated his consciousness, and he felt the touch of the flat of the sword. It was as though that touch broke the spell, for he heard her quite distinctly when she said, "Rise, Sir Thomas."

He got to his feet amid general applause and the sound of cheering from *Heron*'s crew in the waist. The Queen smiled as she returned the alien sword.

"And now, Sir Thomas, I know you are impatient to be at sea. 'The wind commands me away,' Drake once said. But before I depart, ask a favor of me. I'll grant anything within reason."

Winslow reached out a hand and drew Virginia Dare forward. She had already drawn some stares from the dignitaries, and now those stares grew blatant, for she was dressed in her tunic-and-trousers garments of Eilonwë style, scandalous here.

"Your Majesty, you've already broken one tradition today by knighting me yourself. I ask you to overturn another. Allow Mistress Dare to accompany me, returning to the New World where she was the first English child to be born."

A tittering arose among the courtiers, but it died a quick death as everyone saw that the Queen was not even smiling. And de Cuellar, whom Winslow had expected to be among the most amused at the idea, wasn't smiling either. He knew a warrior when he saw one.

The Queen remained serious as she met Virginia Dare's eyes. "Are you certain this is what you wish, Mistress Dare? I would have thought your desire would have been for my leave to marry Sir Thomas."

For the first time in Winslow's experience, Virginia Dare blushed, and her gaze brushed against his. "The thought is there, Your Majesty, and has been for some time. But however I turn the matter over in my mind, the need to cleanse my birth continent of the Grella comes uppermost. Everything—even my dearest wishes —must wait upon that."

The Queen met her eyes, and for a moment it was as if no one was present except the two women.

"It is in my heart, Mistress Dare, that in you the Grella have forged a weapon for their own destruction. I would not keep that weapon sheathed even if I could. And . . . I know what it is to be a woman with a Purpose and a Power within her, in a world where such things are supposed to be the province of men. Oh, yes, I know a thing or two about that! It is what bearing a child must be like—it cannot be withheld. Yes, you have my leave."

The courtiers' looks went from amused to stunned. But Walsingham, Puritan though he was, gave only a wise smile. And a thunderous cheer erupted from the ship's waist, led by those crewmen who had passed through the Void and fought beside Virginia Dare.

The Queen departed and the ship began to clear. Winslow caught sight of Shakespeare giving the ship one last, half-wistful look. "We'll kill some Grella for you, Will!" he called out.

"Kill them?" Shakespeare looked at Virginia Dare, then at Winslow. "I believe, Captain, they're already dead. They just don't know it yet. But the two of you can do me one favor."

"What's that, Will?" asked Virginia Dare.

"You've already given me the makings of a play. Bring me back another!"

She went to his side and kissed his cheek. He beamed, and was gone.

Orders rang out, and the sailors went to the rigging. The wind began to fill the sails.

— AUTHOR'S NOTE —

IN RECENT YEARS THERE HAS BEEN SOME CONTROVERSY about just exactly where on the east coast of Florida Juan Ponce de León first made landfall. I have gone with the traditional view that it was near St. Augustine, just north of the beautiful and evocative Shrine of Nuestra Señora de la Leche, about where the modern tourist trap known as the "Fountain of Youth" is located. Aside from this concession to romanticism—and, of course, the ambiguously successful denouement I have given it—everything in the Prologue about Ponce de León's 1513 expedition to Florida is true to real-world fact. This includes all the individuals I have named (a fascinating lot, unaccountably neglected by historical novelists), so don't blame me for the fact that there are so many Juans. In fact, except for Thomas Winslow and the rest of the ships' companies of the imaginary *Heron* and *Greyhound*, all the humans named in this novel actually lived. Even St. Antony of Padua (not to be confused with the better-known St. Anthony the Great) is an authentic saint, and for the fictive use to which I have put him I may need the intercession of St. Francis de Sales, patron of authors, who must already have his hands full.

My portrait of the Duke of Medina Sidonia may come as a surprise to some readers, brought up on his image in popular history as a ridiculous poltroon. They may be assured that it has been half a century since any serious historian has bought into that view of him. I hope to have done my part to counteract this and various other entrenched misconceptions about the Spanish Armada. On that subject, everything I have written—except, of course, matters relating to "Father Jerónimo"—is as reliable as conscientious research can make it. The only liberties I have taken with the known facts about the Armada campaign are trivial ones. For example, I cannot prove that Martin Frobisher was not present for the English council of war on the morning of August 7, 1588. But his absence from the next such council, following the Battle of Gravelines, is attested, and it was probably for the reason I have suggested: that he and Drake would very likely have done King Phillip of Spain a service by killing each other.

As to why the colonists led by John White (no known relation) were in effect marooned on Roanoke Island, I am indebted to Lee Miller, author of *Roanoke: Solving the Mystery of the Lost Colony*, whose conspiracy theory I have adopted for narrative purposes despite certain reservations. (Giles Milton's *Big Chief Elizabeth*, published in 2000 like Ms. Miller's book, reaches very different conclusions, which should give an idea of how contentious the whole subject of the Lost Colony still is.) Stephen Budiansky's *Her Majesty's Spymaster* should be read as a corrective to Ms. Miller's Snidely Whiplash-like characterization of Sir Francis Walsingham. In fact, it should be read, period. Both views of Walsingham agree on his loyalty to England—and to Elizabeth, even though her chronic vacillation nearly drove him to vice, Puritan or no.

Some would dismiss John Dee, who may or may not have had the right to style himself "Doctor," as a con man—or, worse, as a dupe of the undoubted con man Edward Kelley. But his linguistic and mathematical abilities, not to mention his services to the Walsingham organization in cryptography and other fields, cannot be honestly denied. There is also no denying his mystical and occult susceptibilities. Like many Renaissance geniuses, he still had one foot in the Middle Ages. (Also some post-Renaissance geniuses—I cite Newton and Goethe.)

Oceans of ink have been spilled over the question of Shakespeare's whereabouts and occupations during the "lost years" between the mid-1580s and early 1590s. Some would place his arrival in London as late as 1591, but a date of 1587 is supportable. The latter seems more likely given his attested status as a budding playwright by 1592, with at least *Henry VI* to his credit. There is no reason to suppose he was ever in any way connected with Walsingham's intelligence network, but his friend Christopher Marlowe certainly was.

The North Carolina Outer Banks have changed over the centuries under the relentless assault of the Atlantic waves. Croatoan Island probably comprised what are now Ocracoke Island and the southern end of Hatteras

Island. Hatorask Island almost certainly included today's Pea Island and the northern end of Hatteras. Roanoke Island, inland from the Banks and sheltered by them, is more or less as it was. Incidentally, at the time of the story the entire area was included in what was called "Virginia."

As regards dialogue, I have deliberately made no attempt to reproduce sixteenth century English, with its unavoidable air of affected quaintness. Elizabethans didn't know they were being quaint; they weren't consciously trying to sound like Elizabethans.

1635
THE TANGLED
WEB

VIRGINIA DeMARCE

Available from Baen Books
December 2009
hardcover

Window of Opportunity

Section One: In the beginning . . .

The morning and evening of the first day
Mainz, March 1634

Eberhard was asleep. Rather, he had been asleep until the drumming started. What in hell?

Tata stood up on the bed and poked her head through the tiny third-story window of the Horn of Plenty. "Just some soldiers."

"They're not for me. I'm not late. The world may be full of sunshine, but it's my day off and I don't even have a hangover." He reached up for her wrist and pulled her back down.

She plopped onto his stocky body, wriggled, and told him to quit it right now because he might have the day off, but she didn't.

Reichard Donner's wife Justina also heard the drum. She looked out the front window of the main floor, more than a little warily. Her husband wasn't famous for his attention to submitting paperwork in multiple copies or keeping track of the details, so she thought that her wariness was fully justified. The Horn of Plenty had a record of too many times that its proprietor hadn't, quite, complied with those abundant city regulations designed to ensure good order and civic peace.

"What events do we have scheduled for the coming week?" Anything that will cause problems with the *Polizeiordnungen*?

"Nothing unusual," Reichard answered from behind the bar. "The two wedding parties are the largest functions. I have the written authorization from the city council for both of those. Well, it's almost approved. Everything will be ready by Thursday, certainly. Since both the groom and the bride's fathers for the Koster-Backe reception are local artisans, the families are bringing in a lot of the food and drink themselves, which is making a bit of trouble with the pastry shops and our regular sausage vendors. Fifty guests approved. Up to thirty guests permitted for the Biel-Braun wedding. I have the extra military paperwork for that, since Jost Biel is a soldier and so is the bride's father. It's . . . "

Reichard scrabbled around in his piles of paper. "Well, I did have it, right here, somewhere . . . "

Justina nodded. Marcus Pistor, Brahe's Hessian chaplain for the Calvinists in his garrison, would perform the

Biel-Braun ceremony here at the inn, in the public room, since Mainz had no Calvinist church or chapel and they were all, in this family, good Calvinists from the Palatinate, subjects of the unfortunate Winter King's heir. *May Elector Karl Ludwig's soul be preserved from the influence of those Spanish Papists in the Netherlands who took him prisoner*, she thought. *Chaplain Pistor will have made sure that Reichard received the permissions. Now, if he hasn't misplaced them . . .*

Reichard, who hadn't even glanced up, was still talking while he sorted more paper into various piles. "Here it is. Right here, under the receipts. Everything's in order. Why? Is there a problem?"

"Lift up your head and listen. There are soldiers headed our way. That's what the noise is. Hear the noise?" She turned around, waving her hands at him. "There are four or so of them, Colonel von Zitzewitz's men from the uniforms, with a drummer. Also with a corporal and probably they're not just looking for a drink at this hour. What regulation have we offended now? Well, at least the children are at school, so I don't have to worry about having them mouth off and cause trouble. Except for Tata, of course; she's home. Anyway, four soldiers aren't enough to do too much damage, usually."

Kunigunde Treidelin, Justina's widowed sister and the tavern's main cook, came out of the kitchen, complaining as usual about a world in which a woman could live for half a century and still not be permitted by the authorities to finish out her waning days in peace and tranquility. "It's your fault entirely, Reichard, for getting involved with those Committee of Correspondence people and letting them meet here. The Swedes and the city council both keep a sharper eye on the Horn of Plenty than they would otherwise, just because of that. You know that as well as I do."

"I am the *chairman* of the Mainz CoC," Donner pointed out rather mildly. "It would be rather ridiculous if I didn't let the group meet here. According to the theories of Althusius, since—"

" 'The Mainz CoC'—as if that means anything. It's not as if you have anything like they do in Magdeburg, with toughs and enforcers. You get all the grief and what do you have to show for it? Nothing. It's not as if there's a CoC-raised regiment anywhere near Mainz. They're all up north with the emperor. We've got Swedish regulars, German mercenaries, and maybe a dozen soldiers scattered among them with even the slightest interest in politics. Hah!" Kunigunde turned her head. "Something's boiling over." She stomped back into the kitchen.

Tata, more formally known as their daughter Agathe, who had pulled on her clothes and come down instead of going back to bed, took her place at the window. "*Pffft.* That's Corporal Hertling. You know him. He's been here often enough. He's in Eberhard's company, so it shouldn't be a problem, whatever it is."

Walther Hertling motioned for his little troop to stop and rapped sharply on the door.

Tata waved her parents back, opened the door, glared at him, and asked, "Why are you bothering us?"

"Look, Tata, it isn't my fault."

Justina relaxed. Interventions by one's social superiors that were likely to lead to measures of harsh oppression were rarely accompanied by plaintive apologies or the use of nicknames.

"It may not be your fault, but you're here. With your goons."

"They aren't goons," Walther protested, looking as firm has he could. Which, considering that he was barely twenty, was not particularly firm. He had gotten his rank because his father had once upon a time been Duke Eberhard's father's bootblack. "They're . . ." He tried to think of some term more martial, impartial, and less embarrassing to his captain than *babysitters*. "They're, uh, the Captain Duke's personal *Leibkompanie*. Bodyguards, sort of."

Lorenz Bauer, Jacob Kolb, Ludwig Merckel, and Christoph Heisel strove mightily to look as un-goonlike as possible. Since all four were long-time mercenaries in their thirties, with the scars to show for it, this was not particularly easy. Still, if Corporal Hertling, otherwise known as the immediate conduit to their now-reliable paymaster, urged them to look harmless, the least they could do was try.

"Eberhard says that he's off today."

"That's not the problem. At least, the problem isn't about anything he's not done. It's about something he's supposed to do next. It's, uh, about Hartmann Simrock."

"Theobald's friend?"

"Yeah. Uh, Theobald Pistor took home a copy of some of the speeches that Simrock has been giving here at the CoC meetings."

"Ouch. Dumb, dumb, dumb, stupid. University student or no university student, Theo has no sense at all. I can't believe that he's Margarethe's brother."

"And, of course, he left them on the breakfast table where they're quartered. At least, that's what Margarethe told Lieutenant Duke Friedrich. He left them on the breakfast table where their father, Chaplain Pistor, found them. And read them. Especially the one about . . . well, you know. He is a military chaplain, after all, so he took it to someone on Brahe's staff. And we've been ordered to investigate."

Reichard swept up his various piles of receipts and stuck them into a cubbyhole under the bar. " 'We' being?"

"Uh, well, the captain's company. Him. Us. And his brothers."

Hertling wasn't worried about Donner, but he was a little intimidated by Frau Justina, so he turned around so he could talk directly to her. "Uh, that wasn't the brightest thing Simrock could have done, you know. Calling for the equivalent of a Ram Rebellion in Mainz and the Rhine Palatinate. Especially not criticizing General Brahe the way he did. Captain Duke Eberhard has the highest respect for the general's military talent and bravery. So it's just lucky that . . ." He stumbled, not quite sure how to phrase what was coming next in a manner that might be interpreted as mildly tactful.

Merckel was less concerned about tact. ". . . damned fucking lucky that the captain is actually fucking Tata here, or you'd all be in a deep pile of shit, you stupid assholes."

Justina winced. It wasn't that Reichard was unhappy about the attraction that led the young German officer on General Brahe's staff to regularly attend meetings of the Committee of Correspondence at the Horn of Plenty, in the company of his brothers and then spend the night, even though he had finally been allotted a much nicer room in the new unmarried officers' quarters. He was perfectly aware that Eberhard's interest did not lie entirely in the realm of radical political theory. Or even primarily in the realm of radical political theory.

No, Reichard was a practical man. His comment on the arrangement had been that this was the greatest stroke of luck the Donner family had ever had and was ever likely to have.

Still, there was such a thing as tact. Maybe not where Merckel was concerned, though.

Besides, with increasing exposure, Eberhard was gradually becoming more interested in the political portion of his evenings. Still, though, the Horn of Plenty's primary attraction for him had a neat figure rather than a lot of economic figures. Feminine cooperation rather than the need to establish a purchasing cooperative was the crucial element that led to the extension of the captain's regular presence at the inn and the protection that resulted from that presence.

It was protection that they needed, in Justina's opinion, as long as Reichard kept flirting with those radical CoC ideas. She intended to take full advantage of it as long as there was a window of opportunity. Which meant, in effect, as long as Eberhard remained interested in their daughter. Which would be long enough, she hoped, to get the protection in some way institutionalized and make the continued existence of the Horn of Plenty and the Mainz CoC somewhat less precarious.

"Uh," Hertling said. "The captain will have something to say about it, I suppose, once he talks to the boy."

The subject of their discussion, having dressed somewhat less hastily than Tata, wandered into the taproom. Duke Eberhard of Württemberg yawned. "Which one of the boys is in trouble this time? About what?"

Hertling duly saluted the square-faced, brown-haired, slightly long-nosed young man. Personally, he thought that his noble captain looked more like most people's idea of a sturdy peasant than a dashing cavalier, no more aristocratic than anyone else on the streets of Stuttgart or Mainz, including, for what it was worth, himself. That wasn't an opinion he was given to sharing with other people, though. *Der gute Walther* was prudent for his years.

"Neither of your brothers, sir. Simrock. If you could come down to General Brahe's headquarters with us . . ."

"I suppose that's not a request?"

Tata's eyes followed their departing backs. "So much for the idea of taking a boat down the river to Bingen with Friedrich and Margarethe and looking at Castle Ehrenfels today."

"Castles," her father said. "Castles, bah!"

Reichard Donner surveyed the room. The view was depressing. Mainz just wasn't a hotbed of revolutionary fervor. Perhaps he would have been better advised to move to Heidelberg. However, to be practical, there hadn't been an inn for him to take over in Heidelberg, whereas, in Mainz—owing to a fortuitous series of childless marriages and deaths from smallpox and plague, not to mention dysentery and measles, running through several imperial cities and tying all the way back to his long-ago godfather, one Reichard Wackernagel, belt-maker in Frankfurt am Main, husband of Justina's Aunt Maria—the Horn of Plenty had become available.

Even so. In addition to the two students, Pistor and Simrock, the attendees were not politically promising.

Pistor's sister Margarethe only came because her brother and her boyfriend did.

Philipp Schaumann, perpetual belt-maker's journeyman, aged about sixty-five, the hapless and hopeless perpetual suitor of his sister-in-law Kunigunde, came because Kunigunde lived here as well as because he was the younger brother of Justina and Kunigunde's late uncle's equally deceased wife. Also, he had been an acquaintance of Reichard's own late godfather back when they were both journeymen.

Sybilla Binder, about fifty and never married, was a friend of Kunigunde and the unhappy daughter of a belt-maker. She faced being thrown out of work when her father retired or died—one of which was certain to happen soon—and had no wish to spend her declining years spinning in the municipal hospital.

Ursula Widder, about fifty, Sybilla's friend, also never married, was the equally unhappy daughter of a tanner who had died and left her no option but to go into service. So she was now Kunigunde's general maid-of-all-work in the kitchen of the Horn of Plenty. It wasn't as if she had to put forth much effort to attend the CoC meetings.

Plus four soldiers and a corporal who were definitely not from a CoC-raised regiment and who attended because they were tasked by Gustavus Adolphus's commander in Mainz to see what they could do to prevent problems with . . .

. . . three very young dukes of Württemberg, one of whom was sitting with his arm around Tata's shoulder and twirling her reddish-tawny hair and fondling the various bits and pieces of her rotund body that he could conveniently reach.

The rest of his children were already in bed, which was some comfort.

"It's *not* an up-time idea," Simrock was insisting. "It's in Montaigne's *Essays* and they've been around for, oh, at least fifty years." For Simrock, not quite twenty himself, fifty years was ancient history. "How did he put it?

'No matter that we may mount on stilts, we still must walk on our own legs. And on the highest throne in the world, we still sit only on our own bottom.' "

Theobald shook his head. "I don't think that Montaigne thought it up all by himself. He probably swiped it from the Greeks or Romans."

A revolutionary's lot in Mainz was not a happy one. Maybe he could trade the Horn of Plenty for an inn in Magdeburg.

Bonn, Archdiocese of Cologne, March 1634

"We simply can't do what you want us to," Walter Deveroux said. "You're out of your fucking mind."

This wasn't the most prudent thing to say to the personal confessor of the archbishop-elector of Cologne, said archbishop-elector, Ferdinand of Bavaria, brother of Duke Maximilian, being at the moment the man who was paying them. Walter Butler sighed. It was true, though. The idea that they should take their dragoons on a *razzia* through Hesse, or if that route would not work, past Mainz and Frankfurt-am-Main, up the Kinzig valley to Fulda, was ridiculous. Absurd. A recipe for disaster.

Now the Capuchin was suggesting that just the colonels go in. Some of the Buchenland imperial knights were far from being happy at being placed under the administration of the up-timers. Upstarts, it was more accurate to say. They could provide a couple hundred men. Ferdinand's confessor got up. "You're the professionals. The archbishop wants to damage the prestige of the USE administration in Fulda. Figure something out and let me know what you decide."